FUTON FEVER

Dawn Anderson was born in 1970 and grew up in East Kilbride. After studying at Bell College she worked in Glasgow as a health food assistant, librarian and archivist. She now lives in Edinburgh where she works in an academic library. She admits to wearing Lycra, has never been a florist, and likes to keep flat-sharing with psychopaths to the bare minimum. *Futon Fever* is her first novel and was written on a single futon. Her second is being composed on a double.

FUTON FEVER

Dawn Anderson

HarperCollins*Publishers*

HarperCollins*Publishers*
77–85 Fulham Palace Road,
Hammersmith, London W6 8JB

www.**fire**and**water**.com

This paperback edition 2000
1 3 5 7 9 8 6 4 2

First published in Great Britain by
Black Ace Books 1998

This novel is entirely a work of fiction.
The names, characters and incidents portrayed in it are
the work of the author's imagination. Any resemblance to
actual persons, living or dead, events or localities is
entirely coincidental.

A catalogue record for this book
is available from the British Library

ISBN 0 00 651448 0

Typeset in Meridien by Palimpsest Book Production Limited,
Polmont, Stirlingshire
Printed and bound in Great Britain by
Omnia Books Ltd, Glasgow

ACKNOWLEDGEMENTS

Thanks to
the library staff for living through this with me;
especially Susan for the title
My family for their constant support
&
A very special thanks to Paul
for his tolerance and patience

For Mum & Dad

1

EVE He's nothing more than a slouched ball, sitting there on my doorstep. Quite the thing, he is. Not a care in the world. A crumpled mass of wounded testosterone.

I knew when I saw the flowers. I just knew it. By the way the artificial jobs propped up the aisles, I knew we were not talking class as much as trash. Nowadays some artificial flowers look really good, but these must have been bought as a job lot at Ingliston market. On many an occasion, I had said to Will, 'Let me do them. Let me make the bouquets.' And as usual he just nodded his head and did the complete opposite.

You see, I knew the frills and flounces were an omen

of things to come: the Wannabe was most likely a Maybe, which probably, let's face facts here, was a Neverbe.

So now he sits with head in hands on my doorstep, a well used and abused lump of hormones and blubber. I rattle my keys to get his attention. He looks up with those big pitiful eyes of his and I don't know whether to hit him or hug him.

'Have you been here long?' I say.

He shrugs. He stands up. God, he looks good in his kilt. McIntyre tartan, he told me. For his dad. 'Where have you been?' he asks.

I put it down to disorientation, but it's pretty obvious. 'At the church.' It's only now I can smell him: a mixture of beer, fags, whisky and farts. This is bad. This is very bad.

On his lapel is a sprig of white heather bound together with a tartan ribbon. He unpins it and hands it to me. 'Lucky white heather,' he says with a forced laugh.

'Uch, Will, look at you.'

'Just hurry up and open the door, I'm desperate for a piss!'

WILL Bloody shoes! I've got a blister on my heel the size of Gibraltar. Jesus, how in hell's name was I supposed to dance in the bloody things? They don't tell you that at Moss Bros, do they?

This piss is the longest in history. Bet I've got a chill in this kilt. All that free-flowing air circulating under the skirt. One gust of wind and my bits would have withered down to nothing more than a walnut. They never think to tell you that either.

They never even tell you how itchy it is, just let you

find out and suffer for yourself. And by then, well, it's just too damn late.

Jesus, I feel sick. I'm going to spew.

I feel dirty.

I want a shower.

I'm so tired.

I want to sleep.

I wonder if Eve has any Valium? Maybe I could take the whole bottle and that would be the end of it.

'Will?' I hear her say through the door. 'Are you all right? Will? Talk to me.'

I mumble something but even to me it doesn't make any sense.

'Ian's dressing gown's hanging up behind the door. See it? If you want to change, it's there, okay? I'm just going to make some tea.'

I look to the hook behind the door. It's pink, and not even towelling. More cheap-thrill satin. 'I don't drink tea,' I tell her.

'Well, it's tea or nothing. Camomile or Earl Grey?'

What kind of man wears a pink dressing gown? I ask myself. The kind seen in those dodgy adverts in the *Sun* – if you've got a bit of an imagination – is the answer. I put it on over my boxers, thinking on how such shite keeps me from thinking about other things.

Relief is not the word to describe it, when I take that bloody kilt off.

Ian? Who's Ian? I've never met any Ian. Fuck sake! He must be the weirdest shape. And a perv! Look! This hardly covers my arse. Look at the arms, barely covers my elbows, for Jesus sake.

Right, so, we're sitting in the kitchen opposite each other, me in Ian's slip of a dressing gown, and Eve still in her wedding outfit, over a pot of Earl Grey. 'Lemon or sugar?' she asks.

I don't reply, so she dumps both in the mug. 'Now drink.'

Daylight still comes in through the window. Or maybe it's hallucinations from too much booze. Nah, it's definitely the sun. Least we had a good day for it.

In fact, I can't believe it is the same day. So many hours must have passed, it must be tomorrow. It must be Sunday. I'm scared to look at my watch in case it's not.

'I like your dress,' I say, fighting mugginess in my head.

'Mm. I bought it specially,' but she smiles at me at the same time, so I know she's not mad at me. It's important that she's not mad at me. It means a lot.

'Don't you want to know what happened?'

'I know exactly what happened. You chickened out. I can read it on your face, Will.'

Fuck, am I so obvious? Here, I'm thinking I'm being so dramatic, and something major has happened to change my life for ever, when really I've just done something that everyone expected me to do anyway.

Is this when I'm supposed to say, I just couldn't do it 'cos I knew it would be the biggest mistake of my life? Big, big mistake: the same size as the blister-on-my-heel kind of mistake.

Before I get the chance, the phone rings and I almost jump out of the window, in a complete frenzy. 'If it's someone looking for me, then I'm not here. Please, Eve, I can't face them. Not now.' Not ever. I can hear the whiny pleading tone creep into my voice. I can't control it though, and I don't even have the decency to feel embarrassed about it.

'God, Will. Calm down. You're safe here.'

She leaves the kitchen to answer the phone in the living room. 'Yes,' I hear her say, 'that's right. One box of tulips and one of white roses.'

I breathe a sigh of relief. It's work. Good, the guns aren't aimed at me yet.

'No, Nathan, we don't need any chrysanthemums. Listen to me, Nathan, no!'

I want to sleep now. No, that's wrong. I want to die. Right now I want to die. This may seem a bit drastic, but I want to do it myself before anyone gets the urge to do it for me.

I don't even want to start feeling anything. Numbness is fine. I can cope with that. Yeah, numbness is good. 'Cos if I start to feel anything, I know it's going to be guilt, and then dread, which is guaranteed to give me a stomach ulcer, so I can never bloody forget. God, I feel sick just at the thought. Can you die from a stomach ulcer though? When I say I want to die, I don't really mean it. I don't really mind my penance as long as it's not fatal.

'Well, why did you phone then if you thought I'd be out? Yes, I was. No. It's a long story. I can't talk now. I'll tell you on Monday.'

So that's enquiry numero uno.

I go and collapse on Eve's bed.

EVE We met last Friday in 'The Monty'. It's actually called 'The Montgomery Arms', but it's nicknamed 'The Monty' by its friends. It was a typical Friday night, with crowds of people meeting up to celebrate the beginning of the weekend. And it was the last Friday of the month, so naturally everyone had just been paid. Tenners and twenties were flashed around in abundance. Everyone was there for a good bevvy and to eye up the local talent. They would all drink too much, flirt too much and wish they hadn't by Saturday morning.

Will acted a bit strange. What I mean by that is that he didn't have his normal *joie de vivre* about him. And that's what everyone loves about Will. His *joie de vivre*.

'You know,' he said, 'this will be the last drink you'll ever have with me as a single man. From next Saturday, my life sentence begins. So if you want to make your move tonight, then it's fine with me.'

Will always winds people up like this. I have known friends of friends to be offended by him – or by his attitude, to be more precise. It normally happens after everyone has had a wellie-full, granted, but noses have been put out of joint for months.

I take him as I find him, so normally I just laugh or tell him to shut up. However, on the occasion of last Friday night, I have to admit the warning bells started ringing – chiming, to be exact. But he wouldn't talk about it. Just clammed up. You would have needed a chisel to get into that oyster. I approached the subject tactfully many times but never once got a straight answer. Not once.

'Well,' I said, 'are you all organized then?'

'Organized for what?'

'Next Saturday? Your wedding?'

'Well, it's like this. Suzie's organized everything. All I have to do is turn up.' He smiled at this point. 'So, who do you think will win the Cup Final then?'

Evasion is Will's answer to everything. Dentists, doctors, exams at school, trouble, questions; anything. Will made up this policy at a very young age and sticks to it like glue. Yes, according to the or[...] is the best line all round.

Even when we were saying goodbye, I a[...] loved Suzie. He smiled that lopsided grin of h[...] he said was, 'She's a right good fuck, if that's wha[...] mean.' He knew fine well I didn't mean that!

Then I got a jumbo hug before I climbed into my taxi. My last view of him was from the rear window. His shoulders were hunched, his jacket collar wrapped tightly around his neck. His hands were in his pockets and I watched him shuffle away up the road. I put it down to the bitter east-coast wind but I have to admit those alarm bells were chiming even louder.

I made up the spare bed, just in case.

He comes into the kitchen when I'm chopping an onion. 'This is very touching,' he says, 'but you don't even know Suzie.' He hands me a bit of kitchen roll.

'It's these onions,' I say, wiping the tears away and blowing my nose. 'You know, people who wear contact lenses don't cry when they're peeling onions.'

'That's because they get someone else to do it for them. They've got this great excuse of damaging their lenses with onion fumes and wiping eyes, and the whole big carry-on.'

'No, you've got the wrong end of the stick as usual. It's something to do with the lens acting as a coating over the eye, so they don't cry like wimpy non-contact-lens people.'

'Did you see her?' he asks.

This is all a bit too abrupt for me, and I get into a bit of a flutter, dropping the knife in the sink, making a huge

...nk and then dropping the onion on the floor. I shake my head though. 'She didn't come into the church. Colin must have stopped her.'

'Colin's going to kill me.' He sits down at the kitchen table and begins to pick away at the embroidered flowers on the table-cover.

I don't say anything because I bought it at some junk stall down the Grassmarket last year during the Festival.

'He's probably got the lynch mob outside the door, even as we speak.'

Somehow it just seems so normal for Will to be sitting in my kitchen with nothing on but Ian's dressing gown, talking about being murdered:

'I told the driver to stop because I thought I was going to be sick. He stopped and you couldn't see me for dust. Colin was shouting my name, and I just ignored him. Can you believe I did that? Jesus! Take a good look at this face, Eve, 'cos this is the last time you'll see it like this. My nose will stick out the back of my skull and for the rest of my natural days I'll be chomping away on falsers.'

I pass him a glass of Alka Seltzer. It fizzes up and I watch him swallow it in a oner. While he's swallowing I take a quick look at my tablecloth. One yellow thread from the daffodil has already begun to unravel, and the stem looks as if it is about to disintegrate with one more tug on the green thread.

'When it came to the crunch, I just couldn't do it. I didn't have to get married, right? She wasn't pregnant. I thought about the mortgage. I thought about growing old with Suzie, and I don't want to grow old. I'm the eternal Peter Pan, me. I didn't want to go and sell myself short, understand? I kept asking myself if I loved her, and I honestly didn't know. I thought of how she got on my nerves with her constant nail filing and eyebrow plucking.'

'What do you want?' I ask him. 'Shepherd's pie or chilli?'

'Chilli.'

I start browning the mince and wonder if chilli is the most sensible thing, considering the state of Will's gut.

'I'm a bastard, but at least I know it.'

'I never was a Suzie fan, and you always knew it. And I think you did the right thing in not marrying her, but –'

'God, I knew that was coming. You're just like my mother, always leading up to a *but*,' he interrupts.

I talk louder to make myself heard:

'But you should have sorted it out long before now.'

'As I said, I'm a bastard. I know it.'

I don't disagree.

'You've got this table-cover on inside-out.'

'Just leave it alone, Will, for crying out loud. If you're going to take your frustrations out on something, do it to one of your own possessions. That was my granny's heirloom, and now look at it. You've ruined it with your pick-pick-picking.'

Well, might as well make the most of it. Might as well pile the guilt on in a oner. Make him feel *really* bad.

WILL 'Who's this Ian?' I ask Eve.

'Someone who's been hanging around for a while, that's all.'

Now I won't say I'm Mastermind potential, but I am aware of Eve dodging the question. Dodge city, I would

9

say. 'Is it serious? You've not always had a dressing gown hanging up on the bathroom door.'

'It's hard to explain. He comes, he goes. When he comes we have a good time. That's it. That's all there is to it.'

'I'm not prying,' I tell her. 'I'm honestly not prying, but look at the state of me. I've got to believe there's someone out there in that great big world who's got it right. Call me an old romantic fool, if you like.'

And you know what the cheeky bitch says?

'Parasite's more like it. You're just wanting to know all the juicy bits because you don't have any yourself at the moment.'

'I just don't want to tread on any toes while I'm here, that's all. If, for instance, Ian comes by for the odd evening or two, well, I'll leave you to it. Don't worry about me. I'll walk the streets.'

Eve picks at her chilli. 'What are you saying? Are you planning on staying here?'

It kinda takes me by surprise, I have to say. But I can think of worse things for sure. Suzie springs to mind. So does my mother, with her toast cut into fingers and the smell of Dettol burning my nostrils.

The day hasn't been a complete disaster after all.

Okay, okay, I'll never say any of my family or friends are Mastermind potential either, but for Christ sake, with a wee bit of nous they might have realized that I was at Eve's.

Not one lousy phone call! Not one! And it's way past midnight by now.

I'm on the bed in the spare room. Except it's not exactly

a bed. It's one of these futon things. Right, and since I'm suffering from a major crisis in my life, my sleeping patterns are a bit erratic to say the least.

I would die for a bed, just a normal bed. I need the reassurance of springs. When I turn over for the hundredth time at 4 a.m., then I want to bounce, not thud.

EVE Why, for God's sake, was I talked into this? Why on earth didn't I just tell him to pick up the phone and talk to his mother himself? Oh no, that would just be too simple. Remember, we're talking about Will here. And anyway, why do your dirty work when you've got some other mug to do it for you?

I ring the doorbell again. Still no answer. I know someone's in, because I see a blur of movement through the double-glazed door. A bit of apple blossom flutters on to my face from the tree at the bottom of the garden. When I look down, around the garden, everywhere is covered by these pink and white petals. It almost reminds me of confetti, but I force the thought from my mind.

The bottle of Dettol in one hand and the orange J-cloth in the other is the first thing that catches my attention.

'Hello, Mrs McIntyre. Can I have word?'

Will's mum's face is red and she puffs, a little out of breath. After a few furtive glances at the neighbours' windows, I am admitted into the living room.

I hear her wheeze as I follow her, and not once do her slippers come off the ground. Scuffle, scuffle, scuffle, she goes until she plops herself down on the sofa. I'd never noticed how old she was before. But today it's all too obvious. It's times like this I just want to kill Will. The poor woman's got Tesco bags under her eyes. As I watch her remove the Marigolds from her hands, the shakes are uncontrollable. God, I hate him. Sometimes I really hate him. No wonder he wouldn't come himself.

'I've got to keep busy, so I don't think about it, you see,' she says. Her hands still fidget with the rubber gloves. 'I've been meaning to clean out those kitchen cupboards for long enough, but with one thing and another . . .' Her voice falters a little. 'I'll go and put the kettle on.'

I notice a photo of Will on the mantelpiece. He must be no more than three years old. Even now he gets the same mischievous look when he's up to no good.

'He'd been crying you see. Just before the photo was taken. He didn't like his jumper. The neck was too small, so I had to pull it down over his ears with a tug. Come to think of it, I didn't like it much either, but his gran had knitted it for him and sometimes it's easier to just get on with it rather than cause a scene.' She shrugs. 'Mind you, after one wash it wouldn't have fitted a new-born baby, so as per normal he got his own way in the end.' Shaking her head, she places a tray on the table and passes a cup to me. 'Would you like a piece of cake? I'd bought it in for my sister and her hubby who were staying here for the wedding, but they left soon after . . .' Sadly she eyes the cake plate. 'It seems such a waste.'

The house seems empty, hollow even, as if the life in it has been taken away. I half expect my voice to echo.

'Will is all right. He's staying at mine at the moment.' All the while I'm saying this I'm checking her face for shock or disapproval. And when there's none, I have to admit I'm kind of disappointed. 'He's asked me to come round and tell you. He thought you might have been worried about him.' The Madeira cake tastes like sawdust. 'He would have come round himself, but he didn't think you'd want to see him.'

'Well, he's right there. Just as well his dad ain't here to see it. Poor Jim will be turning in his grave.'

'I'm sorry. I honestly am.'

'It just seems such a *waste*, you know?' Is she talking about the Madeira or the wedding? 'Are you two "together" now?' she asks. 'He dumped Suzie for you? Is that it?'

I knew she would ask this. My heart starts beating faster and I'm sure I blush to the gills. So I tell her that we're not together, as she puts it, and I'm not the reason for the wedding not taking place. 'He just needs a friend right now.'

'Mm.'

'He's feeling really bad about this.'

'He should.'

'I know. I know.'

'He should have said something long before now. He should have acted like a man. But that's not Will.'

I try not to laugh.

'I just keep thinking of all the *money* wasted. Suzie's parents took out a loan for it, you know,' she says, touching her nose with her forefinger. 'Sometimes I loathe him. Isn't that terrible? My own flesh and blood. The only family I have left. But sometimes I'm ashamed to say he's my son. All of those people . . . how could he do this?'

'He had a good reason, Mrs McIntyre. He realized he didn't love her.'

'Love?' she almost shouts. 'Love? I'll give him love. Marriage has nothing to do with love.'

Forever the peacemaker, I say:

13

'Well, he's young, he's still thinking idealistically.'

'Have another slice of cake, dear.' And she passes a wedge of sultana cake over to me on a clean napkin.

It's only now I notice the design: silver wedding-ring jobs with a white dove displayed in one of the corners. So this is where Will gets it from.

'Waste not, want not,' she smiles, going on to slurp her milky tea. She's a noisy eater as well. I can't take my eyes off the slice of Battenburg she's just popped in her mouth. Even when she's chewing, it never closes. Pink and Yellow. Yellow and Pink, until it binds together to make a mismatch of colour. Round and round it goes, accompanied almost musically by saliva tuts. 'I'm glad you came. I've not seen anyone since the fiasco. I'm too embarrassed to go to the corner shop. I don't want to see curtains twitching and hear conversations stop.'

I almost interrupt, *You must be used to it by now, with Will*, but I manage to restrain myself. 'Things will die down soon enough,' I say.

'When push comes to shove,' she says, 'he's my son. Here, my mind's been working overtime, thinking of him jumping under a train or into the Forth or something. Wishful thinking, eh?'

WILL Say what you like, but it's always looks that attract you to the person in the first place. Rightly or wrongly, that's the way it is. Don't bother arguing with me, 'cos you know I'm right. Don't give it any of this I'm-a-modern-man shite. When the shit hits the fan you're going to go for the blonde with big tits rather than the one who makes good scones.

I'm not even saying it's got to be Cindy-Crawford

beautiful. It could simply be a smile, the colour of her nail polish, the bra strap slipping off her shoulder and falling down her arm. Anything, really.

Lycra. What a beautiful word. What a beautiful invention. The man who created Lycra in my book is a genius. I'm saying it's a man because I don't honestly think a woman would have created something so earth-shatteringly revealing, especially in this day and age, when they're screaming about equality and women's rights all the frigging time.

That was the thing that drew me to Suzie in the first place. Lycra. Not every girl can wear it, but she could. Right, everyone's got leggings now, even Linford Christie. But see, when you think about it, most of them shouldn't wear them at all. Take for instance the other day, there I was walking behind this girl on the way to Princes Street. Really pretty, she was. Long blonde hair and a nice whiff of perfume from her. But she had on a pair of cream-coloured leggings, kid-on jodhpurs type of thing. Her jacket didn't cover her arse. As she walked I could see every ripple of cellulite wobble through the leggings. It started at the arse and quaked all the way down her thighs. I tell you, it put me off my lunch. Leggings are all well and good when the legs are thin and the arse is covered, do you know what I mean?

That was the thing about Suzie. I wouldn't necessarily say she was skin and bone, but boy, could she wear Lycra. It showed off her tight bum and Big Bristols. A few eyebrows raised, no matter where we went, when she wore those skintight clothes. What a vamp! I was proud of her then at those moments.

I miss that already and it's been less than a week. I miss the power she would have over me at times like that. She could be so sexy and so bloody vicious in the same breath. Whatever she told me to do, I did it without qualms. Jesus, that power, and it all came from Lycra.

But alas, I looked at her mother about a month before the wedding was due, and I mean really *looked*. And, for fuck sake I couldn't face waking up with that every morning. There's a big difference between a spud and a tattie. I had the jitters, then the skitters, and then back to the jitters again. I thought of cellulite and Playtex bras. No. I've definitely done the right thing. Forever is an eternity too long for me.

I could picture it in my head. Okay, the first couple of years would have been tolerable. Then kiddies would come along. Then the sex drive would go. The tits would go, the looks would go. We'd eat fish fingers and beans every night because the purse strings would go. And I'd still be driving my clapped-out Ford Fiesta. She'd be bound to love the kids more than me, so in my piqued neglect I'd start having an affair, then get dragged through the courts for every penny I'd ever earned. Then I'd be back at Square One again with nothing but debts and grey hair. And I'd still be driving my clapped-out Fiesta.

No thanks. I didn't like her that much.

EVE 'Listen,' I tell him. 'Let's get one thing straight, while you're here, we've got to have a few ground rules. You need to take your turn to buy the bare essentials like washing powder, washing-up liquid, and toilet rolls.'

'Okay, okay, Evie,' he says (he always calls me Evie when he's after something), 'is this a permanent arrangement then?'

'Permanent-stroke-temporary.' As soon as the words are out, I panic. What have I done? What have I said? Why am I so stupid? 'You realize within six months I'll probably be in a straitjacket, but hey, never mind, I'm not important in this world anyway.'

Now, I know for a fact Will is more a lager man than some pretentious prat moseying about with a glass of house white, but I only have a bottle of Soave in, plus it's a week before pay day.

I ask him:

'What about the house with en-suite shower and a utility room in Dalgety Bay?'

He shrugs:

'Suzie's there. Needs time to think, she told Colin. I suppose we'll sell or she'll stay there. I don't have a scooby.'

I suppose I should tell you at this point that Colin, the best man, appeared two days after the 'reprieve from death row' (Will's words, not mine). Okay, he ranted and raved a bit for almost three minutes and then they went to the pub to commiserate – or celebrate, I don't know which.

The bare-faced cheek of it. We women could learn a thing or two from these bastards. Why be on the verge of a nervous breakdown when you can go down the boozer for a swally and a game of pool? That's it, no hard feelings. No personal vendettas. Not one word will be spoken about it henceforth. Just a shrug of the shoulders and a nod of the head in acceptance and that was that.

Will drinks too much Soave, until he minces his walk and his words, but I tell him straight there's no way a picture of Ally McCoist is going up in the living room.

He cries, and I put it down to alcohol. It certainly isn't to do with Super Ally. I don't know what to do. It was bound to happen at some time, and bang! It's happening now. No big deal. I think the proper thing to do is not say anything, just let him be. I go and get the last toilet roll from the bathroom and pass it to him. 'It's definitely your turn to buy some, you know.'

2

EVE Ian isn't the kind of guy who's around all the time.

He's certainly not the clingy kind. Meeting me after work every night to go home and watch Neighbours together. It's just not his scene. 'Quality time,' he calls it. 'Quality instead of quantity.'

It's nice being in a relationship where the well of conversation has not completely dried up. I've always said I never wanted to end up like one of those couples you see often enough in restaurants and pubs. They're spruced up to the nines and then sit opposite each other with not one word to say. They play with the ashtrays, the candles, the beer mats, the stem of the

19

wineglass; anything apart from look at each other and have a conversation. It doesn't need to be a political discussion about nuclear disarmament, just a simple, 'How was your day, dear?' But I can hear them sigh from across the room, their tongues dried up, apart from the buttering of alcohol.

I haven't seen hide nor hair of Ian since Will moved in. This doesn't affect me, not in the slightest, this is normal, but boy, my tenant seems rather perturbed about it.

'What do you mean, he hasn't phoned?'

'Will!' I say. 'Give it a rest, will you? It's none of your business. He'll phone when he's good and ready. That's the way it works with us. We don't live in each other's pockets.'

'What are you insinuating here, lady?'

'Oh, for God's sake, stop being so touchy. Make yourself useful by cleaning the bathroom, or watering the plants, or something. Don't just sit there and fidget.'

Let me explain: it's Sunday afternoon, the Sunday afternoon Will was supposed to come back from his honeymoon in Tenerife. It's work tomorrow, and he's panicking like a January sales-goer.

He moved in permanent like, he says. Permanent temporary, I say. I still don't know what's happening to the house in Dalgety Bay with its utility room and en-suite shower room. I don't suppose I ever will. All I know is that Will arrived at the door last Thursday with a bin bag full of clothes, a CD player and a garlic crusher. 'My mum had an extra one,' he said, 'So she won't mind if she doesn't get it back.'

WILL I lurked about the housing estate making sure

she wasn't there. Like a common thief. I was peering in the windows and checking the doors. Trying to look low-key. But the more I whistled and furtively looked about, the more I looked *high*-key! In fact I'm sure someone phoned the police, 'cos a panda car kept circling the area.

Anyway, being arrested would have been easier than talking to Suzie, that's for sure. I'm no fool. I want to live to see my next birthday, thank you very much. So, believe me, being thrown in a cell with nowhere to piss seemed a much better future than facing Suzie. Those flaring nostrils and freckles as big as moles, when her temper was in fourth gear, are enough to give anyone nightmares. She said it was because of her red hair. But I knew it came out of the bottle. I remember those evenings when I'd go for the nibble on the ear and smell cow dung from her scalp. Yes, I remember licking that self-same ear, and having a henna strip down my tongue for a day. I knew the Titian hair was just an excuse for being a moody cow.

For a minute I thought she'd changed the locks just to spite me, but I was just sticking the Yale in the wrong hole. God, was I shaking, praying for fuck that neither the panda car nor Suzie would come round that corner.

The house smelt new, which considering it was, it should have done. Everything just looked so perfect, not like a home at all. Somehow it reminded me of a hospital, with that new, plasticy, emulsion-paint smell. I tell you, I was in and out like a shot, took the vital and vamoosed. Nothing to do with me. She was the one who wanted everything. She was the one who sent out a wedding list, for God sake. She can deal with all that.

Anyway, I've got a touch of the Paul Youngs: 'Wherever I Lay My Hat, That's My Home.' Easy come, easy go, that's me. I'm not one for possessions, as long as I have my CD player and Jazz aftershave, well, I'm a happy man.

I'd parked the car half a mile away from 'Sycamore Boulevard' and to avoid the wrath of Suzie I climbed over the garden wall at the back. I stopped a minute and imagined myself in forty years time: scuffling about in my beige cardigan and tartan baffies, watering the tomatoes in the greenhouse, using the 'trim-mower' to tidy up those grassy borders, patting the Labrador 'Pookie' or some such name before planting the hybrid rosebush I had created and christened Suzie Wife.

Boy, I had a lucky escape.

EVE There's loud music now where I would have silence. I wouldn't mind if it was decent stuff, but it's all this techno garbage. And the boom base is always on, and the graphic equalizer is always at 10, and it's got PBS and soft touch mechanism and auto this and remote that, and it still sounds like shite. I think I'm living in a heartbeat with the boom-boom-boom all the time.

It's nice though to walk into the kitchen and see the pulley balanced for once. It used to worry me that all that hung there were bras, knickers, tights. You know, feminine things. And no matter how I arranged them, it would always hang lopsided. Will hangs his stuff up at the same time, so we've got boxers, jockeys, T-shirts, socks, the masculine on the other side. And it hangs in balance now.

He's restless though. He can't settle. He's always been

the same, so I can't blame it on this nervous stress he insists he's going through. No, he could never just sit and read or watch TV or something. His attention span is equivalent to a doorknob. He sits down with *GQ* and I think, Yes, some peace. But within two minutes he's pacing up and down pretending to be swatting invisible flies on my head, or throwing cushions at me, or sighing if he's feeling sorry for himself, or farting just to get attention, or tapping his fingers on his leg.

He's always been a one for going out, hanging around the streets instead of staying in. For however long we've known each other, he's always been the same. He's never quite got over the phase of drinking Thunderbird in the swing park and puffing on the cigarette stolen from his mum's packet earlier.

Mind you, he's got his room sorted, I'll give him that much. All this black-and-white photography hangs on the walls now. Okay, it's not my cup of tea, but for Will it's quite tasteful. I half expected Pirelli calendars to be hung up in the kitchen, and call it art instead of soft porn. But he blissfully failed on that one. I'm saying my prayers every day just in case he gets a picture of Pamela Anderson from somewhere.

He's upset about Ian. Not that it's any of his business, mind. But Will has this habit of making anyone's business his own. He's a nosy bugger. Thinking he's the centre of attention in everyone's lives, even the poor shop assistant he buys his Clearasil from. 'Not that I get spots, but, you know, prevention's better than a cure,' he says with a cheesy grin, in-between launching his patter and bedroom eyes on the unsuspecting soul.

Let me inform you about a few of his irritating habits. When he has a shower, not once has he thought about cleaning the plug hole after him. Okay, I'll mention this before he does, but one of my pet hates is pubic hairs in the bath. Now, unless he's moulting then he's doing it deliberately to wind me up. I bet he's out with a comb, brushing his widget bits just to annoy me. Well, it's working, Will. So quit it, okay? Everytime I go into the bathroom I have to don the Marigolds and remove them myself. He says I'm obsessive. He says I'm pyschologically scarred, but still doesn't clean them up,

I've got a good excuse though. I've been living on my own. It's hard for me to tolerate dribbles of liquid soap running down the bottle, making a puddle. That stuff is stronger than superglue – even Domestos wouldn't unstick it from the sink. And toothpaste – squeezing from the top instead of the bottom. And towels left on the floor. And dirty mugs left in his bedroom until there's none left in the cupboard. And not noticing dishes need washed, or not caring, I can't decide which. The case of the disappearing teaspoons, or stains appearing on the carpets.

Believe me when I say: I think Suzie's the lucky one.

WILL She's mentioned the pubes, hasn't she? Jesus Christ! The woman's obsessed. She never thinks they could be hers. No. They are always mine. She's got a real thing about the bathroom. And the kitchen. And the living room. The woman's a walking bleach advert!

And she changes into her pyjamas as soon as she comes in from work.

'Why do you do that?' I ask.

'It saves clothes,' she says.

Well, I have to say I'm stumped by that one. I put it down to depression, myself. Sometimes she acts like an old lady. You know the type – those sad grannies always in the gas adverts leading up to Christmas. Well, there she is, shuffling about the place, with her jammies on, her dressing-gown belt flapping about after her, making endless cups of Earl Grey.

I was in my bed by 8.30 last night. God, Eve's habits must be rubbing off on me. The worst of it was that I couldn't sleep. Above me, the ceiling shook from thudding for over an hour. Thump, thud, thump, thud, thud, thud, thump, it went. I lay there and watched my light swing back and forth, trying to hypnotize myself into believing that they weren't having a good time up there. It started off fast, and then got progressively slower and slower. But it wasn't what you think it was. Pity. Eve told me this morning. Our neighbour is a step-aerobics fanatic. One hour steady she lasted. Not bad if you're counting the stairs on your way to your office. Not bad at all, considering.

'What's she like?' I ask Eve over the cornflakes, trying hard not to think about taut thigh muscles.

'A bear,' she replies. 'East German. Doesn't shave under her arms.'

'How do you know that?'

'A woman knows these things.'

Eve always comes out with sweeping statements like this. Maybe she's trying to build up the wonder of womankind for my benefit. Waste of time. Listen, I've watched one wax her facial hair. I've got women sussed. A bag of chips and a pickled onion before going for the slip of the hand, and well, my best mate is Johnny.

Thinking of this, I have to ask:

'What's Ian like?'

'Shut up!' she says.

I think she's made him up out of her depressed imagination. I used to have an invisible friend when I was a boy. Nothing funny, like. My mum tried to stop it, but I've seen the photos for four place settings for Sunday dinner.

And Eve has always been a late starter.

Well, what do you know? Ian has just arrived at the door. All as nice as nine pence. Flowers, wine, God knows what else. I mean to say – flowers for a florist? One out of ten for originality.

With just a peek out my bedroom door, I know it's him. It's pretty obvious, with Eve screaming, and those soft giggles she puts on when someone is chatting her up. I hear his voice and I'm trying to decide whether it's manly enough. Yep! He's definitely all man.

I hear him say, 'Black or white today?'

'Well, grey actually. I accidentally mixed them with the towels,' Eve giggles. 'If I'd known you were coming round, I would have shaved my legs and put the black lacy ones on.'

'Well, sweetie-pie, they're not going to be on long enough for me to notice.' Then it's the sighs and chewing noises while he forces his tongue down her throat. I get to thinking that he's a man with a mission, and we might get on quite well after all.

Eve tizzies about in the kitchen, rustling up some guacamole in her Moulinex blender. I walk in and catch them in mid clinch.

'Oh,' she says, all surprised like that I'm there. 'Ian, I'd like you to meet my lodger, Will. You know, the one I'm always telling you about? Well, at long last, here he is.' She poses like a magician's bimbo. 'Den-na.'

He shakes my hand. I have always said you can tell a lot about a person by his handshake, and I'm not just talking about the Masons here. First it's a limp fish, lulling me into a false sense of security, next it becomes a Stallone special, and then back to a limp fish. Temperamental, I'd say.

And Eve is still tizzing about, in her element. The two men in her life have finally met. I'm aware of the expectant excitement in her eyes. Her voice automatically moves up an octave. I'm aware of it, even if Ian is not. Well, looking at him, he's probably aware of it too. We smile (or rather, grimace awkwardly) at each other.

'So, you work in insurance then?' he asks.

Small talk. God, how I love small talk. 'Yeah!' I reply.

'Oh, oh,' Eve interrupts, 'tell Ian about the parrot. I swear it's just like the Monty Python sketch.'

'Eve! That was years ago. I'm in car insurance now.'

'I know, but it's still funny.' She passes me a glass of wine, and I promised myself I wouldn't accept any. I'd just say hello, and then leave them to it. However, it's placed in my hand. It seems rude to refuse.

At one point she says:

'Living on your own is so quiet. It's insubstantial, somehow. The effort to do anything just for yourself gets harder and harder every day. You just sink into a routine of eating toast and beans. Every day.'

Now, this could be due to a number of things:

1. too much plonk;
2. making a point to Stud Ian;
3. a sudden nasty reaction to the mixture of garlic and avocados.

But, translating from Eve-speak to plain English, it's a plea for Ian and myself to get on, be mates, go down the local for the occasional pint. Forget the hippie incense-burning cheesecloth-and-sandals thing. We're talking Eve-speak where east never quite meets west. Reading between the lines is a millimetre or a mile out.

I notice Ian's hand on her knee, working round in a circular motion. Time to skat, I think. As I say good-night I can't help wondering how Ian manages to squeeze himself into that pink dressing gown. He's not a weird shape at all. In fact, all things considered he's pretty normal.

Talk about disappointment.

EVE I love lying in bed, knowing that someone is going to flush the toilet and be back beside me in less than thirty seconds. Me, being ever so daring, I even stretch my feet into the ten-centimetre cold border around the pit of bent and stretched springs where him and I gravitationally end up. I love reaching over at four o'clock in the morning to find flesh, skin and bone there. It may snore and fart. And his backside may force me into the cold ten centimetres in the middle of the night, but it seems something wonderful at the same time.

You know what it's like after sex: it's always a race

to see who can get to the loo first. Well, I won the gold medal tonight. But unfortunately it's me who has to try and keep the bed warm. The time it's taking Ian, I'd say he was the ass. But what a cute ass at that.

Watching Ian, as he comes in the door, I see how ridiculous he looks in my old silk robe. How come I've never noticed before?

'I just met Will in the hall,' he says.

'I bet he had a smirk on him from ear to ear.'

'Just about.' He takes off the robe and climbs into bed beside me. His feet are cold and he warms them against the back of my calves. 'You know, I don't like him living here. I don't trust him.'

'Put the green-eyed monster away, Ian.' I've been waiting for this since he came in the door tonight. 'Will's Will. He's more of a brother than anything else. I'm fed up struggling with the mortgage. Just think of all the exotic underwear I can buy with the extra cash.' I'm stroking his thigh.

'I'd help you, if you needed it. Just ask.'

'No! I always said I would never take anything from you apart from your body.'

His feet are warm now, and he snuggles down behind me, in the spoon position. I hate this position. I'd rather see his face. I'd rather my back wasn't to him. It seems rude. I can feel his widget against my thighs, tucked there like a hot-dog in a finger roll. It's nice. Like a mini hot-water bottle.

I say:

'You know, when I was seven one of the boys in my class chased me around the playground with his widget hanging out. I kept screaming and screaming, hiding my eyes against the bars of the school gate.'

29

'I bet it was Will.'

'Nope. He had bright red hair and loads of freckles. I can't remember his name now.'

'What's this got to do with Will?'

'Nothing. Just thought I'd mention it.'

I feel his breath against my neck. It's tickling, but nice. The smell of garlic lingers in the air between us, but it's not offensive. I hear him sigh. He's dropping off to sleep, fighting against the snores.

Sleepily I hear his voice in the darkness:

'Is it permanent-temporary? Or temporary-temporary?'

'Don't know yet. I'll play it by ear.'

'I just want you all to myself, that's all.'

'Well, come around more often then.' I hate to say it, but Ian is a creature of habit. Without even looking at the calendar I can tell you what days Ian is going to appear on my doorstep, with duty-free perfume, flowers, and bottles of gin. Normally it's the 28th of every month. Apart from December 1995, when we went for a dirty weekend in Paris on the 13th and 14th.

He says it's work. I say it's routine.

Ian's a routine freak. Everything has always to be in the same order. Like when he's undressing. First it's the socks, then the tie, then it's loosening the top button of the shirt before taking off his trousers. God forbid if it's any other way. I'm just another part of the routine. He probably has me marked down in the 28th box of every month in his Filofax, noted under *Must floss teeth*.

This is the man who lives by that book. The Filofax is his bible. I know it's not for show. I know he's not posing. He just can't live without it now. From my menstrual cycle (a red cross in the top right hand corner) to the normal boring things like meetings and dentists, to what days he gets petrol in which garage, so he can monitor how long it lasts. 'This car drinks petrol like you drink Earl Grey,' he says. I told him to swap his Saab for a Cinquecento, but somehow that didn't appeal to him. He'd rather mark down how many times he buys petrol from the Shell Garage on the City Bypass at Dreghorn Link. I wouldn't mind, but he forgets about the saving tokens. All we've got so far is one replica crystal glass and the equivalent to the left earphone of a personal stereo.

WILL Her back is to me, looking out the window. She's got nothing on but her dressing gown. I check for the VPL first. Not one thread of knicker elastic in sight. Secondly, I look closely at her bum. The disappearing wedge shadows a thin dark line on the material. Her hair isn't combed.

As I go and stand beside her, I have a sniff, just out of curiosity to see if the smell of sex is still there. Not that I heard them, mind. I mean, it wasn't as if I had a glass to the wall or anything, but the toilet treks themselves made it pretty obvious. It could have been too much guacamole on the digestive system, but that I very much doubt.

I put the kettle on.

And she turns round. 'Beautiful morning isn't it? If you look really closely out here on a good day, you can make out Arthur's Seat.' She looks at my feet. 'Can I have your slippers? My feet are freezing.'

I kick them off and she begins to flip-flop about the lino floor.

She gets the mugs. I get the milk. She reaches for the coffee, and I reach for the sugar.

'There's only two here,' I say, when I see she's only got two mugs from the draining board.

'One each.' She looks at me carefully. 'He's gone. He left about seven this morning. On his way to New York, he said.'

I want to find out all the ins and outs of last night's extravaganza, but don't want to push too hard in case she goes ballistic.

Saturday morning's fry-up day, so I put square sausages and bacon under the grill. 'What does Ian actually do? He was a bit evasive last night.'

She shrugs. 'I've never thought of asking. Something to with finance, but it sounded too boring to go into.'

'He could be a drugs baron, Eve. Think of all the time he isn't here. He's a drugs baron.'

'No! And stop being stupid.'

Damn, least that would have made him interesting.

'And anyway, I resent that remark about my lover.'

'He's not . . . married, is he?'

'No time for that either.'

The grill spits a yellow flame out in a temper. I turn the sausages over.

'What's the time?' she asks, looking at her watch. 'Shit! I'm going to be late for work. I always am, the morning after the night before – if you know what I mean. It must either be the twinkle in my eye or Nathan's telepathic powers, but he always says when I walk in the door five minutes late, 'Was Ian there last night?' Never a good-morning or how-are-you, always insinuations about my sex life. Why is everyone so interested in my sex life?'

'Because you've got one, that's why.'

3

EVE Do you know what I love most about being a florist?
The smell.

I love nothing more than being the first person to
open the door in the mornings and take a deep breath.
Even before the lights are on and I can see the colours.
Forget caffeine, it's that first gulp of perfume that wakes
me up.

For those few seconds I think I've walked into heaven.

Then I start moaning about Nathan not being on time,
and all that crap. It's just me and Nathan here at the
moment, you see. And it's Nathan's shop, so he swans
in and out as if he owns the place – which, considering
he does, he's allowed to.

Flower Power is on Newington Road, situated between Oddbins and R.S. McColl. 'Perfect siting,' Nathan's famous for saying. 'It makes perfect sense.' He holds up three fingers. 'Firstly the wine.' He folds down one finger. 'Secondly, the chocolates.' Another finger folds down. 'Lastly, and most important of all, the flowers for what one might call the perfect evening with your lady love.'

'And there's a chemist across the road for the condoms,' I say. He always tuts. Then sighs dramatically, raising his eyes heavenward at my comments. Secretly he enjoys it. It passes the time.

Mostly I have free reign in Flower Power. If Nathan's not delivering the bouquets in his Range Rover, then he's concentrating on his bistro, Woodstock. I know, I know, the names are so superficial. He says it's to do with his mis-spent youth in the sixties. He believes when you reach the time of your life when you're happiest, then simply stick to it.

The problem is, though, he's a bloody hypocrite. The eighties and nineties have been very kind to him. He has flourished and the business has bloomed (forgive the pun). He's the one in designer clothes and always walking about with a mobile phone stuck to his ear.

Single-handedly, Nathan was the one to relaunch the sun-flower on the unsuspecting public. It was that display of sun-flowers that won us the 1994 cup for most original floral arrangements in Scotland. Now he thinks he's Van Gogh:

'We're still painting a picture. Granted it's without paints, but nevertheless a picture is achieved.'

Still, I can't imagine him in Jesus sandals preaching about free love, especially since I've had to suffer his nineties jargon about the Internet and British Rail privatization. Some of his time is spent driving round Edinburgh in a Y-reg Range Rover with *Flower Power: Forget the psychedelic and reach for the idyllic* plastered all over the place.

'The sixties sell, Eve. Just think of all that Beatles memorabilia on sale in Sotheby's last month. Besides which, all the customers we want to attract are instigators of the sixties. Okay, now they've settled for middle-class suburbia, but with memories comes profit. Remember that, Eve.'

The thing is it's a big con. It's not as if we sell incense sticks and daisy chains. We are completely middle-class, middle-of-the-road mass-marketeers of the carnation.

Today he says:

'Now, Eve, I know we are the John and Yoko of floristry, but really I think we should extend our happy little family. Imagine . . .'

I'm getting this while wrestling with a bunch of gypsophila. It's looking a bit brown, even though it's just a day old. I'm tempted to get the Tipp-Ex out to touch up the ends. Just to get a reaction.

'And I know you're overworked, with business picking up and all. And Mother would simply love to come back if it wasn't for the bridge tournament. So I propose – and mind this is just a thought to get the grey matter working – that we could get a youngster in.'

'You mean a Youth Trainee?' I interrupt.

'No,' insists Nathan. 'I pay my staff a wage, not a pittance. This is no Victorian workhouse environment here, Eve. It's my theory that if you pay more, you achieve more.'

I wonder if this is a good time to ask for a pay rise.

He sits down, crossed-legged, as he always does, with

the turn-ups of his trousers slightly above his ankles so a brief glimpse of his colour co-ordinated Argyll socks can be seen. Today they're black and red, matching his trousers and red cashmere crew-neck.

I'm still wrestling with the gypsophila and roses, which have to be delivered ten minutes ago. I wrap them in Cellophane and hand them to him. 'Number 121 Grange Road, pronto.'

'For pity's sake! I'm not asking you to part the Red Sea! Just give it a thought, if you don't mind.' He says before stomping out in a flounce.

I can tell it's Will from a mile off, by the cloud of ozone-unfriendly fumes. I open the door, trying to decipher if the bodywork is actually orange or rust.

'Well,' he says, 'What's the script?'

I'm too angry to talk to him, and I know he just wants me to ask him how was his first day back as the notorious jilter. But I know he wants me to ask, so I don't. Anyway, I'm still too pissed off with him.

'So, what's the script?' he asks again, this time a bit louder in case I've turned deaf since 9 a.m.

I shrug. 'Put your seat belt on.' He's just gone through a red light.

'I can't. It's broken.'

Gazing out of the window, I see Nathan opening up Woodstock for the pre-theatre trade. He's whistling.

'She turned up, didn't she?'

I turn round to look at him. 'How do you know?'

'How the bloody hell do you think I know? She turned up at mine as well. Waltzed right up to the third floor of Life Insurance, came over to my desk and started beating me up. So much for security guards. The bitch must of planned it. It was their lunch hour. Meanwhile four of my workmates had to pull her off.'

'Well, she turned up at Flower Power when I was there on my own. I didn't think I was going to get out alive. First she accused me of stealing you away from her, then she accused us of – well, you know – then she slaps me across the face. And just as she was saying her farewell line of, "Don't expect him to stay with you when you've got a face like that. He's probably fucking someone in your bed right at this very moment," in walks Mr Morton, the manager of Life's Necessities, for his table decorations. I was so embarrassed.'

The pseudo-turbo exhaust makes such a racket. Will turns up the radio so we don't hear it. Between the latest Boyzone single and the echoing of the underside of the Fiesta, I'm shouting at him. He comes to a sudden halt outside the flat. 'Will, sort it. I mean it. I don't have to put up with that behaviour.' I change tack and sigh. 'Do you never think about the ozone, Will?'

'The ozone isn't going to get me to and from my work, is it?'

I can see his pout starting. 'Look,' I say, 'don't get all stroppy with me. None of this is my fault – Suzie or the exhaust.'

WILL So, we open the door, and Eve starts lifting the junk mail tossed through the letter box while we were out. I step round her, wanting to go to my room and slam the door. You know, the mature thing. But I hear her scream, so I run back and look to where she's looking.

There must be at least twelve white mice scurrying about up and down the hall.

'I lifted the *Herald and Post* up and then I saw them.' She's crying by this point, clutching the mail to her chest. 'I must have woke them up.'

The only shoe box I can find is the one from my Caterpillar boots. I wanted to keep it. But when you've got a hysterical female and a dozen albino mice peeing and shitting in your hallway, there's not a lot you can do. Drastic times call for drastic measures.

Lucky enough, all the doors leading off the hallway into other rooms are closed, so it's just a matter of myself running up and down the hall like a complete prat, shovelling and cajoling the wee bastards into the shoe box. All Eve shouts in pantomime mode is:

'It's behind you!'

It's not until I'm driving to the nearest pet shop to give them a donation of twelve white mice that I get to thinking of 'Fatal Attraction'. I think of the rabbit in the kitchen and how when you use your imagination there's really not too much difference between Glenn Close and Suzie, except maybe a bad perm.

I look down at the Caterpillar box, bound tightly with elastic bands, and air holes poked in the top. And laugh to myself. Jesus, that's just like Suzie. I used to love it when she was immature like that. There were so many things she did to get back at people, without any remorse at all. And I used to think, Well, why not? Life's too short. Once, at one of my staff dances, I was chatting to this girl I used to work with. It wasn't as if she was worth a shag, or anything like that, but the next thing I knew, Suzie had lunged at her, nails full out and attacked the poor girl, leaving holes as wide as the Channel Tunnel in her tights. She used to remind me of Joan Collins, that way: all those scenes with Linda Evans and shoulder pads.

Funny enough, I didn't expect her to get back at me. I thought I was above her wrath. Stupid, really. But it's done now, over and done with. She's had her pound of flesh. She'll feel better now. I know her. That's it, finito.

EVE The interviews are today. 'Both of us should be involved, you know, Eve. You're the one who'll have to work with the persona. I own, you run, that's the way it works here. And we're both happy campers. I make money and you get oodles of job satisfaction without a narky boss always on your tail. So, relatively speaking, you should have the ultimate say.'

It's all waffle. I know it is. I know for a fact I'm not going to get to say one simple thing, have any opinion or even be allowed to ask whether they have any relevant experience with pot plants.

When he smiles, a row of slightly tobacco-stained teeth is exposed. And his breath always smells of percolated coffee, even though we don't have any in the shop. But these are his only flaws. Everything else is immaculate. The Argylls are blue and green today, to match the blue trousers and what looks suspiciously like a green golf jumper. The white cuffs – which incidentally manage to stay white for the entire day, without those horrible grubby bits drawing attention, shouting 'Dirty Bugger!' to every customer – peek out from under the jumper, with matching tartan cuff links.

The third girl is sixteen. (The first two aren't even worth mentioning.) And shy with it. Every time I look up

I see the girl's mum pace up and down over the same bit of pavement in Newington Road, stopping every so often to ogle in the window to make sure we're neither raping nor murdering her precious baby. If Nathan notices this he conveniently ignores it.

My mind wanders until I hear him prattle:

'Now, we've got some very big clients, and with the right training from my able assistant here . . .'

All I can do is smile lamely as he points to me. I'm being downright unco-operative, but I can't help it. Well I can, but I'm too busy thinking about the wedding bouquets I have to make up for tomorrow. White lilies, lots of foliage. A table decoration for the Women's Institute annual dinner for tonight. Spring Seduction, they want to call it. To go with their talk on teenage love and pregnancy.

Nathan's now on Woodstock. 'Now, any member of staff gets twenty per cent off their meal, and I note from your CV that it's your seventeenth birthday in two weeks' time. Now, wouldn't that be nice?'

Uh, come on! No! I can't bear it! Surely not? So I give him one of my *Don't Push It* looks. The young girl, who I believe is called Jennifer, hasn't said a word since she came in, apart from hello. She nods, and shakes her head. I know she's thinking, He's gay, how do I deal with this? Which, let's face it, is a difficult concept for any seventeen-year-old to cope with. I know she's thinking that. She's all jittery and can't look at him straight without her eyes being drawn to his crotch every now and then.

Saved by the bell, when I hear its gentle but persistent tinkle as someone enters the shop.

'A dozen yellow roses, long stem. For my girlfriend, please.'

I try to hide my smile, and act all demure, but it slips with eye contact.

'Hiya, sweetie!'

He leans forward to kiss me, but I shake my head, seeing Ma, Pa and the weans stare in at us through the window. 'When did you get back?'

'About half an hour ago. I'll take the roses while I'm at it.'

Not that I'm biased, but I take my time and choose the perfect petals, with the most fragrance. 'Do you want the discount?'

'Why else do you think I come here?'

'Come round tonight?' I say, wrapping the roses.

'Usual time?' When he leans forward to whisper in my ear I can smell Eternity aftershave mingled with cigar smoke. Must have been a good business deal.

'Wear the black I like.' His breath is warm on my ear and I fight the urge to kiss and grapple him on to the table.

He leaves, almost as quick as he's been in, and I stand and watch his navy raincoat saunter back out of my day in the meantime. The urge to run after him and tell him to just whisk me away from all this is reinforced when Nathan walks out of the back shop with Jennifer.

Everything is always so dramatic with Nathan. He would have made a perfectly divine Lovey, drinking cocoa with Gielgud and sipping Dom Perignon with Olivier. He sighs, thrice, to make his point. 'It's up to you, Eve. On your head be it. You're the one who's going to have the ultimate control.'

I stick another fern into Spring Seduction. It's kind of long, and tall, and a bit too phallic for its purpose. Ferns and a few sprigs of gyp will do wonders, I reckon. I can't think of anything worthwhile to say, so I don't.

'Don't fret. We'll see. There's not much point making our minds up until we are one hundred, nay, one hundred and one per cent sure. Not one of them showed any artistic flair, and that's what this business is all about. Art. It's not just about sticking some flowers in a jug of water. One has a reputation to maintain. One must not settle for second best, not when we hold the 1994 cup for Most Original Floral Arrangements of Scotland. We must hold out, for that person with that extra something. Just that bit of *je ne sais quoi* to emphasize their artistry. You wore a pair of burgundy tights which matched your lipstick, I remember that, when you came for your interview. And your status was achieved. Eve, my pet, we must hold out for the burgundy tights.'

To end his soliloquy, he hands me a piece of teasel and flounces into the back shop. I hear him yell:

'Was that Ian I saw earlier?'

There are times when the effort to talk to Nathan is too much. In fact, most times. He exhausts me. By three o'clock every day it's almost automatic to reach for the gin bottle or the Prozac. I have no energy to talk or even answer politely, especially when I know he's just fishing for some juicy titbit to go home and tell his mother over the glass of port.

'Well,' he carries on regardless, 'if it was, then go, my fair maiden. And deliver that glorified penis on your way, will you?'

WILL Male bonding is a fucker of a thing. Either it's seen as a homosexual display of devotion or a lads' football day out. Going to watch an Old Firm match is a male thing. Not for one minute would I even begin to mull the possibility of Eve coming with me – for a start, she'd moan about the pie crusts and peeing in the stands.

We went to an international match years ago when she practically begged me to take her. Scotland versus Greece. Mo Johnston and Super Ally up front, Jim Leighton in goal. It should have been one of the matches history's made from. But what do I get? Eve in my ear-hole:

'What side are we? What colour of strip is ours?'

And, of course, she's completely shut-eyed to the guys around her, tutting, giving it a wide berth, and male 'typical woman' malarkey. Then someone throws a pie crust and hits her on the head. I then spent my whole time picking bits of pork from her hair, explaining the offside rule and how there was a half-time.

'Tennis is more my game,' she said. 'They don't whip it out and urinate down the tramlines.'

This is all coming out, 'cos you know what she's done now? Acquired, begged, stolen or (even worse) *paid* for two tickets for the Hibs/Hearts match on Saturday. And God forbid I should take Eve. No. It's part of her male-bonding scheme for Ian and me.

Now at heart I'm a bit of a Westie. My dad supported the Teddies, his dad supported the Teddies, in fact, all my forefathers supported Rangers, so it's only right that I wear their scarves with pride and non-religious bias.

But lo and behold the bold Ian is Edinburgh born and bred, so Hearts it is.

'One team's like another,' Eve says. 'It's only their strips that are different.' Hazel Irvine, watch out.

He brings her flowers, champagne, underwear, Belgian chocolates, the list is longer than my overdraft. She gives him a football ticket with a paid companion thrown in as a bonus. I should be grateful, but somehow it sticks in my throat.

She thinks men are men, and should enjoy a bit of crowd/team participation. She's lost the reason (if she ever had it, that is) why we like it. She just doesn't get it – that there are teams and there are teams. Team spirit is all well and good when the team is the right one in the first place.

Besides which she said she'd tell Ian about the mice if I didn't go. And I'm not saying I'm scared of Ian or anything like that. But lets be frank here, my bum is moulding the seat of the chair quite nicely, thanks very much, and I don't want to give it up. Okay?

EVE My dips are famous. I can rustle up a Guacamole, Garlic and Herb, Peanut Satay, with the click of my fingers and the spin of my Moulinex. It's the surest way to a man's heart, I say. Dips and lots of nibbles. Don't overdo it with the carrot sticks, though. Men on the whole avoid things that are too healthy. Use tortilla chips instead.

I make dips for Ian coming round. He says all that nibbling makes him randy, so I put on the black as I promised. My hold-ups don't hold up though. I can't say my legs are too skinny, because there's enough cellulite on them to keep me warm throughout the winter.

Must make the most of things since he's coming around twice in a fortnight, I guess.

It's Will. He says it's nothing to do with Will, but it is. Of course, he denies it. There's no way on earth he'll admit to being scared of Will getting his feet under the table. And as for sharing a tube of Colgate, well, you'd think he's given me herpes the way Ian carries on with his phone calls every alternate night and his constant, 'Are you sure you're all right?' Just goes to show that a little bit of competition never did anyone any harm.

Nathan got these Hearts tickets from one of our clients, a Dr Blue from the university. Anyway, to cut a long story short, Nathan doesn't like contact sports (his words). He believes sport should be a private thing behind closed doors. I asked him what he meant, and he said he had arthritis and couldn't stand the cold. So I took them for the men in my life – Ian and Will, Will and Ian. Why shouldn't they go together? Stop all this threatened-territory bullshit that's going on at the moment.

You should just see them, nerves a-twitching and grimacing into each other's corners before the bell goes and war begins. The terrier and the dachshund – work out for yourself who is who – one yapping, the other barking, ears straightened, teeth snarling, you throw two sticks and they both go for the same one.

WILL Apart from a bad pint, and being at a match you didn't want to be at in the first place, there's nothing worse than a draw. Talk about boring. Nil – Nil. Well, wake me up when the punishment is over, Ian mate.

Nah, I'm messing. It's not that bad, honestly. Male bonding doesn't really come into it apart from the pre-match and post-match 'to get to know each other better' pint.

And what's my verdict?

A control freak. A tuned-in guy, to what he wants. An all-round, complete, content, life-in-control kind of guy.

Nothing wrong with that, I hear you cry. Take a page out of his book. Well, yeah, remember I've seen how wee his dick is in the urinals.

Anyway, I think he's a bit of a lad. 'No harm in looking,' he says, sitting there in The Broken Arms supping our pints and eyeing up the barmaids. 'Lookie-lookie, but no touchie.'

Do you know what it's like, though? Remember those awkward moments when you're in a lift with someone: first it's the smile and then it's the hello and then polite and insincere discussions about the weather, the lack of air conditioning in the building, and how many days it is to the weekend? Meanwhile praying to God that the fart you're holding in won't let rip until they get out at the second floor?

Well, it's a bit like that.

EVE I hate Mondays. Not as a national institution, or the Boomtown Rats song, but Mondays are known as Nathan's enthusiastic days. I agree enthusiasm is a much needed thing. But when it's Monday morning and you're waiting for the kettle to boil for the first of the week's coffees. And it's taking too long. And you're contemplating just eating the Nescafé granules instead. Then you can see how it's all a bit too much for one human being to stand.

Well, in he minces. Nathan's one of life's mincers. I sometimes think he would have been an ideal air hostess, with the flawless appearance and patronizing voice to match. 'Our worries are over,' he sighs, languishing in the prospect of no more traumas. 'I have found the individual who will salvage the sinking ship.'

I think that's a bit strong, but laziness has always been

a fault of mine and I can't be bothered disagreeing with him. Besides I haven't had my caffeine fix yet. Pouring hot water into two mugs – mine says 'Caffeine makes the world go round', his is 'World's Best Son' – I tense myself for the weekend's revelations.

'Well, in she comes to Woodstock on Saturday evening for the pre-theatre special at £8.95, if you're interested. And believe me, I was looking out for the burgundy tights, but she didn't have them. She wore a beret though, so that's a plus. Anyway, I'm getting off track here,' he gulps a mouthful of coffee. 'She came up with what I think is a very poignant and enchanting suggestion for the table decorations. You know how, always upon always, we have a single white candle bedded on a base of leaves and yellow carnation buds? Lo and behold, she advises me to go beyond that and have the centrepiece of the garnish as a single carnation bud, surrounded by a circular array of miniature candles. Now what do you think of that?'

Knock me down with a feather. All problems of the world are solved, and all because of some carnations and half a dozen birthday cake candles. 'Well, Nathan, it certainly shows tremendous aplomb.'

'I knew you'd approve. Good. Good. Art, you see, Eve, is a whirlwind business. You're lost if you stop. So she tells me she used to work on that barrow in Waverley Market, doing dried-flower arrangements, and we both know what we think of that kind of business, don't we? "Uncouth" is too kind –!'

Saved by the bell.

I know as soon as I see her. Today it's a cloche, not a beret. She smiles, the kind of smile you wear when you're trying to make a good impression.

49

'Oh, good, my girls have met,' he says, condescending as ever. 'Did you bring a mug with you, Poppy? The kettle's just boiled, so we can all have a cuppa and a good wee chinwag to break down those preliminary barriers.'

I don't know if I care that much to be angry or not. But I'm damn sure I'm not making the coffee.

First impressions are important. They linger long in the mind, and in my experience you never quite get rid of them. They're there, just sitting there, gnawing away at your otherwise logical mind. It's not as if I dislike her, but I don't necessarily like her much either, from what I've seen.

A good florist knows never to wear a heavy perfume – it affects the flowers and their scent. Well, there's enough Poison in the air now to kill off Day of the Triffids. I pray to God that's it just the perfume, though, and not the kind you put in your boss's morning coffee.

On second thoughts . . .

Her hair's long. That's what it is. *Long* hair, *pale* complexion, *neat* figure. Everything us normal women hate, and everything every guy loves. It may boost business a bit, but she's going to do nothing for my self-esteem.

'Give me a break, Nathan. What happened to "you have the ultimate say so"? God, you men are all the same, thinking of your widget first and common sense later. Not that you have any, mind. You could at least have told me five minutes before she arrives on the doorstep, tinkling the bell the exact same way the customers do. But no, you were just talking mince as always. I should at least have been given fair warning.' Once I start, it seems I can't stop.

'Eve, precious Eve,' he says as calm as ever. 'You deal

50

with the flowers, and leave me to deal with man management. I don't mean to upset you, but man management is not your forte.'

'You fancy her,' I put my hands over my face. 'That's what it is, isn't it? You want to get into her knickers.' And in my own sense of panic and dented self-worth, I'm scared to ask how much he's paying her.

Before I had met Will, I used to have this friend, Frances, at school. She was everything that I wanted to be. All the boys thought she was a complete *wow!*, with her long hair and figure that I would happily have sold my soul to the devil for. My dream was to wake up one morning and *be* her.

Sometimes, though, when I would look at her I would ask, What does she have that I don't? She could have done with a good brace for those gaps between her teeth, and her jumpers – always upon always – had long skinny baubly bits from too much washing at a high temperature.

But she had the wiggle, and in those days that went for a lot in school, with the long hair and fully made-up face.

It was pure Grange Hill stuff.

Except the real sting in the tail was that she never did like the boys in the first place. I always found it funny when we would go to the Youth Club disco, and there they would be flocking around her like vultures, dirty wee sods that they were, offering her a sook of their Kwenchy Cups and their last Salt and Vinegar crisp. But she would just shrug her shoulders and laugh at them. Naive, foolish me just put it down to part of the game, the game in which I was always the last to be picked.

'These are *boys*,' she would say to me, and while all the time I thought she was meaning they were boys instead of *men*, when she wanted a mature grown-up of twenty, who would buy her a vodka-and-coke and order extra pepperoni on the pizza.

It all came to a head the Saturday night we thought we'd go and buy our own vodka-and-cokes down the pubs in the Grassmarket. On came the glad rags and a bit too much blusher – to get pass the bouncers at the door. Actually after one drink I didn't need any blusher, since my face was bright red from the alcohol. After two I was flying. After three I was throwing up in the Ladies, and Frances was right there behind me, rubbing my back and cooling my forehead with dampened rolled-up toilet rolls.

It was soothing in a way, you know, just the way your mum treats you when you're being sick, just like that, and I didn't seem to mind it. So she must have seen this as a come-on and kissed me, full on the mouth like, with the stench of sickness still on my breath.

She really must have loved me.

That's what I've decided because there's no way on earth I would even be in the same room as some-one else spewing their load, never mind going for the snog.

But since then I've always been wary of girls who wear foundation lighter than their natural skin colour and need bridge work on their upper teeth.

The funny thing is, I met Frances a couple of years back. I didn't recognize her at first; all that weight she'd put on. A glandular problem, she said. I thought it was from too many sooks of other people's drinks, myself. Anyway she married a man twenty years her senior and has a couple of sprogs named Dora and Danny.

Poppy doesn't need bridge work, I'll give her that, but some serious neckline blending of foundation is required. Even with the cloche, and the non-baubly jumpers, I just know that she wouldn't have needed to buy any drinks or crisps herself at the school discos.

I say to her:

'Do you have a real name, or does everyone call you Poppy?'

She smiles, gurgles a laugh, and I can see the emergence of a spot appearing on the tip of her nose. We must take pleasure in small things.

'Well, actually it *is* Poppy, you know,' she says. 'After the flower. Isn't that fab? Being called after a flower and working as a florist?'

Don't they make heroin from poppies?

I go through to the back room to get the expectant-puppy look from Nathan:

'Well? What do you think? Did you see the posy she made for someone's first communion? Wasn't it good? I admit she needs a bit of cajoling with the oasis, but that's no problem, and we wouldn't want to take away all your little tasks now, do we?'

'Sometimes I wonder why I bother turning up at all, Nathan. In a week's time, I bet, she'll be able to run the shop better than a Timex, do thirty bouquets in twenty seconds flat, and have time to run round the corner to the deli for your blue-cheese bagel at lunchtime. Now – not that I'm clock-watching or anything, but – it's five p.m. precisely. So I'm out of here first for once. You can teach Poppy how to lock up.'

I don't like change, that's my problem. I don't like the evolution of things. Try as I might, I can't figure out why it's necessary in the day-to-day running of things.

Change is all well and good when it's on your terms; when you *want* the change to take place.

But, but.

But.

I just don't understand why things have to change when they seem to be working perfectly well *without* the change. Why must people always interfere with things? *Why?* Is it something to do with boredom? Is Nathan bored with my table decorations? Does he want new blood for old, with new ideas, new methods, and just as much pomp as he's capable of? Have I shot my last sarcastic remark?

And, as usual, it doesn't just involve work. It includes the whole picture. I get to thinking about things and thinking about myself. Here I am, approaching thirty, with nothing to speak of but a mortgage and a jewellery box left to me by grandmother which may or may not be worth a couple of hundred quid.

In a way, that's why I stick it out with Ian. Maybe. I would hate to call myself a 'routine sort of person'. Ian would see it as a compliment, but I don't. Now with a few gin-and-tonics sloshing about inside me, I can see that perhaps I am after all. Better sticking with the devil you know . . . etc.

I am old. I am one of these people who was born old. I am the one who wore sensible shoes when they weren't in fashion. I am the one whose mother thought a revolution would start when her daughter began wearing her shirt outside of her jeans. I am the one who wanted a Laura Ashley dress for her eighteenth birthday.

Now this could just be me picking up the wrong end of the stick, but on Princes Street I always walk by McDonald's with green cheese coming out of my ears. There's forever laughter erupting on to the street and crowds of friends in jeans and labelled shoes making a whole lot of noise eating their chips and sharing gulps from their strawberry milkshakes. It could be something to do with too many mad-cow burgers but even so I would really enjoy that, just occasionally, instead of a pot of tea and a sticky bun.

WILL 'Poppy, you say?' I have to ask. Okay, Eve's being a pain in the arse, but if needs must. All I want is to find out some gen . . .

A heavy sigh. 'So she says. After the flower.' Another sigh.

'It just so happens that poppies are my favourite flowers.'

'No, Will. Please. No.' She's practically begging me. 'Anyway, she's not your type.'

'How do you know what type I like?' I don't really want to tell her it's been so long since a shag that all types are my type. It's about time the salami was dusted and given a good airing.

'Well, she's not exactly Pamela Anderson.'

'What? No chest?'

'Double AA cup, I would say.'

'Jesus!'

55

The bitch sees the disappointment on my face and smiles:

'And she wears baggy clothes.'

'Jesus!'

'She's not exactly what you'd call trendy. I asked her if she'd heard of Lycra and she thought it was a hybrid rose. And she's never heard of Oasis or Blur.'

Jesus! Forget I asked. Then again, I could be just the man to educate her.

Eve's dragging the ironing board out from behind the fridge and setting it up like a deck chair right bang in the middle of the kitchen. Maybe, if I just conveniently leave my shirts there and disappear out the door, then she'll do them for me.

'Don't even think about it, Will,' is all she says.

4

WILL I have shed the black armbands.

Suzie's not dead and neither am I. As from today, the rest of my life begins. Fuck it, I say. I made the decision. Life's too short. Fuck it.

I've been suffocated. Nope, not by the Tesco carrier bag over my head. None of this sexual asphyxiation for me. Not like those Tory pervs. No. I'm talking about guilt here. Waking up in the middle of the night not being able to breathe and my heart thumping so much I think I'm having a heart attack every time I think of Suzie. I tell you, this guilt business has just fucked me up good and proper.

I'm a complete shit. I know it. I'm a complete bastard,

and boy do I feel bad about it. But fuck it, I say. Fuck it. Life's too short.

I've had this stomach ulcer for too long. I'm dosed up with peptide-something-or-other, that must be shaken before swallowing. I'm fed up with its chalky taste and what feels like clay drying in my stomach. I tell you, if I jumped into a swimming pool after swallowing that stuff, I'd sink faster than Robert Maxwell.

I've had enough sleepless nights and dreams of the dreaded 'S' with a pickaxe.

I'm not putting up with the cold shoulder or sniggering from anyone any more. Not that anyone has had the balls to say anything to my face. It's more like conversations stopping when I walk by the girls at work. Then the sniggers behind my back. And this is not paranoia. This is the facts of life in Golden Lifetimes.

All the lads do is smile that knowing smile, take me out for a pint at lunchtimes and I don't have to buy a round. The man would buy the pint and the woman would pour it over me. Maybe I should do this more often.

But just drink quickly . . .

Guilt . . .

God . . .

I mean, why did I call the wedding off? Was it to sit in and watch Brookside and Coronation Street every night? And get hooked on Delia Smith cookery programmes? So I can tell a sun-dried tomato from a tinned tomato? If I had wanted to know how long to poach a herring I would have got married and had her to do it for me, wouldn't I?

As it is, I'm free. So many young ladies just dying to get into my boxers, and it would be cruel to deprive them.

And tonight is Saturday night! Saturday night, as in

the-first-Saturday-night-after-payday night! Tonight is the liberation of my bachelorhood!

'Don't you think bachelor sounds a bit stuffy?' Eve asks.

On goes a dab or twenty of Jazz aftershave. She's sitting on top of the toilet, watching me get ready to go out. I gaze into the mirror, pulling my hair back from my forehead.

'Doesn't it remind you of Cliff Richard? Bachelor, that is? You should have got married, Will. Husband doesn't sound like Cliff Richard.'

'Do you think I'm going bald?' I turn round to show Eve my forehead.

'No.'

'I am, look! Can't you see it? My receding hairline? Jee-sus, my dad was bald. He told me he remembered the exact day he woke up and realized he was bald – seventeenth of May 1964. He was only thirty-two.'

'You've got a few years yet, so calm down.'

'But look!' I grab my brush, some hair gel and push it all forward, puffing my fringe out a bit to give it some body. I'm not exactly panicking, but I get to thinking: maybe I was a bit hasty to call off the only option I had.

'Some bald men are very distinguished. Look at Jean-Luc Picard, or Andre Agassi.'

'Yeah, but I don't play tennis and I'm not partial to Klingons, thanks very much.'

They might as well hammer the last nail in my coffin. That's it. I'm kaput, finito. I'm going to be one of those guys left on the shelf who wears brown and a tweed cap when driving. In a few years true desperation will set in. Picture it: there I'll be buying a wig to go on a blind date with a red carnation stuck in my top buttonhole and all because her personal ad says, *All men considered (including balders)*. 'Evie, sweetheart, come out with me.'

Or even worse, end up with just one strand, which I'll sweep over my forehead like some sad baldy fucker and when it's windy, it'll stand on end and wave hello to everyone going by.

Her knees are hunched up beside her, her head rests on them and her arms cuddle round them. She looks cute in an Eve kind of way, sitting there in her pink jammies, and dressing gown with the belt flapping about as normal. Her feet are bare. Her toenails could do with a good trimming. And a bit of red polish. Her short hair spikes as she sweeps her hand through it.

'Give me a break,' she says. 'Do you think I'd get any pleasure at all out of ten pints of Newcastle Brown Ale, a snog and grope in the corner of some dive with someone who's chewing Hubba Bubba and then, to top it all, a late night Lamb Vindaloo? Call me a spoilsport, but I could just stick my fingers down my throat now, throw up, and save all that money.'

This waistcoat is my pride and joy. Some people say it's pink. Salmon pink, Eve says. I don't really care what colour they call it. I've not got a problem with pink. Yeah, maybe with a pink dressing gown, but not with a waistcoat. There's a big difference between a dressing gown and a waistcoat. Just think about the overtones of a pink dressing gown. That's much more a part of you, it belongs to you, it covers up the scuddy bits, whereas a salmon pink waistcoat is just part of the floor show.

Pink to make the girls wink.

My manhood seeps out of every pore in this waistcoat. I don't need to be a complete extrovert about it. Pink shows sensitivity. A man in touch with his feminine side.

That's the look I'm going for tonight. Pink to make the girls wink, drink, and maybe a bit of the other.

'Your bum looks good in those jeans,' she says. 'I wish my bum looked as good as yours.' She's still eyeing up my arse. I can see her reflection in the mirror. She sighs. 'Do you suffer from cellulite?'

'Nope! Now go and put some music on the boogie box? Get me in the mood. And none of your shite, okay?' When I say shite, I mean *shite*. I mean to say, you'd think she was a granny the way she carries on. Straight to the Easy Listening department in HMV. Frank Sinatra's her all-time favourite. But I can't be bothered with 'Come Fly With Me' tonight. If she puts that on, well, I swear I'll go and throw the hi-fi out the window. Well, I would do if it wasn't mine. Just throw Frankie-boy out instead.

'Why is it only women who get cellulite? Here am I eating bran flakes and fruit, and there's you eating mars bars and sausages. Life's a bitch.'

'Either Oasis or Pulp, please.'

Completely ignoring me, she asks:

'I take it you're on the pull tonight? Normally it's just a squirt of Lynx, but tonight it's gallons of Jazz, I see.' She sniffs the bottle and sprays a bit on her wrists and neck. 'It's quite fruity, isn't it?'

The mirror's a bit too short for me to see my whole reflection. I'd quite like to see my arse, just to make sure it's as fab as Eve says. Let's be honest, her opinion means fuck all. A footballer's arse, that's what you aim for. An arse like Paul Gascoigne's – meaty but in a firm way. Something to hold on to.

'I don't want to sound mumsy here, but it's a long while since you've been on the pull. Take precautions.

This is the AIDS capital of Europe, in case you didn't know.'

I tut in my Most Exasperated way. 'You're right, you are mumsy. Give it a rest, will you?'

'Okay, okay, forget I said anything. Just don't come running to me when you get the clap. I'll go and get a couple of Tennent's.' She pads out of the bathroom. And I hear the slap sound of her bare feet on the lino. It's a sound I've got to know. I can set the clock by the sounds of Eve's feet on the lino. I know it's morning because it's loud and fast, the heels thundering down on the poor cement beneath. Big cracks to be revealed when she decides on carpet. By night, the slaps are lethargic, with the heels hardly being lifted off the ground at all. You'd think she was Quasimodo the way she carries on sometimes:

Slap, draaag, slap, draaag, slap, draaag.

'Disco 2000' comes in by the speaker above the shower. I've not been a complete idle bastard since I moved in here, you know. No. You'd be surprised by where I've managed to wire speakers into.

EVE I'm like a wee squirrel hoarding snack things under my bed to eat when Will's not in, or even worse when he is. I just sneak into my room for a quick fix and then go back into the living room with a mouthful and crumbs down my front.

I find a wrapper for a packet of Abernethy biscuits there, and immediately the guilt feeling starts in the gut. It always starts there, with the sick feeling, and the ugly feeling and the I-want-to-throw-up-in-disgust-with-myself feeling.

62

I'm practically right under the bed now, and I find a couple of empty packets of crisps (reduced fat, though), and an empty box of Mr Kipling Almond Slices. And a nectarine stone. That must have been one of my righteous phases on healthy eating.

Secrecy is the best bit about it, not the actual eating of the stuff. No, that's a lie. Eating is the best part of it. I just don't see why I should share it, so I don't.

On the odd occasion I eat and eat and eat until my sides are sore. I don't make myself sick or anything like that. I don't have an eating disorder, except the guilt starts almost when I start. They go together, food and guilt.

Why? I reason with myself. Why shouldn't I have treats? I have enough hassle to cope with, without worrying about how many calories are in a Cadbury's fruit-and-nut.

And I could eat as many salads as any rabbit, but would then want to order Banoffi pie for pudding.

I'm not fat.

Okay, I have as many fat days as any other female. As well as bad-hair days and ugly days and I-hate-myself days. But I'm a standard size 12. Nothing unusual in that. Yes, but my point is that one of my sexual fantasies has always been to open the door one day in a rubber mini dress. Just to see Ian's face. At the moment, he'd laugh: I'm no Tina Turner. Or Will. I'd love him to see me in a rubber dress, just to realize that I'm a woman like any other.

Just a woman, a normal woman.

Not his Evie.

Anyway, I stashed a French stick and some brie under here earlier. I put 'Sleepless in Seattle' on the video and I'm wishing I was Meg Ryan, or at least had her husband.

I'm not even past the Hogmanay scene when this noise of rabble comes from the hallway. My heart sinks, and it's not because I have to share my French stick. I want my flat to myself. I know it sounds selfish. But it's my home, and occasionally I don't want Will to inflict himself upon it. It needs a rest as much as I do.

'Hiya, Evie,' he says, all innocent-like, that comes from too many pints. 'Let me introduce you to my mates here.'

'What happened to your lads' night out?' I know I'm not making enough effort to keep the disappointment out of my voice. He's unaware of it anyway.

'Plan A dumped, plan B in operation – a lads' night in!'

'All fuckin' students,' this guy says. He's small, with short, stubby fingers. I guess he's got a chip as big as a frying pan on his shoulder. 'All DMs, English accents and milk-bottle glasses.'

'Where d'ye go?' I ask, tightening the belt around my dressing gown.

'Grassmarket.' This comes from a six-footer-plus with long eyelashes and small buttocks. The kind I could hold in my hands and do my melon testing routine.

'Bertie's is good, so I've heard. It's trendy.'

'Piss!' This comes from Will.

Everyone laughs, apart from me. Everyone's still standing and I tell them to sit down.

Melon Buns says:

'Willie here was chatting up this girl there. A bit of alright she was too. Anyway, she asks him what he thinks the meaning of life is. And he says, "A fuck, a fart and a good shit." And we were all pissing ourselves, but she was having none of it. Just turned her back on him and marched off.'

'Students, fucking students.' This comes from Stubby Fingers. 'Twats and teases, the fucking lot of them. "You'll no respect me in the morning," they say in their snooty voices. Too fucking right. That's what's wrong with this city. Too many students. Too many twats and teases.'

'Anyone like a drink?' I ask. The toilet flushes and I quickly look at Will. I can hear the pipes from the cistern overhead. His back is to me, choosing a CD or something. Colin walks into the living room, smiling politely. The mummy's boy. There's one in every group. He takes his jacket off and asks:

'Where can I put this? It's real Valentino, and I don't want anything to happen to it.'

I point to the dining room table:

'It's real MFI and if anything happens to it, then I'll personally dissolve your Valentino originale in acid, okay?' Aggression is a good policy, I think, given the circumstances of my video night being disturbed.

Will gets the drinks. They're all sitting on the floor, drinking straight from the cans of Tennent's or McEwan's. Will is the only one sitting with a can of Stella Artois. This just about sums him up, the big poseur.

'We could make cocktails,' he says.

Melon Buns, otherwise known as Paul, says:

'Ya dancer!'

I look in the direction of my drinks cabinet, wondering if I should run and get a padlock. I wouldn't exactly say it was a drinks cabinet, more of a cupboard under the sink.

'Margaritas. Multiple Orgasms. Sloe Comforting Screws. What do you say, lads?'

Well, out come all sorts of concoctions from the back of the cupboard, that I had forgotten were there. I never drink on my own. It seems kind of sad. Desperate, really. It's a statement saying: I've given life my best shot, and this is all it's got to offer.

The way I see it, I've still *some* time left. Maybe if I reach the age of forty and have neither a husband nor children, then I can concentrate on self-destructive twenty-four-hour binges.

But the way things are going now, I'll not need to worry about it tomorrow, never mind in ten years time. Old Mother Hubbard already, so I am. And the cupboard was bare. All that's left in the corners are wisps of fluff and bits of crisps. With the back of my hand I quickly brush the crumbs on to the floor. I don't want them to think I'm unclean, or that the cupboard hasn't been opened for a long long time. Whichever is worse.

Anyway, I leave them to it in the kitchen, mixing this and mixing that. At one point I hear my Moulinex blender going and I'm almost in tears. Bang go my dips. I turn down the music, some weird drumbeat kind of thing that I just know the neighbours won't like.

In they come with smug grins from ear to ear. I'm pretending to flick through the *Radio Times* or one of Will's *GQ* magazines, I don't know which. I'm just turning the pages while listening, in fact, straining to find out what they're up to. I'm worried about my Moulinex.

They hand me a glass of something I can hardly describe as awe-inspiring. The colour's a bit like the inside of an avocado, except there aren't any in the house. I just know my Moulinex is ruined. I taste it. I taste it again with a cheer from the gang. 'Get it down, Get it down, Get it down,' sings Craig (aka Stubby Fingers), chanting as if on the terraces. My tongue sticks to the roof of my mouth before the inevitable cough, and I begin to think

I'm in dangerous territory here. There's no recipe book for cocktails in the kitchen and I guess they're just making them up as they go along.

Noise.

I wish it would just disappear. Why must they be so bloody noisy? Have a few beers, yes. Have a few laughs, but just do it quietly. The volume goes back up to full earthquake-disaster intensity, but I let it pass. Let Will deal with it, although I know he won't. I consider changing out of my PJs into jeans, but when I try to stand up, my legs give way.

WILL Ah, fuck! My head's stuck to the pillow. Ah, shit! Christ, my mouth is like a cow's backside! Fuck! Fuck! Ah, Jesus! And I'm desperate for a piss! My bladder's about to explode.

I get up slowly. Very slowly. Very, very slowly, and put on a pair of joggies and an old Batman T-shirt. During the terminal illness of my youth I used to want to be Michael Keaton. With both Kim Basinger and Michelle Pfeiffer in tow, he was in a much envied position. But, like any other Joe Bloggs Public, I sold myself short and bought a T-shirt instead of joining the fan club. Still wouldn't say no to knobbing Michelle or Kim, mind.

The cistern sounds even louder than normal when I flush. The flat is silent apart from Craig's snoring. He's lying on the rug on the living-room floor, with Colin's Valentino jacket over him. Jesus, I hope he wakes up before Colin does.

I head straight for the fridge. I remember putting a can of Irn Bru there yesterday, right at the back so no-one could see it. Well, would you credit it? It's gone, disappeared, vamoosed, and I just want to give up on living.

A funny smell catches in my throat. It's only then I turn round to look at the kitchen. I see the empty Irn Bru can, squashed and tossed into the corner. The work surfaces are covered in all sorts of things. A shrivelled-up lemon, egg shells still leaking yolks, half-bottles of booze with lids cast aside, Kit Kat wrappers, half-eaten bags of crisps, stale beer, flat Coke, stains as big as your armpits on our one unexpected hot day of summer when you're still in your winter woollies.

And Eve's Moulinex blender, all crusty and looking dead. I don't even reach for the power button 'cos the noise will be too loud if it works. But really, it doesn't look as if it'll work.

Ah, fuck!

I wonder if I should pack my bags now.

EVE I don't know if it's the catch on the door going or the sound of snores that wakes me up. Reaching over, for a fleeting moment I expect to find Ian there.

There is a body, right enough, so I turn over and cuddle into its chest. It's a different kind of a chest though. Normally I can scratch the stubbly hairs with my nails, like you do with a cat or you did with your favourite teddy bear. I like rubbing my nose against it and getting that tickly feeling. But there's no chest hair here. And although on the whole I would say that I don't like chest hair on men – especially when it works its way down the back and just makes me think of Charles Darwin, evolution, monkeys and bishops – still I miss it now, now it's not there.

And then I come out in goosebumps!

Paul lies with one leg and one arm trailing out of the bed on to the floor. He sleeps with his mouth open, and I watch his chest expand and contract with every new snore. I peek under the covers, and see the other hand protectively cover his widget. It's not until I leap out of bed that I realize I'm totally starkers as well.

Discarded clothes are scattered all over the place, in what I imagine people to call a strewn and passionate way. One arm of my pyjama top is the right way, the other inside out. The buttons are undone. I *never* undo the buttons on my pyjama top. I *always* just pull it off over my head.

My head hurts, and I want to cry.

Rummaging amongst the clothes, and on my bedside table, I try to find the box of condoms. I can't even see the shiny red cover of one.

My head *hurts*, and I want to *cry*.

I get this thing for clean knickers all of a sudden. I want a pair on. I grab the first pair I find in the pile of ironing on the floor, and then grab my dressing gown. As I open the door I curse myself for not having oiled it. I want the cotton wool away from my head before I have to talk to him.

The bathroom is empty. Sleeping bodies are spread about and I expect to find one in the bath – but I don't. I look in the mirror for telltale signs. I didn't have any make-up on, so it can't be smudged. I examine my lips for swollen bits. I pull my dressing gown back to check my neck for love bites – even my breasts, for Christ's sake. And all the while I'm crying.

Silent tears of why-why-*why?* fall down.

Anything to give me a clue, but nothing.

Nothing.

I'm nothing but a great drunken tart.

A loofah brush is just the thing to get rid of any dead cells on the surface of your skin. It said so on the packaging. Now I'm using it to clean away every cell that there can possibly be. I'm not panicking, just going through the motions, I suppose. I must look as if I've got sunburn by the time I'm finished, but I don't care.

Maybe I could become a nun. Okay, I have this problem with God, but I'm sure my doubts can be ironed out. Or maybe I can take up celibacy. You never know. Ian might approve.

Oh, God. Ian.

Nothing seems to have changed much by the time I come out of the shower. I'm sure, though, that I hear the front-door latch. With a bit of luck, it might be Paul leaving.

Bodies are still snoring heaps about the floor. It's a bit strange to see them on the floor when there's a perfectly good couch lying empty. On the other hand, though, I'm a bit relieved: what if they were sick or something? I once heard this story of a guy, a falling-down-drunk kind of guy, who peed over someone's white leather sofa.

Will's room is empty. He's been there though, cos there's a distinct smell of stale beer in the air. Plus the quilt is on the floor.

He's in the kitchen. 'That yellow blind is unhealthily bright on mornings like this,' he says. 'I should put my shades on, in here.'

I bought a yellow blind because I thought it would be cheery. Normally it is, but today it seems a bit false, especially since the sun is streaming right through.

Besides, I don't feel too cheery. And when something else is cheery, it just pisses me off even more.

I want to die. Now. Not later. *Now.*

'I thought I heard the door,' I manage. My voice is a bit hoarse, and I hope it's not glandular fever from snogging the wrong types of boys.

'It was me. I ran down to the corner shop for bread and some Irn Bru. It's freezing out there.'

He's dressed in his old joggies and Batman T-shirt he sometimes sleeps in. His trainers are untied, the ends of the laces damp and muddy-looking. He wears no socks.

'Did you go out like that?' I ask.

'Yeah!' He shakes his head at me, as if to say, 'Are you stupid or what?'

I don't bother saying that *I* should be looking at *him* like that.

'Irn Bru, the best hangover cure.' He pulls the lone clean glass down from the cupboard and begins to fill it. After downing it in a oner, he burps loudly.

'Pig!'

He burps again. 'Want some? It's the business, this is.'

'I'm going to make tea,' I say, coughing a bit. 'I need some Camomile tea.' I'm at a bit of a loss. I don't know what to do. I don't know what to say. My hair's wet, and I didn't towel-dry it properly. A drop of water falls over my face. I sweep my hair back, making it stand on end. But I don't care.

'A wee bit under the weather, are we?' He laughs. We move into the living room and sit on the couch. Or rather, he sits and I lie there with my legs on his lap. We look at Colin and Craig lying on the floor. 'Look at them, just a couple of kids.' He shakes his head. 'It's funny, even

71

though we're the same age, and we'll always be mates, etceteras, etceteras, I feel so much older than any of them. When you look at my life compared with theirs, I've been through so much more.'

'Yes, but it's all been self-inflicted.' I'm sorry but I've got too much on my mind to worry about a Will crisis right now. I mean, why should any crisis in this flat revolve around Will. Why can't I have a crisis for once? It's my turn.

'I suppose . . .' he starts, but I interrupt:

'What time is it?'

'Half past seven.'

'God. Is that all? No wonder I'm shattered.' Yawning, I rub my hands through my hair.

'Your feet are freezing,' he says. So he begins to massage them. I smile at him with what I'm very sure are puppy eyes. He smiles back, with what I'm sure are puppy eyes. And I feel at peace. We're sailing on the couch out in the pacific ocean, with only the seagulls and the odd shark or two called Paul for company.

'Will?'

'Mm?'

'What happened last night?'

'What do you mean?' His voice is low and husky. All I'm aware of is the massaging of my feet.

'Well,' I pause, stuck for the right words. Drama is always the best policy in these circumstances, so I sigh, a huge big one full of Woe. 'Paul's in my bed.' I muster another sigh. I look at the floor, checking the twosome are asleep. I whisper anyway:

'Naked.'

Will laughs, a deep throaty one. 'You dirty bugger.'

'Don't. Please don't.' I cover my face with my hands.

They're feeling pretty cold as well now, and they could do with a massage too.

'Look, Eve, I doubt if anything happened. He was pissed. He wouldn't have been able to get it up, never mind keep it up. Too many beers and that happens, you know.'

I want to hit him. I want to shout. I want to order all these strays out of my house.

'Not unless he's some kind of superfuck!' He laughs again.

'Don't.'

'And anyway, so what? It's only a bit of fun.'

'That's just typical of you, Will. It may be okay for you, but it's not okay for me, okay? You don't have to worry about being pregnant, or something.'

'Listen, don't get ratty with me. It wasn't me who was calling him Melon Buns.'

'I called him that?' I cringe.

'Yep, before you groped him and sat on his knee.'

'I wouldn't have done that. You're pulling my leg. Really, I know, I would never have done that. You're just pulling my leg.'

'You were pulling a lot more than that last night, lady.' He laughs, shaking his head. 'Don't look at me like that. I don't know what happens behind closed doors. Come on, loosen up.' He shakes my leg in the air.

'How come you don't get hangovers?'

'Connoisseur of them.'

We sit in silence for a long time, while he stills rub my feet. It's erotic in its own way, and if it had been Ian I'm sure I would have pulled his trousers off by now.

'It's your fault, Will. You're a bad influence on me.'

He looks angry, but doesn't say anything.

It is his fault. It is. I'm not being unreasonable. You didn't know me before he filled up my fridge with Chicken Tikka Masalas and a dozen cans of Budweiser.

Before he moved in, I had nothing. Well, maybe I had some peace. But too much peace turns you into a lentils-and-sandals type. Anyway, I had nothing concrete in my life.

Okay, okay, I have Ian. I admit that. But I wouldn't call that concrete. I'd call it more . . . rough casting. Ian's like a kettle, when I think about it – sometimes hot, sometimes cold, but most of the time not even switched on.

So, out goes the mineral water, and in comes the Irn Bru. Out goes *Scotland on Sunday*, in with the *Sunday Mail*.

It's fun, don't get me wrong. But sometimes I would like time on my own, to watch what TV programmes I want to watch, listen to my Frank Sinatra records, and read without constant interruptions.

I'm dozing by this time, in the state between dream and reality, when I see a white speck of a thing move from the red Valentino jacket and end up at Craig's nose. I think originally it's a white tissue, but then tissues don't have tails.

The scream brings reality into everyone's dreams, as Craig jumps up and leaps about the place. It's under the sofa now.

'What the fuck?' Will shouts.

'A mouse on my face, eating my fucking nose, that's what the fuck!'

'I got rid of them all,' Will says, scratching his head, somehow in slow motion. If I looked closely enough, I'm sure, I'd see the cogs going round. 'Fuck, one must of escaped. Wee bastard!'

'Unlucky thirteen,' I say, trying not to do the hysterical-female bit.

'Yeah,' Will says, still scratching his head, 'I thought it was a bit funny, thirteen being her lucky number, and all. She was superstitious like that.'

At this moment Craig holds up Colin's Valentino jacket, that's been mauled, chewed and basically been made into a comfy bed for the escapee. Colin wakes up and looks immediately at his jacket. And so an argument starts. Will chases about after the mouse. I stand and watch all this as if it's not happening to me. It must be the hangover. This place could drive me to drink, if it wasn't for my new vow to never touch another drop.

I want to go to my room, sleep and then wake up to realize that this has all been a dream.

'Come here, Steve, come here,' Will says, taking the mouse in his hands. Its red eyes and pink tail make me want to scream. Not because I'm scared, just out of frustration, just because of the hangover. Its eyes look almost as red as ours. He's probably been on the cocktails as well.

'Steve?' Craig asks. 'No-one calls a mouse Steve.' He rubs his chin from where Colin has decked him with a pathetic attempt at a left hook.

'Do you have a needle and thread?' Colin asks, practically sobbing into his gnawed sleeve.

'Steve McQueen from The Great Escape. The one who got away.'

'But he didn't.' This is Craig, now completely unaware of the Colin crisis. 'Don't you remember? He was caught again at the end, on the motorbike.'

'Listen, mate, you'll need more than a needle and thread for that.' This is to Colin from Will. 'Yeah, and

75

this Steve McQueen has been caught as well.' This is to Craig from Will.

'He wasn't on a motorbike though.'

'Have you not heard of artistic licence, ya fucker?'

I'm fussing about trying to match burgundy thread to the colour of the jacket. Even I can see it'll need more than a few fancy embroidery stitches.

'This jacket cost me over two hundred quid,' wails Colin.

'You're a lying bastard, Colon!' This is Colin's nickname since he admitted last night that he has trouble with his gut and that's the reason he's still living at home with his mother. 'I was with you when you bought it. It's just a cheap imitation, cost you no more than fifty.'

Colin and Craig start arguing again. Will stands oblivious to the noise, stroking Steve McQueen in similar motion to the way he was massaging my feet not ten minutes ago. I'm glad I was first.

'Get rid of it, Will,' I manage as my final say-so on the subject.

How could I forget about Paul, lying there in my bed? But I do. And it's all Steve McQueen's fault. So, when I open the door to my room and see Paul buttoning up his jeans, I want to escape myself.

WILL Something good comes out of everything. This is what I'm thinking at the moment. Steve McQueen's doing well. He's in this wee cage in my bedroom. And I like putting him in one of those ball things and kicking it around the place. God, don't phone the SSPCA. He likes it as well. Only last night I'm sure I heard him laugh.

Or maybe that was his bones breaking. That's a joke, by the way.

And to cut a mini-series down to an advert, Eve is giving it her all:

I'm nothing but a tart. How can I look Ian in the eye again? What will I tell him?

'Look,' I say, 'if you get an embarrassing itch or the red flag doesn't fly by six weeks time, *then* panic. But until then, chill out. You had a good time. Don't fret, pet!'

'I don't know if I had a good time or not, that's the annoying thing. I can't even remember going to bed.'

I tell you, though, what a fucker that Paul is. Jeez, I thought I was going to piss myself. You should have seen Eve's face. It was a bloody picture.

Right, out he comes from Eve's bedroom, not looking at all as if he's been shagging like a rabbit all night, and whistling What's New Pussycat? 'Ah, fuck it,' he says. 'Is that the time?'

This is in the hall. Eve's standing there, not knowing whether to cry or propose marriage.

'I've gotta go,' Paul goes on. 'My wife's going to kill me. It's her birthday, see, and I promised I'd look after the wee ones, while she goes to get her hair done. See ya, lads.'

Course, we all know he's not married, but Eve doesn't. She just stands there, saying nothing, her face white as Steve's and her eyes almost as red. Then she turns a distinct shade of green before going into her room and slamming the door.

We both get the munchies about three o'clock. My lady and mistress sends me to McDonald's for a whopper. How is it you always crave junk food after a night on the piss? It's the amount you want, as well. It's shocking.

77

So, basically, we sit and eat our mad-cow burgers and then phone out to Mamma's for a pizza. Eve thinks the cravings have already started.

Good day, all round.

Rangers won as well.

This is the way Sundays should be.

I'll keep it in mind for the next time a girl asks me what the meaning of life is. I'll say:

'Eating junk food, having a laugh with your mates, and Rangers winning an away game.'

5

WILL I've started to give Eve a run to and from work. Take from that what you will. She's says it's because of Poppy. I say it's because I'm passing it anyway.

Okay, so we all know that's not the reason.

Poppy's a bit of all right. Put it this way: I wouldn't throw her out of bed for eating crackers, that's for sure. As far as I'm concerned she can eat more than that.

It's just a bit unfortunate the way we meet. The car breaks down and Eve and I have to run to Flower Power 'cos of the pissing rain. Well, lo and behold I look like a drowned rat. So does Eve, but that's hardly the point.

And Poppy laughs. She throws her head back and laughs so much at the state of us that she starts crying. I don't think it's that funny, myself. But it's a nice laugh – all gurgles and giggles. I like it. She gives me a towel and phones the AA for me. It's hardly the way I wanted to meet her. But she seems to like it all the same – having a laugh at my expense.

'You'll be needing to change out of those wet things. You'll catch your death otherwise,' she says, biting her lip. I know what's she's getting at but I'm hardly going to sit starkers with only a carnation covering my dick, am I?

Then she makes me a mug of tea. Now, I hate tea but it seems a bit rude to decline.

'So you're Will, then? Eve's told me so much about you.' The bad things, I'm sure. 'Sorry to hear about your wedding.' Christ, is nothing sacred with Blabbermouth Eve about?

'C'est la vie.' There's loads of eye contact. 'It was the best thing all round.'

She slurps her tea and passes me a packet of Digestives. 'Oh, I know exactly what you mean. There's nothing worse than being in a bad relationship.' She shakes her head and tuts as if she knows all about it.

Well, she must have been an early starter, that's all I have to say. Jeez, she's no more than a baby. Actually babe is more like it. Okay, the chest could do with some padding. But as for the baggy clothes, Eve's a bloody liar! We're talking Lycra Goddess here – fitted T-shirts, short skirts, knee-length boots . . . the business! This girl is heaven-sent. This is the very reason I didn't marry Suzie.

She's young, granted. Could be a virgin for all I know. But I've never been a one to turn my back on opportunity. She's a bit too orange for my liking: that look as if she's just been let loose in her mum's make-up bag. But then again, she can't be all bad if Eve doesn't like her much. Besides, beggars can't be choosers.

So I decide to become a regular fixture at Flower Power, much to Eve's annoyance. Least she's getting a run to and from work.

'What do you want for your tea, then?' We're in the Fiesta, and believe it or not, it's colder inside the car than outside. I don't see a face. All I see is a hood with a fake fur trim. I see her breath when she speaks.

'Dunno,' I say. It's Eve's turn to cook. Joy to the world! 'As long as it's not that vegetarian stuff. I'm a man, sweetheart. I need some protein.'

'Well, I'll make eggs then.'

'Eggs? Eggs? I want meat. Do you hear me? I want *meat!* Jesus, when it's your week to cook, haven't you noticed the distinct lack of dogs roaming about the place? And do you know why that is? Because I'm out there when it's dark, drinking their blood and eating their hearts.'

'You said protein. Eggs are one of the richest sources of protein you can find.'

'I meant meat, and you know that. I hate eggs. I bloody hate eggs.' I'm a cranky bastard first thing in the morning. 'Jesus!'

'Jesus nothing, Will! At least I make things, not like you who just makes do with toast and beans or bungs a Birds Eye curry in the microwave.'

The Fiesta is cold, and chugging along is describing it too kindly. Forth FM plays in the background.

What makes me feel even worse is the queue of bus after bus, hogging the whole street, blocking everything solid. They stop in the middle of the road to let some prep schoolboy carrying a rucksack, a tennis racquet and a trombone case on board.

'South Clerk Street's always like this, and they never mention it in their road reports.' I give a blast of horn, and nobody's more surprised than me when I hear it honk.

'Maybe that's *why*. If it's like this *every* morning, then it must be *normal*, so there's no point in *mentioning* it –'

'Shut the fuck up!' I honk again. I like showing my frustration, I'm sure it gives my personality definition. 'Come on, get a fucking move on!'

Eve fiddles with the heater buttons. She's wearing red gloves with a green duffel coat. I remember my mum telling me, 'Red and green should never be seen, except upon an Irish colleen.' For someone who works with colour all day, it's strange to see colour co-ordination go out the window when it comes to her own clothes. I'm not going to say anything though, 'cos she'll just think I'm in a bad mood and wanting to take it out on someone.

'What you doing? It's a waste of time doing that. It's broken. I told you yesterday!'

'God! Sorry for breathing!' She sits back in the passenger seat, wrapping her arms tightly around her body. A week ago, when I started giving her a lift, she said, 'You should take your jacket off when you're in the car, so you feel the benefit when you get out.' Right, so I laugh, but I know better. And she's never taken her jacket off since then.

The seat belt is hooked through her left arm, for the 'clunk click every trip' illusion. But the police would know as well as I do that it's knackered. 'It doesn't matter what's it's like, Will, as long as it gets you from A to B. Nothing else matters,' she says.

Right, as if that makes any sense. I read in one of my magazines that a car is an extension of your manhood. Burning rubber is a fantasy when it comes to my Y-reg Fiesta. And you don't hear of girls having fantasies about doing it in a Fiesta. A Jaguar or Rolls maybe, but somehow a Fiesta doesn't conjure up any erotic images. Least with the exhaust falling off, I can pretend it's actually a turbo.

I'm trying to strain at what Eve is looking at. All I can see is one training shoe lying there in the gutter. There are a few shop windows: Pizza Express, Marie Curie Cancer Research, but nothing of any interest, just the shoe.

'I wonder where the other one is.'

'What?'

'Look.' Right enough, she points to the shoe. 'A trainer. I was just wondering where the other one is. What do you think?'

'Dunno.'

'Don't you think it's weird that on every road you travel on there will be one lost shoe. Just one. Never two. Never the pair. You can just imagine all those people hopping about because they've lost their other shoe. It's not like socks, you know. If the worst comes to the worst, you can wear two different socks and put it down to colour blindness, but with shoes it's a completely different ball game. How do you think they lose them in the first place? Don't you think it's really strange? And look at it, Will. *Look* at it. It looks new. It's so white. And I bet the person who lost it in the first place would never think of looking in the gutters of South Clerk Street for it.'

'Mm.'

'Or a bit of carpet. That's something else I've never

understood. Why are there always bits of carpet on roads? Never big enough to cover a floor. Just about the size of a tea towel. How on earth do they get there? Do you think people just toss these things out their car windows?'

'Probably . . .'

'I Don't Like Mondays' by the Boomtown Rats is on the radio. The first record I ever bought. I think I've still got it some place. Bob Geldof and the gang. God, those were the days. When music was music and we still had half pences.

'But why?' Eve pulls her hood down. 'Do they look down at their feet and say to themselves, I don't like these shoes, let's toss one out the window? I doubt it. Or see the bit of carpet on the floor of the car and think, this doesn't co-ordinate with the interior of my hatchback, let's toss it out the window?'

'Evie! For Christ sake, shut the fuck up! I can't be bothered with this at half past eight in the frigging morning, okay?'

I see her look at the shoe once more. It's simple. The guy's mum has bought the trainers in Poundstretchers or What Everys for their 'bargain price' of £2.99. This guy doesn't have the heart to tell his mater that everyone at school will laugh at him, that they're not trendy, so he conveniently loses one on the way home.

Been there, done that, bought the T-shirt.

It's quite frosty this morning and I get to thinking that maybe I should get the tyres checked. While I'm thinking this, I'm watching this youngish woman toddle along on her tiptoes, not letting her high heels touch the ground.

'Why don't people wear sensible shoes in this weather?' Eve says. 'I mean look at her, you'd think it was Saturday night at a club, instead of a Monday morning. Skirt with a beard, and black patent shag-me's.'

I look closely at High Heels' bum. It wobbles more than a boil-in-the-bag curry, but at least she looks like a woman. Not like the normal student scumballs you see around here, with their Doc Martens and the kind of smug, superior look on their faces that you'd just love to wipe off.

'Eve,' I say, 'I think you should grow your hair long.' I look down at her DMs. 'You know, you're beginning to look like a militant lesbian, in that get up.'

She puts the hood of her jacket back up and as she breathes, I can see the bits of fur wiggle about.

EVE Wait till I tell you this!

Fridays are always busy. Beginning of the weekend. Payday, or any other excuse you can think of, really. Mainly I think it's either so the men can get the leg over that night, or so they can get permission for getting pissed with the lads. But that's beside the point. Roses are always a big seller, and then carnations for the cheapskates. Red roses or pink carnations. No imagination, when it comes to flowers. Nine times out of ten, men'll opt for the predictable red rose or pink carnation. On the very odd occasion when a man chooses irises or freesias, well, Nathan thinks he's found a soulmate. He says, 'Flair wi' ra' fleur,' trying to be oh-so chummy with the customer. All the while he's full of simpering smiles and putting his hand out to touch their elbows or shoulders.

He's totally oblivious to the fact that the male customer thinks he's gay and giving it the big come-on. Another customer bites the dust, I always think.

'Is Nathan gay?' Poppy asks. She's practising with

snowdrops and a glass vase. I didn't think you could do a hell of a lot with those ingredients, but I was informed I was just being obtuse.

'No. Though he's abnormally close to his mother, I believe. Takes her out for a drive to North Berwick every Sunday, rain or shine, to have a flask of coffee and egg mayonnaise sandwiches at the seaside. When they really push the boat out, then they opt for ham and cucumber. His mum's very old-fashioned. She used to come in on a Wednesday morning to help out. That's how I know the goss.'

'Has he got a girlfriend then?'

I nudge her. 'How? Do you fancy him? Eh? Eh?'

'No! It's just . . . well . . . you know, I thought he was queer, that's all.'

I've decided that working with Poppy isn't so bad after all. It's good to have someone else to moan with. We're different, but variety is the spice of life, or so I hear. Anyway, we've decided to join forces against the management. Even if it is only Nathan. But most of the time he deserves it. She giggles a bit too much for my liking. But she's young. She'll learn.

I even told her about the Paul crisis.

'Oh, I know what you mean,' she tells me over a mug of coffee. 'But at least you woke up in your own bed. Something similar happened to me, but I woke up in his bed. Turned out nothing had happened, but waking up with a complete stranger in a stranger's bed is not a happy experience. Can you imagine?'

Yes, I can imagine. And I don't like it. 'I'm just so ashamed of myself. It shouldn't have happened. I have never ever been unfaithful in my life.'

She nods her head as if she understands. 'I may give

the impression that I've been about a bit. But I haven't, believe it or not. There are just some things you don't do. But when the devil drink is inside you, well, nothing is sacred, is it? Not even your bed.'

I told her I washed the sheets. I wasn't going to admit I threw them out.

She's certainly worldly wise, I'll give her that. 'If you're worried we can do a home pregnancy test when Nathan's out delivering – if you like.' She shoves another Kit Kat finger in her mouth in one go. She's partial to a bit of chocolate. Pity it doesn't make her put on weight or give her acne.

She must see the look of panic in my eyes. 'Or I'll come to the doctor's with you. What about an AIDS test?'

This is just getting out of hand. I mean, I don't even know if we 'slept' together. Doubt it, somehow. Surely I would have had enough self-restraint to not do anything.

Anyway, shouldn't the roles be reversed? Shouldn't I be giving my junior some advice, rather than the other way round?

The next day we scream and hug a lot when, in Will's words, 'The red flag flew.'

'Thank crunchie,' she says. 'I don't think I could have coped with Nathan when you were on maternity leave.'

A few single red roses have been conveniently forgotten about at the counter since Poppy arrived. The poor guys rush in, drop their jaw when they hear the price, then drop their money in an attempt to pay quickly before they change their minds. Then without leaving their names or telephone numbers, they run out the door in a tizzy.

Our – or should I say Nathan's – arch enemy's van (The Purple Gladioli) stops outside the shop and in rushes this middle-aged woman wearing what looks suspiciously like a Margaret Thatcher suit:

'Anyone called Poppy here?'

Mouth agape, Poppy nods.

'Well, this is for you.'

Inside the box lies a single poppy, for originality, and a card tucked there beside it. Out rushes Nathan from the back shop thinking World War III has been declared and grabs the box from Poppy's hand. 'Inferior quality,' he screeches, his face purple. 'Just look at those leaves. Greenfly, I tell you. *Green*fly.'

Poppy grabs the box back and hugs it to her chest. 'I think it's lovely.'

'Open the card, open the card.' God, I'm almost as excited as she is.

There's a phone number under the words:

A poopy for a Poopy.

Spelling has never been The Purple Gladioli's selling feature. I burst out laughing.

'What? What is it?' she asks.

'Well, all I have to say is that it's my phone number, but it wasn't me who sent it.'

Thought he'd be romantic, the fool. Stupid fool. And do you know what else? He used my Access card. Fraternizing with the enemy in Morningside Road, with my Access card. Nathan will never talk to him again. Will says, 'Well, you've got to be thankful for small mercies.'

Poppy still hasn't phoned him. She asks about him, but I don't tell him that. His head's big enough as it is, thank you very much.

We're doing this new window display. This big orange

Japanese thing. Looks a bit like an orchid, or more likely something Nathan's conjured up in the back shop.

'What do we do with it?' asks Poppy.

'Stick it in a chintzy bowl, I suppose.'

'Girls, girls, have you left your creativity still snugged up in bed this morning? This is a chance for you to shine. Show the world what you're made of —'

'I don't like it,' Poppy interrupts. Boy, she's got a mouth on her. And the problem is, she never closes it.

'It's ugly. Nobody's going to be impressed with that.' She waves it in the air and some pollen sprinkles to the floor.

'The Grange crowd. Think of the the Grange crowd,' yells Nathan.

She looks at me, torn between murdering the plant and murdering her employer.

'You know,' he continues as if talking to a three-year-old. 'The *Grange* crowd. Lawyers, accountants . . . well-to-do's, basically. People who think it's less pretentious to live in the Southside than the New Town. Think Big, girls of mine. Give them what they don't expect, and then they're loyal followers of fashion.' Nathan walks away, muttering under his breath.

'You know,' Poppy carries on, 'he's nothing more than a walking cliché.' She snorts in disgust.

So we stuff the monstrosity in a bowl and stick it in the window. Never mind that Halloween is approaching and everyone else is decorating their displays with pumpkins and black cats. No, never mind all that. We've got a huge orange weed in a bowl to attract the arty-farties.

'We could tie some of that ghost hair stuff round it.' We're standing in the doorway looking at the window display. A flying witch with an extended broom springs to mind, and I know just the place to stick the broom.

Poppy goes to serve a customer. I'm still contemplating some leafy reeds, when I smell Eternity aftershave behind me.

It's funny how a bit of competition brings out the man in Ian. I really should thank Will for it. Boy, his kisses are so passionate now. So passionate. Here, in the street, which we have never done before – because Ian is definitely a behind-doors type of man – he sticks his tongue down my throat and I actually quite enjoy it.

'Very Habitat-ish,' he says. I assume he's talking about the plant and not the kiss.

Well, who comes rushing out at this moment but Poppy, going on about Billie on the phone. 'He says his van's broken down and he can't deliver the irises until tomorrow.'

I think of Nathan fainting and farting about in the shop all over a dozen bunches of irises. When I'm on the phone to Billie, sorting out the mess, I'm able to look out past the orange tiger lily to see Poppy and Ian chatting away like old friends.

I want to run out and tell her to keep her claws out of him. But it's not easy when you've got a motorway in one ear and a hysterical Nathan flapping in the other. 'Tell him this, tell him that,' he says, while I stand there, ignoring the dramatics, and watch Poppy and Ian chat.

I didn't think he'd like girls who wore black eyeliner. No, no, I'm being stupid. They're just talking, just making small talk. Polite small talk, that's all it is, until I go back out. Nothing else. They don't have anything in common. When someone's taking Poppy out to dinner, for God's sake, it's to cheap-but-cheerful Burger King. They're in a different class. They're in different age groups. No, no, they're just chatting politely until I go back out. They're probably talking about the tiger lily and what to do with it.

'Amateurs, that's all these people are.' Nathan's having a tantrum, picking up piles of paper and then tossing them back down in the exact same place. 'Amateurs.' I'd love to see Nathan on ecstasy. He tosses more paper about. His floppy hair, which is normally gelled perfectly in place, is shaking loose and falling over his face. On second thoughts, drugs would be a bad idea. His nostrils are flaring, and he rubs his hands through his hair, patting it back in place. Tantrum over. Billie has run out of coins and will phone back after the AA man collects him. I can tell Nathan's mulling over the pros and cons of driving up the A9, looking for Billie to get the boxes of irises. He's muttering to himself.

No, drugs are definitely a bad idea.

And then I think about Will and what he sees in Poppy in the first place. Yes, she's attractive enough. Yes, she's a good laugh. Yes, she's got that way about her that men just crave.

Us girls crave a Galaxy bar if we're lucky, and make do if we end up with a Milky Way.

But men, the selfish bastards that they are, always aim higher than they ought to. The entire male population seems to want the girls with that way about them. It's the look of the person. The confidence. The very way she walks and talks. The gurgle of her laugh. The way he can smell her perfume once she's walked by.

And she can be the biggest bitch who ever walked the face of the earth, and it won't matter. Eyes just pop, tongues get all fankled and their widgets suddenly leap to attention.

And I'm thinking of Ian's widget right now: peering out of the window, trying to check his groin is flat.

6

EVE Gothic candlesticks are strategically placed like collector's items throughout the house. Ian likes candlelight.

Apart from that, I suppose you'd call him one of those minimalists. I don't understand it myself. To him it's a way of life. It's a firm statement that he feels he has to make. I never like to ask who he's making the statement to, or why he's even bothering.

All that space in which the odd yucca would work wonders.

I made the fatal mistake of buying him a yucca once. I carried it all the way down to Stockbridge. 'Eve,' he said when he saw it. 'Don't leave that thing here. It'll sap my oxygen.' He moaned so much about it I ended up carrying it all the way back home again.

'Don't the candles sap your energy too?' I ask. I'm lying on the king-size futon in his bedroom, surrounded by tall black iron candlesticks and thick creamy-coloured candles. I'm sure there's something phallic about the whole thing, but I suppose you could say the same thing about hot water bottles if you put your mind to it.

The walls are cream too. Everything matches. I nickname him Mr Next Interior Man, but he takes it as a compliment.

'Mm?' he says dreamily, which means basically:

Shut up, Eve. I want to sleep.

Klimt's 'The Kiss' watches me from the opposite wall. It's the only splash of colour there is, and even then it all looks a bit too bland for my liking.

He says it's classy. He says it's sophisticated. And I suppose it is, for a bachelor. But really, men are no good at soft furnishings. I've always said it, and I don't think I'll ever change my mind. It always either '60s fluorescent purple paisley curtains and a brown candlewick bedspread or it's this right-on minimalist crap.

What's wrong with the odd pile of old Penguin paperbacks? Okay, the spines are orange, but so what? The world isn't going to end because orange clashes with the wallpaper. What's wrong with the odd wicker basket, pilled up with old magazines (*Hello!* always shoved to the bottom, *Homes and Gardens* on top)? What's wrong with cushions and valance sheets?

'I don't like fuss.' He stifles a yawn.

'It's so cold though,' I say. 'You need a bit of warmth about the place. The odd plant. The occasional table with photographs. Anything at all, to give people a clue about you. As it is, you're a complete stranger, hoarding everything away, hiding it in cupboards.'

He moves over and his chin digs into my shoulder when he talks. 'You've heard of paperless offices, haven't you? Well, I just want a clutterless home.'

'God, you're worse than a woman.' The other day I caught him putting his kettle away in a kitchen cupboard. 'I like clear work tops. There's not much point calling them work tops if you can't work on them,' he said.

This is the man who doesn't buy bananas because they clash with his 'touch of apple green' Dulux-special kitchen. Apples are okay so long as they're Granny Smith's. Likewise kiwis and avocados, but as for bananas and the poor tangerine . . . forget it.

'I'm going to buy you one of those Braun mini-vac thingies.'

'I think you'd be better keeping it for yourself,' he says all of a sudden coming to life.

'What do you mean by that?'

'Maybe then it'll eat up some of your junk.' He's a prickly one, so he is.

Truth be known, I've been trying to pick a fight since the moment I walked into his house. Not trying to kid myself on here or anything, but it's got something to do with guilt and this Paul business. Not that there's anything to worry about, I keep reminding myself, but still it stays put in the forefront of my mind, probably planting roots and enlarging twenty-fold every time I think of it. And the cherry on top of the icing is this jealousy factor about Poppy. All I've heard about all night is how wonderfully witty she is. How mature she is for her age. How fortunate I am to work with her.

Well, join the queue, Ian.

'You know, Eve, while we're on the subject, do you know why I'm never round at your house? Do you know why I always like coming back here to spend the night?'

I'm waiting for this, with my customary pout and jutting chin.

'Because I get a headache from all your clutter everywhere. It's hard on the eyes, you know. Everywhere you turn there's another picture, another photo, another plant. There's always something. It's claustrophobic.'

I have at least to be defensive, I reckon:

'Well, at least I show a bit of personality. The way your house is, you don't have a personality.'

'Yes, but there's a difference between a bit of mystery and laying bare your soul. Think about it.'

I leap out of bed before he has the chance to grab my arm. I kind of skip in the air, and I'm all too aware of my breasts bouncing and making a flapping sound when gravity pulls them back down. My stomach protrudes like a rugby ball after that Indian takeaway. I can't find my knickers, so I put on Ian's boxers. It's funny how at time like this you're aware of the strangest things. My DMs are smelly. There's a hole in my tights, where my big toe peeks out. My cardigan has a hole in the pocket. Plus there are half a dozen used Kleenex covering it up. My fringe is in my eyes. It needs a trim.

He's still lying in bed, on his stomach, his head covered by the pillow. His elbows look really bony. I hate to see guys with big Adam's apples and these elbows look like two. I expect a swallow any minute now. He farts, just as I look at him, and that about sums it up.

It's all silly. Really silly. I'm just about out the door when he mutters something. I look at his head keeking out from beneath the pillow.

'Eve?' he says.

I'm waiting for an apology or even a bit of a whimper of a single word that I can pounce upon and make a big deal out of.

'What are you doing next Friday night? How about being my partner to this big office do we're having?'

Well, progress indeed. I can see his head now from under the pillow. And I have to say this changes matters considerably.

'What?' I demand, kind of lost and kind of excited in the same breath. 'Me? You want me to come, as your partner, to your dance? Well, well, well. Wonders never cease.'

'Uh huh.'

Sitting back down on the edge of the bed, I hold his hand. His thumb strokes mine so tenderly I almost wonder if this is love. 'I should have hired Will years ago.'

'What are you talking about now?' He tosses the pillow away from his head, and then takes my hand once more, with the exact same touch, and again I wonder if this is love.

'Well, to get some action. We're into relationship territory now, Ian. No longer just foreplay and the occasional shag.'

I think he almost regrets tossing the pillow away, because now he wants to hide his head again. I can tell by that frightened-rabbit look on his face. Partly because I said the *R* word and partly because he hates it when I'm crude. The laughter is a bit forced. Then:

'Are you coming, or not?'

97

'I suppose so. Can I get a new dress?'

'Do I have to come shopping with you?'

'No. I'll take Will. He's got more style than you.'

'Remember, though: I've got a bigger bank balance.'

WILL We're addicted to The X Files. Eve fancies Mulder, but she won't admit it. I ask her:

'You fancy him, don't you?'

'No,' she says, a bit too coyly, taking a sip from her Shapers Hot Chocolate. All through the programme she sits there on the couch, stirring the mug until the noise drives me up the frigging wall. Every so often taking a gulp or a spoonful with a huge slurp. Then she says:

'Look at that spiky bit of hair at the side. Don't you think it looks so cute? I like his raincoat. I think men look good in raincoats. None of this dirty mac business. Nice raincoats. It gives a man stature, don't you think?'

Personally, I think she misses the plot with her ogling of David Duchovny.

Well, tonight she comes in quite early, really. Just past eleven. I'm watching some programme about gorillas mating. Seemingly the mothers in this species seduce their sons to keep inbreeding to its optimum. 'Incest, a game for all the family.'

'Did you see The X Files tonight?' I ask her. 'It was a really good one. Eugene Toomes got released from that mental hospital. Remember him? The one who could metamorphose himself to get through different sizes of holes and then ate human livers to survive – remember?'

'No.' She's untying her DMs, and when she takes them off, her feet and legs look like skinny liquorice sticks apart from the her big toe peeking out. 'Ian doesn't have a TV. I've told you before. A thousand times. Just listen to me for once, and then I won't have to sound like a British Rail Tannoy.'

'He doesn't have a TV? That boy's strange, Eve. Dump him. What is he? A vegetarian?'

'No, he just never watches it, that's all. He prefers to talk or listen to music.'

'Jesus, Eve, why do you always go for the strange ones? Just once I'd like you to fall for someone normal. Remember Dilatory Dope?' I watch her cringe, which makes me laugh and laugh. 'His head was too big for his shoulders. Wasn't he into trainspotting?'

'Tropical Fish.'

'Mm, enough said.'

'Tropical fish are very soothing, I'll have you know.'

'Then there was Vance. Remember Vance? All teeth and skin-tight jeans.'

I can see she's trying to ignore me and appear engrossed in the gorilla's sex-life. She takes her coat off and throws it over the chair. Next comes the scarf, and it's not until it's completely unwound that I see the ginormous hickey right there on the middle of her neck. I don't say anything. All I do is wonder if there are more elsewhere and if gorillas get hickeys as well.

'He's asked me to be his partner at this dance thing next Friday.'

'Eve, I should have moved in here years ago. You'd have been an old married woman by now, permanently pregnant, smelling of Johnson's baby powder and the proud owner of a family allowance book.'

She plonks herself down on the sofa with a huge sigh. I can't decide whether it's a happy or sad sigh. 'Well, at least he's decided that he wants me and not some chocolate-box girl with firm tits and thick pouting lips. Now all I've got to decide is if I go for the wee black number or the romantic look.'

'Black!'

'Oh, that's just typical of a man. You all just want a glimpse of cleavage and thigh. You're all the bloody same.'

'What I meant to say, before I was rudely interrupted, was: don't wear those horrible tights you've got. Have you never heard of Lycra? Your tights are always hanging there baggy at the ankles, for Christ sake.'

'Ach, shut up! That's all I ever get from you. Lycra this, Lycra that. You're such a sad git, Will, do you know that?'

'Listen to you! Stop this melodrama bit, for Jesus sake. Make the most of it. Get the wee black number. Get tights with Lycra in them. Nothing more than fifteen denier either.'

'All right, all right. I get the message. Give it a rest, will you? Anyway, how come you know so much about women's tights?'

'I always find the sixty denier best for over-the-head when I'm robbing the bank, and the five denier for my red shag-me's.'

'Jesus, Will. One day you're going to be arrested.'

'And body-searched, hopefully.'

'You're a perv.'

'And you wear baggy tights, so we're even. Go for the black, be different. Or should I say, be like every-one else.'

'My mum's advice was always, "Just be yourself and everyone will love you."'

'Mmm,' I say. Then one more dig. Just one:

'My mum always told me that rubbing salt into a hickey makes it disappear faster.'

Over the next few days she's wearing polonecks and disappearing a lot into the kitchen, seasoning her neck for vampire Ian. She comes back with a bag from Laura Ashley on Saturday.

I say to her:

'Let's see it, then.'

Well, it's blue and silk, short and slinky (in an Eve kind of way) and not one flower in sight. Well, as you can imagine, I'm gobsmacked that she actually found this by herself. On the other hand, I'm a wee bit piqued that she did it without me.

It's pity the way things work out, because she walks in halfway through a vital try for Scotland. She thinks I'm not paying attention to her. I can tell by the way the door slams behind her. I let out a cheer as our heroic captain's successful conversion brings the score to 21–17.

'Don't you like it, then?' she says.

I notice she's not eating her chips. I steal one from her plate.

'I thought it was nice. Do you not think it gives off the right vibes, or what?'

There's vinegar on it. There's one thing I hate in this world and it's vinegar on chips. I eat another one though. 'Aren't you going eat these?'

Eve shakes her head. 'No. I'm on a diet.'

'Then why the fuck did you put vinegar on them? You know I hate vinegar on chips. More than anything else in this world, I hate vinegar on chips.'

'Jesus Christ, living with you is a nightmare! All you ever think about is yourself. I've still to get a straight answer: do you like my dress or not?' Her voice is high, screechy like, and I put it down to PMT.

Before answering, I take her plate and pour brown sauce over the chips. 'Yeah, I do. It's the best dress in the whole world. Now are you happy?'

'Right, that sums it up. You don't like it. You think it's frumpy, just because it doesn't start at my neck and end at my ears.'

'I do like it. It's very . . . you.' Diplomacy is never my strong point.

'You hate it.'

'Have you shown it to Ian?'

'I wanted to surprise him.' She puts her head in her hands, elbows on the table. Now, my mum always told me never to put your elbows on the dinner table, especially when someone's eating, but I let her off.

'Why wouldn't you come with me? If you had come with me, it would have been all right.'

'I hate shopping on Saturday afternoons, when the shops are full of loiterers just wasting time until Blind Date comes on. Especially with girlies who window shop, rack shop and then disappear into the changing rooms for half an hour while I'm left outside hoping to God none of my work mates catch me skulking about the lingerie department in Marks and Spencers. What a slagging that would be! Then you come out to show me the first hellish outfit, which you will probably end up buying after trying on another forty things, just to take it back the next day because it doesn't match your handbag. It's either that or taking a whole afternoon to choose a lipstick: the exact same lipstick you bought the previous weekend.'

She yawns. I see her look at her watch. I look at mine. 7.00. Blind Date time.

Recently I've been dreaming about the night on the Fenwick Moors in my Ford Fiesta. Jesus, what a night that turned out to be. I always thought catsuits had zips in them, but Suzie taught me otherwise that night. It's not easy doing a strip tease in a three-door Fiesta, but she managed it in such a way that I thought either my head or my willie was going to fall off. It's amazing how handy the hatchback comes in.

I've been thinking about Susie a lot. And I know it's just because I don't have anyone else at the moment. But it doesn't make it easier, you know. Okay, okay, I'm trying the subtle approach with Poppy, but subtlety won't raise its unnecessary head tonight. Of that I can assure you. Anyway, the subtle approach doesn't seem to work with me. I've not even got one of those shy come-on looks from her yet. She's a tease. But that's just part of the game. Gimme time, gimme time. Plus, there's plenty more trout in my loch until then.

Inviting Sonia, the new clerkess in Business Insurance, is a great ploy on my part tonight. I know it's really tacky, but I've been using my traumatic experience as an icebreaker: going for the sympathy vote. I tell you, Sonia was eating out of my hand in thirty seconds! Beat that! Bring out the maternal in them and they're yours to play with.

With a bit of luck.

She's got terrific nails. Long sculptured things. And nothing so common as bright red. No, siree. More of a subtle pink, actually. I bought some of that aromatherapy oil out of the Body Shop in case a massage is on the cards.

And Eve's left the place in a mess. Talc footprints on the carpet, dirty knickers lying on the kitchen floor and I'm beginning to think Chanel No 5's an air-freshener. The amount she's sprayed and missed her neck with is record-breaking. Even if I did decide to don the Jazz, its aphrodisical qualities could never compete with the clouds of stuff already floating about this place. I mean, she's hardly ozone-friendly, is she?

I did think about tidying up – you know, getting the Hoover out, opening a few windows – but I changed my mind. Keep them keen, you lean mean sex machine, Will.

There's this vision in my head of Sonia turning up at the door wearing nothing but a leopard-skin coat. That's it, not a bean underneath. Okay, I'm disappointed when she turns up in a raincoat, but when she takes it off to expose bare flesh creeping out of crevices at her neckline, well, my sexual fantasy zooms up another avenue.

She drinks Budweiser straight from the bottle and I'm cursing myself for only buying six instead of twelve.

'What are we eating?' she asks. It's the kind of voice I used to dream about when reading *Playboy* under my bedclothes with a torch. All husky like, and soft as a Cadbury's Flake.

'What about each other?' I give her one of my best boyish grins. I've been told this is what drives them wild and, if past experiences are anything to go by, I have to say it's a dead cert I'll get into her knickers in under an hour.

My ear is obviously for starters. 'So,' she says, 'Do you need any personal favours?' It's not like a Flake at all, her voice. I've got it wrong. It's more like that honey-and-lemon cough syrup you get from Boots the Chemist.

I can think of a few favours offhand, but I just kind of laugh a bit. All good things come to those who wait. She works her way down to another hors d'oeuvre: my neck. 'No? Are you sure? Really if you need any administrative assistance, I'm your man . . . or woman, rather.'

I can't think what's she meaning. Have I been out of the game so long I don't know the jargon any more? Anyway, the innuendo is lost on me.

'I've heard Joan is for the heave-ho. If you need a replacement, then I'm here, and I'm available.'

By now the alarm bells are ringing and I get to thinking that this isn't Sonia at all. She's just some girl who knocked on the wrong door. But what the hell. In for a penny, in for a fiver. Maybe she's just got Suzie's name wrong. I decide to change tactics a bit, and work in the sympathy ruse for that extra bit of tenderness.

'Slow down, please,' I say. 'I'm just getting over a major crisis in my life, if you remember. I don't want to rush into things. I want to get to know you as a person – you know?'

'Well, as they say, her loss is my gain.' Her nibbles make the hairs on the back of my neck stand on end. I'm beginning to look forward to dessert.

'No, please, really. I'd like to talk for a while.' I see her make a face and I can't help getting a bit annoyed. Jesus, it's not as if I'm paying her by the hour, or whatever! I go and get some more Bud.

'You poor soul. You've been through such a lot lately. It must have been terrible waiting there in the church like that, waiting for her. Just as well you've got your work to take your mind off it.'

I kind of mumble, 'Yeah!' while thinking how I don't think about my job at all apart from when I'm held prisoner between nine and five. And even then I spend most of that time looking out the window. 'But it never replaces friendship, affection, whatever you want to call it.'

'You know, it's such a big department you run. If you ever feel it's getting too stressful for you, give me a call and I'll come running.'

Quickly I review all the lies I told to get her here in the first place, and I don't remember exaggerating about my position in car insurance. Again, another tactic, forget the chat and get on with the business.

Any guy tries. A bit of a touch here, a bit of a feel there. That's the way it works. That's what makes the world go round.

So here I am trying it on with Sonia, her nails digging into my back, her top getting lower and lower, until she asks:

'So, is it mine?'

'Sorry?'

'The job?'

'What job?'

'Joan's. The one in Life Insurance? You could swing it for me.'

Now, I could have lied here, just to get another notch on the bedpost, but I declined the invitation:

'What are you talking about?'

'I want the admin position in your department. Since Thomas was born I've been needing the break, to get back on to the ladder.' She still kisses my chest. Soft kisses, which almost make me promise her the job on the spot, although I have no say in the matter what-so-ever. 'If you play your cards right, then we can have this at work, rest and play.'

Finally the penny drops. They don't call me Quick Draw McGraw for nothing. William McIntyre, Pleb, not William McIntyre, Manager Extraordinaire of Life Insurance. I could have coped with this after the bedroom scene, but not before. After is acceptable for recriminations, but not prior to the event.

'Listen, Sonia, the only ladder you're heading up with me is to the giddy heights of ecstasy, not the boardroom.' Who could turn me down after that?

But she does.

I try to coax her to stay, the opportunity not completely ruined, well, not before I see her slip her wedding ring back on.

'Don't go! We haven't eaten our tortilla chips yet!'

'You're nothing but a devious bastard. God, you knew exactly what I wanted, and I knew exactly what you wanted, you jumped-up little bag of shite. And if you tell anyone about this, then believe me, you'll be eating your balls for breakfast, okay?' All this while she ties her boots up. Thigh-length jobs, they are. Pity. What a pity. The raincoat is grabbed and the door slammed. I should have kept my mouth shut. She never would have known.

So I go to bed with the two leftover Budweisers and the highlights of The British Snooker Championship.

At exactly 3 a.m. I am awoken by a lot of banging and grunting noises. My first thought is Eve and Ian are here. My second is a spasm of terror that Sonia's husband has found me. And I'm completely shitting myself. I imagine him with a tattoo on his forehead and biceps bigger than my waist. He's broader than the door and has to walk sideways into my room . . .

My third thought is that this is all a dream.

But I hear another thud and think of my hi-fi in the living room. No burglar is going to get that.

I grab my squash racket. The noise is coming from the kitchen. Obviously they've got the knives, the toolbox and Eve's Moulinex blender. I've got a squash racket. This is going to be a fair war.

The only light I can see when I peek round the door is from the fridge. Eve throws a bag of frozen mushrooms against the wall.

'What the fuck are you doing?' A logical question under the circumstances, I think. It's not until then that I notice all the food on the floor – frozen carrots, peas, you name it, it's there on the floor.

Eve spins round. Her face is set in a grimace. Her hair's that spiky way it gets when she's doing her utmost to pull it out. Her mascara has run, and the lipstick half disappeared and half smeared over her chin. Morticia doesn't have a look-in here. I can't bear to look at her any more. Don't ask me why, but I just hate to see her look like this. Anyone would. So I glance over to the wall. Now, I can't really see a lot, since the only light we're getting here is from the fridge door. I don't want any more lights on. I'm not tempted at all to reach for that switch. Ice has stuck to the wallpaper, now defrosting, and a trickle or twenty runs down and meets at a puddle below.

Dripping water has slid on to her silk dress. I can make out the thin long lines starting at the neckline and reaching the hem. And I can't help thinking of those moments when it's raining outside and you're watching the drops race each other down your window pane.

'Oh, it's you,' she says, her eyes wide. I can't see any colour, just the deep black of her pupils. 'You gave me a fright.'

'Thought we had burglars there, for a minute.'

She looks down at her bare feet. Her toenails are trimmed and painted bright red. The colour clashes with the vegetables.

'Eve, for Christ sake, what you doing?'

'I saw it on this programme once. Except it was plates. She had just discovered she had cancer and was so angry, and her boyfriend bought her all these cheap plates to throw against the wall to get rid of all her pent-up anguish. It was really good. Anyway, I thought veg would he cheaper. And less noisy.'

She's flipped her lid. She's out to lunch. There are lights on, but nobody's in.

'It's supposed to be therapeutic.'

'Is it working?' I ask.

'Sort of.'

'You don't have cancer, do you?'

Her hands cover her face. 'Will, I'm so embarrassed. It was the worst night of my life.' The only thing left in the freezer is a chicken. She takes some yoghurts and a tin of peaches from the fridge. The chicken bounces off the wall and lands back at her feet. She picks it up to rethrow it. This time it comes straight at me. I duck. You'd think it was a rugby ball the way it lands with a big bounce. 'Must be past its sell-by date,' she says, sighing.

'You're a fucking nutter, you know that?' I can't think of anything to do but laugh. *If you can't beat them, join them* has always been one of my mottoes, so I grab a

109

handful of frozen vegetables and throw them myself. The frozen peas fly back like tiny ping pong balls. Mushrooms waltz to the floor. Strawberry yoghurt congeals with the defrosting ice on the wall, and at a slower pace slops down to cover the lino.

That's the final straw. I catch her wrist in mid throw. The other yoghurt drops and explodes on my foot. Cheers! Pink spray covers her face. Her hands are wet and cold. She looks at the French-manicured nails and then turns them over. Over and over again, almost as if she's just grown aware of them. 'They're all wrinkly like prunes,' she says.

There's a bluish tinge to her fingers, so I rub and rub them, trying to get some warmth into her body. 'What happened?'

'Everything was going well. He was being so attentive. And I didn't make a show of myself. Honestly I didn't. But when I come out of the toilets, I see him standing there with his tongue down some other girl's throat, right in the middle of the floor. I could just tell she was wearing a Wonderbra.' (Eve's near tears, but fighting them.) 'You know the type, Will. No breasts sit at ninety-degree angles. None do.' (The tears start now.) 'I always thought he had more taste. I honestly did. God, how I wished the floor would just open up and swallow me. Everyone was looking at me. I left. Didn't even say cheerio.' She sighs, hangs her head.

'Jesus!'

'Yes, well! Plenty more fish in the sea.' She kind of smiles. 'But I don't like fish. Specially not the smell. Sorry about this mess. I'll clear it up.'

'Don't bother. We'll just add some rice and make a risotto.'

Eve laughs, not excessively, just a bit. She pulls her hands away from mine. It feels as if a wee black cloud is hanging over her. She opens up one of the cupboards and I think, 'Jesus, what's she doing now?' And before I can stop her she throws her Moulinex to shatter against the wall.

Now it's the waterfall of tears. No longer the snuffly ones. I don't know what to do or say. I'm still in shock about the Moulinex. Eve just breaks down completely. Huge big gasps like she's trying desperately to breathe. I don't know what to do, so I give her a hug. Still prune fingers.

I hate women crying. Somehow it always makes me feel guilty.

EVE I wish I had a car. I wish I could drive. Right now I have this tremendous urge to see the sea. Not to jump into it, or go for a swim, or try to catch another fish. Just to see it in the darkness. Just to hear it, I suppose. Smell that salty, putrid air. Feel the wind on my face. I want to feel like someone in an advert, and in less than thirty seconds I can give a coy smile, make a coffee from some gadget I can attach to my cigarette lighter and know everything is going to be all right.

I'm a fool to myself.

Here I was thinking all the while that our relationship was so adult, so extraordinarily different from anyone else's when all the while it's been cheap.

Cheap. That's what it has been. *Cheap.*

Love.

Jesus, that's a joke. I thought it was turning into love. God, how I wanted someone so mature and sensitive after

111

putting up with Will all these years.

Love. Is it such a rare commodity? Is it really so much to ask for?

I want normality. I'm not ashamed to admit it. I want normal things. I'm fed up with these relationships that teeter on the edge of something. I want an eighteen-month-long engagement. I want to marry in an ivory dress. I want my husband to come to child-rearing classes with me. And what do I have? One man with a compartmentalized tidy mind who makes one fatal and very public mistake, and a lodger who thinks more of his pet mouse than he does of me.

I feel sick.

I'm hungry, but I don't want to eat.

I want to sleep, but I can't.

I have an itch in the middle of my back that I can't reach, or don't want to.

She was there when we arrived at the hotel. All sultry poses and pouting lips. A personal administrator. Why couldn't she just say secretary like a normal person? Even when I said I was a florist, I could see the look of triumph on her face. Of course, she had on a wee black number. She flicked her hair and managed to flutter her eyelashes at the same time. Some achievement, that. Wonder how long she practised that for.

Miaow!

Well, what do you expect?

How can I compete with that? I suppose I could have caused a scene, scratched her eyes out, Dynasty style. But I couldn't be bothered. There wasn't any point. I didn't have any shoulder pads on.

I'm lying on my back, watching the shadows on the ceiling. No flats have these shadows like Edinburgh flats.

The covings remind me of Gargoyles, sitting there, laughing at me, and I think of Notre Dame Cathedral and Paris. And Paris makes me think of a weekend I had with Ian there. We were happy then, way back when Andy Roxburgh was still the manager of Scotland football team.

Stragglers from a late-night drinking session pass by my window. I'm watching them closely from behind the curtains. One woman's walking shoeless, carrying them in her hand. The guy's eating a slice of pizza from a plastic tray. They're noisy, but I don't mind. Laughing, having a good time, so they are. And I don't remember having any of that, even when I was a teenager. I don't remember walking through the streets, wearing new shoes that gave me blisters, stealing one of my friend's chips, and singing 'Flower of Scotland'.

It's around four when the doorbell goes. I hear it, but I can't say that I rush to answer it. I know who it is. I know who's ringing my doorbell at four in the morning.

Even if Will hears it, I know he's not going to answer it either, because he knows who it is too.

'Let me in. I know you're there, listening to me. Please. Let me in.'

I worry about the neighbours for near on half a second and then forget about them. Let him grovel a bit more.

The walk down the hallway seems excessively long now. I never noticed before how long it is. Funny, that. I unlock the door, but leave the chain on. 'You took your time.' My voice doesn't even quaver, and I'm proud of that.

'I want to talk to you. Come on, Eve. I'm freezing out here. Let me in!' I see his face through the crack in the door. His jacket collar is wrapped tightly around his neck. As he talks, I watch his steamy breath rise. Pity is a pure excuse for opening the door, but it's a reason, I suppose.

'What do you mean: "You took your time"?' Ian follows me down the hall, but it doesn't seem as long as it did before. How many steps did I take? How many do I need now? One, two, three . . . six, seven, eight, nine. Nine.

'The dance finished more than three hours ago. You must have been busy elsewhere.' I'm reluctant to put any lights on, but it seems spooky in the dark. One table lamp makes all the difference. I see snatches of him sit down, cross legs, uncross legs and run his hands through his hair, lapped in the yellow tinge of the light bulb. I can't see any colour in his eyes. And I'm glad about this, because I've always said he's got good eyes. Blind as a bat, but a rich brown colour to look at. Almost black, really. My man with Guinness eyes, I used to call him.

Used to.

'Eve! Stop this. As a matter of fact, I left soon after you, on my own, and I've been roaming from pub to pub ever since, on my own.'

I'm aware, and so is Ian, of my bare legs when I cross them over. I cover them in the pink dressing gown that used to hang behind the bathroom door. The same dressing gown my lover wore on his infrequent visits. The same dressing gown I can smell his aftershave on.

'You once told me that people fall into two categories, Ian. Those who are naturally untidy and those who are tidy. Sitting looking at you now, I know you're the latter. I'm not. You've been spending too much time with me, Ian, because tonight you were untidy as well.'

'I'm sorry. I don't know what came over me.'

'I would say it was a 40C chest, to be honest. I'm disappointed. I thought you had more taste.'

'I know this isn't an excuse, but she just appeared with some mistletoe. She's been after me for ages, pestering and pestering. She'll have her P45 on Monday morning.'

'Mistletoe in November?' Then in a flash of escaping memory I get to thinking of Paul, lying there in my bed that Sunday morning, his chest rising, one arm and leg trailing out of the bed. God, what a hypocrite I – but I've started so I'll finish:

'Why, Ian? Why? I'm the one who's never asked you for anything. How could you treat me like that? It's not so much the snog with the walking chest, it's the fact that you did it right there in front of me. I didn't expect you to ever treat me like that. No matter what I've done to upset you in the past, I don't deserve to be treated like that.'

He uncrosses his legs again. Runs his hands through his hair, and I think of Will sitting in the exact same position on the day he turned up at my door still wearing his kilt. There's not much difference between them after all. When the shit hits the fan, they look the same, and they make the same excuses.

'You're sitting here, Eve, all prissy, giving it the big martyr act, but maybe I just came to the stage when I gave up on you.'

'Gave up on me! If I recall, you were the one who invited me tonight. I needn't have known about it at all.'

'I know. I know. But it is your fault.'

'Don't go blaming me.'

'I'm not the one with all the barriers up about me.

115

I'm not the one who wants everything on my terms. It was you, you, you – all the way. I tried, but Jesus, I'm tired.'

'What are you talking about?'

'Think about it.'

'Stop twisting things round. That's just typical of you, to twist things round to land in my lap.'

'Think about it,' he repeats.

Uncomfortable with thinking, I wander over to the window, ever hopeful of seeing the last pizza-eating beer-swilling club-goer. I want to see someone smile. The streets are deserted. All that is visible is Ian's reflection, looking untidy and tired all of a sudden. Deflated just like me.

'Do you love him?'

'Who?'

'You know who. The person always standing in the way.'

I don't answer the question. 'Stop twisting things round. We're talking about you, not me. Stop twisting things.' My voice is getting higher, screechier, louder, and I'm all too aware of Will in the next room.

'Do you love him?'

'He's like my brother.'

'Do you love him?'

'I can't answer that.'

'Do you love him?'

'I don't know.'

He's forcing me into an answer. If this is the way he does business, no wonder he's so successful. 'Well,' he pauses, and all of a sudden I want to go to his place with him and lie on the futon and watch the candles flicker in the draughts. 'That's that, then.'

'Yes. That's that.'

Ian looks at his watch as if suddenly recalling a business meeting he's got to go to. Then:

'He's like me. He'll break your heart.'

'Have you broken my heart?'

'It's probably my own conceit, but I like to think so.'

We hug, swaying.

'Give me a phone.'

With our arms wrapped around each other, we walk down the hall and this time it seems far too short.

'Will you phone me?'

Nodding, not able to speak, I open the door. With a brief kiss on my cheek he walks out.

After closing the door I can still smell Eternity aftershave in the air. I sniff the cuffs of the pink dressing gown.

You reach a point in every relationship that goes way past the easy stage. It goes past the polite stage and enters the zone where you know each other too well and can't go back, even if you want to. It's too risky. You'll lose out one way or another.

So you don't lock the door in the bathroom. He watches you clean your ears with a cotton bud. You watch him floss his teeth and clean his dirty socks.

You let him see your Access bill, and he lets you work out his cheque book. He knows what size of bra you take and knows the frilly bits itch your nipples. You know what side he hangs.

You'll let him see you eat and eat until you feel sick as long as he's doing it too. You feign interest in the football results on a Saturday evening. He lets you watch Home and Away when he wants to see the news.

He's got you drinking Guinness, man-size pints of the stuff, when you go to the pub. So much so, you can tell the real stuff from the con. All of a sudden you appreciate Oasis when you've been used to Pavarotti.

He chops the onion while you're browning the mince. He tells you the water's not boiled when you put the rice in the pot. Salt, he says, when you're trying to watch his cholesterol level.

He's the one who smiles at you when you open the door when he's forgotten his keys. A secret special smile just for you. You walk through the puddles and splash him. He walks at a pace you have to run to keep up with. He's the one who tells you that you look a mess one minute and beautiful the next.

He brings out the girl in you and you bring out the boy in him. It's immature, the way it goes round in circles; the things you laugh at, the times when you cry, the shouting you do when the dishes aren't done, or the toilet seat not put back down.

He's everything in your book and you're nothing. He says you're everything and he's nothing.

He tells you the time when you can't be bothered looking at your watch. He massages your feet when you're watching TV. He can answer most of the questions on Telly Addicts, and you're proud of him then.

He talks to your mother on the phone. You remember his birthday and he forgets yours. He wants nose-hair clippers for his Christmas whereas you hope for that ring.

And that's why you can't go back a stage. Ever hopeful, ever optimistic, even though he pisses the hell out of you

118

most of the time. You can't go back. You can't go back. It's too scary.

WILL Well, I always thought the heebie-jeebie zone appeared in The X Files but not in this flat.

It's Sunday morning. The Sunday morning after the night before. It's precisely 11.01 a.m. and 45 seconds and Billie Holiday's voice wakes me up.

Okay, okay, I know I've given Eve a raw deal. I know I turned up here on the edge. I know. But I never – and I repeat, never – woke her up on a Sunday morning with depressing music worming its way under her door.

'Is it not a tad early for Billie?' I ask her, heading straight for the Maxwell House.

'No. When you feel depressed and listen to her, it makes you feel suicidal. And sometimes, believe it or not, you want to feel suicidal.'

The way she's whisking those eggs is a bit worrying. It's a great wrist action, though. 'I'm making scrambled eggs,' she tells me, and I know not to tell her that I don't like eggs.

'You didn't throw them at the wall last night, then?'

'Forgot about them. If I'd known . . .' Her voice trails off. 'It seems much longer than a couple of hours ago, don't you think? Whoever says twenty-four hours isn't enough in one day is a liar. With some days one hour seems too long. And then the good days seem so short, but that's just because there are so few of them.'

'Can't help loving dat man of mine,' wallows poor Billie.

I don't know what to say. Guilt is still eating away at

me, and I don't know why. The nerves on my neck are standing to attention.

'Did you hear Ian at the door during the night?' She's still with that bloody whisk and it's beginning to annoy me.

'Nope. Must have been sleeping like a baby,' I lie. I'm not saying I had a glass to the wall, but you know –

The whisk is dropped in the sink with an almighty clatter. 'Good. Good.' Next, two slices of bread go into the toaster. The lever pulled down with a hefty thwack. I feel sorry for the springs. 'So,' she carries on, 'I don't know what happens now. I don't know if I'm supposed to phone him or if that's it. Things were left a bit up in the air, I think.' She pauses for a moment to push her hand through her hair. It doesn't make it look any better. It's still sticking up all over the place. 'And anyway, I don't know if I want to phone him.' The belt of her dressing gown suddenly becomes fascinating to her and she plays with the few strands of thread. Then she ties a knot in either end of it, tightly. Very tightly. 'I don't know what I want any more. I've got to decide, I suppose.'

I pour some coffee and make her sit down at the table. Normally Eve's in control of things and it's me who's sitting with my head in my hands. I'm the type of person who wanders from one dilemma to another. Eve's the one who has to put up with it all.

I don't know, but I feel powerful watching her drink her coffee, looking a mess, feeling a mess. I end up making the breakfast which means forgetting about the eggs and finding the packet of Penguins Eve hid yesterday.

I never eat the ones in green wrappers. Eve doesn't notice what colour the wrapper is. She just pulls off the wrapper and in two bites the biscuit's away.

'Well, let's start with the basics. Do you love him?' I ask.

'That's the second time in twelve hours someone's asked me that.'

'Oh?' I ask. 'Who else?'

'Forget it. It doesn't matter.'

A look passes between us. A look that I don't quite understand. 'Don't look at me like that,' I say.

'Listen, Will, this big-brother act is very good of you. But – how do I say this without sounding like a narky bitch? – lay off, okay?'

'Moody cow, is more like it.'

'I've to decide what I want, that's all. I'll make this huge plan and then wait for things to happen.'

'Don't plan anything, Eve, if you want my advice. You'll only end up disappointed. Go with the flow.'

'You know something? I don't want your advice, Will. When your life is in some kind of order, then maybe I'll listen.'

I ignore this. 'Ever thought of smoking dope?'

'No!'

'Buying a bottle of voddie?'

'No!'

'Maybe you should.'

'Piss off! I've to make huge decisions about my life and you want me to take on even more addictions.'

'What do you mean? More? What addictions have you got?' I'm trying hard not to laugh.

'You. You are the biggest addiction of all. Just bugger off and leave me alone.'

Right, so now it's not just the nerves in my neck that are standing to attention. And I'm thinking where I can go today to keep out the way of Psycho Bitch here. Even thinking about going to visit my mum, but I'm not quite that desperate. I have a car. Have car, have roads, will travel. The Romans were good for something, you know. Go to the sea, maybe. North Berwick, maybe, and watch the tide. Certainly better than staring at these kitchen walls. I mean, they're still a bit damp from last night.

7

EVE It must be female intuition. Poppy opens the door and looks at me. Probably expects a confirmation of a proposal or a revelation about the best sex of my life. But when my eye catches hers, she knows. You see, female intuition.

Well, she rushes to put the kettle on, hands me tissues and tries to make sense of the garbled muffled words I attempt to say through the tears.

Poppy's the one who rushes out for chocolate at the earliest opportunity. And then cream cakes for morning break. By eleven o'clock we feel sick.

'It's a pity I've forgotten my blusher,' she states while ushering me in front of the mirror. I'm forced to stand

and look at my blotchy face, while she restores a normal tone of complexion with a tube of foundation and a lipstick doubled as a blusher. Once done, and feeling a bit pleased with herself, she eagerly awaits for my cry of delight. 'All done. Ready to face the world now.'

That I'm never ready for. Especially when I look like an orange-faced clown. But she means well, with her patronizing little pats on my shoulder every so often, and doing me up like a Barbie doll.

Besides, it means we're going to the pub at lunchtime to bitch about men over a white-wine spritzer and a tuna baguette. Sometimes we're so bad I think we curdle the mayonnaise.

'Why is it that you always end up doing what *they* want to do? Is it a fluke, or their wily devilish ways – making you feel guilty about wanting to see a romantic comedy instead of yet another meaningless blockbuster?' She shakes her head and pulls the ice from her drink, then plopping it in the dirty ashtray beside her. 'Sensitive teeth, you know.'

I thought nineteen was too young to have sensitive teeth.

'They're bastards. Every single last one of them.'

'I know.' But at the same time think this is a huge generalization. There must be one good man out there. Somewhere.

And is nineteen not too young to be so cynical about the opposite sex? Probably not. I get the impression that Poppy could teach me a thing or two about men's wily devilish ways.

It's all a front of course. She wants to know all the Will stories since they are now, according to her, 'an item'.

She's a bit smitten. But that will soon wear off when she discovers how irritating he actually is.

Meanwhile, things are not going too well in other quarters.

I work for a mincing, money grabbing moron.

The latest is he doesn't want any Christmas trees or decorations in the shop window. I just don't get it. We'll lose trade, but he insists we will be bound to gain from it:

'Eve, face facts, people are sick to death of Christmas. Let them just get on with the day-to-day running of their lives. Let them buy their weekly bunch of carnations. Let them order an Interflora basket for someone's birthday without the synthetic holly and gold-spray fir cones inflicted upon them.'

'But it's Christmas. People *want* holly, mistletoe and all the synthetic stuff. It's traditional.' I want to hit him. 'I'm not talking about tinsel and fake snow stencils in the window. We could go for the subtle effect. Forget the tree, even. Go for a topiary and garland arrangement. They're really popular this year.'

'Excellent! You have achieved what I set out to prove. Artistry is still your best friend, although he must have been on vacation over the past few weeks. Go forth, my petal and NB, no flashing lights.'

'You had me worried there for a minute. I thought maybe I'd be calling you Ebenezer from now on.'

'Oh my, we are a cynical wee misanthrope, aren't we, these days? You're as cheery as a turkey on Christmas Eve.'

Nathan's other problem is that he laughs at his own jokes.

I must be pre-menstrual, because all I want to do is

give the first person that gets in my way a good kicking. Nathan recommends overtime, Poppy recommends yoga and Will recommends a bottle of vodka.

Poppy says I should be going out more, meeting new people, not staying in and brooding. But I'm not in the mood to meet people. What would I say?

I told her I'd rather stay in and clench my teeth.

'You'd be better clenching your buttocks to get rid of some of that cellulite!' she said.

I don't think she meant to be nasty.

I'm grieving, that's what it is.

I mean, what happened to the chance for reconciliation? What happened to one of us crawling back to say, I can't live without you – mm? What ever happened to that first awkward phone call? Ian, you bastard, you never phoned.

WILL I don't know what it is about shaving that makes me think. But see, when I'm scraping away, then a bit of a rinse, then scrape, scrape, scrape again, I'm a happy chappy. I love the sound it makes. I feel as if it's getting right in there and pulling the wee bastard follicles out by the short and curlies. I can hear them screaming.

I suppose it's got something to do with concentration. Shaving gives me these precious moments when I actually use my mind constructively. Okay, the TV or radio or something may be on in the background. But put it this way, I put more effort into shaving off my facial hair than writing insurance policies. Well, I've got to, or else a slip of the hand could mean I look a total prick with a bit of toilet paper stuck to my face.

Believe it or not, I'm one of these people who find

it difficult to concentrate on more than one thing at a time. If the new Oasis song comes on the radio, then I'm sorry, that's it, wave bye-bye to brain space. It's a well-known fact with me that my concentration span is so limited I can't pat my head and rub my stomach at the same time.

Not that I want to, mind.

I can't abide people who introduce such crappy ideas as tongue-rolling competitions as their party trick. Or the type who just sit around and discuss old kiddies' TV programmes. 'Ach, do you remember Dougal? Spaced out, he was. Or the Clangers?' At this point they always make the noise of the Clangers with their forefinger against their lips. Also, at this point I head for the machete. I'll show them my party trick.

However, that was by the bye. Back to the shaving. It just proves the point I was illustrating there.

Last week I go into the bathroom to find Eve cleaning my razor with my toothbrush. 'What you doing?' I ask.

'Oh, God. Typical of you to walk in just now. I might have bloody known! But since you're here, you can make yourself useful. Bring a clean towel, will you?'

A white towel is already thrown in the corner of the floor, dyed blood red. She has another one tied round her ankle, blood oozing out beneath the cotton and covering her feet.

'In the name of Christ, what have you done?'

'Just get a towel!' she almost screams. Her face looks pretty pale, so I decide to panic in case it's an emergency. I mean, I've never been a Boy Scout, so first aid has always been one of those unsolved mysteries to me. The only thing I know I can do is scream for help louder than anyone else, and take false teeth out if someone's having a fit. Neither of these things seems appropriate right now. I pass her the towel, putting the responsibility on to her shoulders.

Well, Eve was a Girl Guide.

She peels off the blood-sodden towel and quickly wraps the clean one around her left ankle, holding it tightly.

'I think I'm going to faint,' says she. 'Hold it tightly, while I put my head between my knees.'

Now, there's two things I'm not good with, blood and puke. So all I can think is: I'll do it, I'll do it, just so long she doesn't pass out on me.

'Eve, I think you should know that this is a complete botch-up of a suicide attempt. I think wrists are a better bet.'

'It was an accident.'

'With my razor!'

Meanwhile, her head's upside down between her legs. Pity she's not a contortionist. Then she could hold her ankle in her teeth.

'Well, Will, you don't use them, do you? Look at yourself. Somewhere between George Michael and David Mellor.'

Even so, it wouldn't have been so bad if she had used one of the disposable Bics instead of my posh Gillette twinblades that I keep for Saturday nights. But God forbid she should think about me for a change.

'I feel sick.'

'Me too.' I'm the one left holding the ankle and looking at blood-soaked towels. 'This is giving me good practice for when my first child is born.'

'No, it's not. There's more blood, membranes and bits then. You haven't seen anything until you've lived through that.'

'You haven't either, so I don't know how you're so up on it.'

'I'm a woman.'

'Jee-sus. This is such arrogance, thinking just because you're the same sex, you know exactly what's going on.'

'Men think a woman's body is a temple. But it's not. It's a platform for fungi, leakages, lumps and – the boss of it all – hormones. Just think. A woman's hormones are the equivalent of the government. Hormones govern the body. And if you've got Tory hormones, then you're in for a shitty time. Men don't have to stirruped and prodded, things stuck up you, things pulled out, examine this, examine that, beware of this, beware of that. That's exactly what it's like being a woman. So the next time you look at the model on the front cover of *Cosmopolitan* and think she's a bit of alright, just remember she's probably got rampant thrush and smeared herself in natural yoghurt or Canesten!'

'Why yoghurt?'

'Forget it. Doesn't matter.'

'You mean, strawberry? Or fruits of the forest?'

'Forget it.'

'I think you've stopped bleeding now.'

We tie one of the cotton handkerchiefs my aunt gave me last Christmas around Eve's ankle.

'Men get piles, though,' I say, proud that I can think of something.

'So do women.'

'Men get genital warts.'

'And pass them on to the woman.'

'Men get hard-ons at the most embarrassing of times.'

'Well, think of smear tests or cystitis and I'm sure your

hard-on will soften up soon enough. Why didn't you tell me you were sleeping with Poppy?'

Well, this catches me a bit unawares since I don't know what connection there is supposed to be between cystitis and Poppy. And I really don't know what to say, apart from Mind Your Own Bloody Business.

'We're not exactly sleeping together.' I say this a bit awkwardly. I don't know why, but Eve is like one of the lads, and admitting that I haven't exactly got the leg over yet seems too close to failure.

'Oh? Right.'

There's a pause in which I'm supposed to tell her the story, but I don't. Instead I have a gander under the handkerchief to check that she's stopped bleeding. 'I think that's you. No more suicide attempts today – okay?'

'How many times do I have to tell you? It, was, an, accident.'

'Just because I'm going out with Poppy doesn't mean that I'm not your friend any more. Don't kill yourself on my account.'

'It was an *accident*. If I was serious about killing myself, do you honestly think that I would slit my ankles? Do you think I'm that stupid? A long lingering death, when a bottle of pills would be much easier.' Her voice gets higher-pitched with every statement, until the ultimate half-squawk half-screech.

And you know what I think Eve needs? I worked it out, see.

A right good fuck!

Not that I'm volunteering, like. But a right good fuck is all she needs.

Fuck, fuck, FUCK . . .

EVE The worse thing about the east coast is the wind. I could be wearing twenty-five layers and still the sod would be able to bite through it all. Sometimes I just want to cry with it, when I'm kind of just rooted to the spot until the gust dies down a bit. Okay, I haven't twenty-five layers on, but enough to make my arms immobile. I can't bend them, can't even put them down at my sides. They stick out at forty-five-degree angles from the rest of my body, and I look like a doll I had when I was a kid.

Chatty Kathy was her name.

If you pulled a cord at the back of her neck, then she said:

'My name is Kathy . . .

'I'm hungry . . .

'Isn't it a lovely day?'

My mum would never let me take her outside in case I broke her. So there I was with the rest of the girls, with their prams and very exotic dolls – compared with my Paddington Bear shoved into the pram even though he was far too big for it.

If anyone talks to me today, all I'm going to say is:

'My name is Eve . . .

'I'm hungry . . .

'Isn't it a lovely day?'

No more than a few inches of snow has fallen over-night. The sun shines this morning though, making it the kind of morning that everyone hates getting out of bed for, but happy once they step outside of their front door. It's still a bit early yet, so the streets are empty. 7.34, to be exact. Besides me, only a few gritters are out and about on South Clerk Street. The delivery of poinsettias won't be affected by the flurry of snow. I

131

know, because I've checked with One Stop Delivery Service.

Truth be known, it's not my turn for the early-morning delivery, but Will didn't get in until well after 3 a.m., which means Poppy'll be the same. She's always late at the best of times, so I don't see this morning being an exception.

Not that I'm complaining, mind, because I couldn't sleep anyway. Will's snores are always earthquake intensity after a few pints. I shouldn't moan. At least he's home. Not that I see him much. Don't really see much of Poppy now either. The pub lunches have stopped. She says it's because she can't afford it. More likely because she's heard all my Will stories now.

Flower Power is freezing. I have learnt from every news bulletin possible that:

'The gas supply in the Lothian region is minimal due to the increased demand in this freeze.'

Or words to that effect.

Just ask me, and I'll be able to tell you practically verbatim what every weather report has said over the past twenty-four hours. That shows you how interesting my life is.

King's-Cross-to-Edinburgh trains are cancelled due to frozen points. Edinburgh Airport is under a frozen fog. Roads are blocked due to snowdrifts. Old people are suffering from hypothermia.

Oh yes, it's another winter wonderland up north.

John, the delivery man from One Stop, knocks on the door. Maybe it's my imagination but I'm sure when he sees me instead of the exotic Poppy his face shows signs of disappointment. He's pleasant enough in a workman kind of way. Pleasant enough, I suppose, for someone who has tattoos on his right arm (visible in the summer, not today) and teeth in bad need of repair. Funny, though, how I haven't seen him since Poppy has taken over some of the deliveries.

'John' – she has been known to say – 'delivered the lilies this morning. He's a bit of alright, I suppose, if you forget the halitosis.'

Maybe it's my own conceit, but I used to think he had a wee passion for *me* in the pre-Poppy days. Or then again, maybe it was just relief when he saw my face instead of Nathan's.

'I'm off to Aberdeen now, but I don't know if I'll make it through,' he says, clutching his mug of tea in both hands. Big hands, he's got, big enough to carry one large poinsettia in each palm with ease.

This is when I get all in a fluster, making sure I get my geography right. 'Oooh, I'm not so sure, John,' I start gushing. I always find when I've been watching the news that I'm desperate in a very self-indulgent way to let everyone know about it. 'Most of the roads are blocked. Aberdeen seems to be the worst. Did you know the River Clyde is frozen?'

'The River Clyde isn't in Aberdeen.'

WILL Nat the Rat must be into the Christmas spirit all of a sudden, 'cos he lets Eve away early from work. Okay, it's only an hour, but it's better than a slap in the face.

'Time off for good behaviour,' she says. 'Fancy a walk?'

'A walk?' I'm astounded. Walk? I don't know if I can do that any more. 'Is that when you put one foot in front of the other?'

'Uh huh.' She sees the I-don't-know look on my face.

'Forget it. Forget I spoke. I'll go on my own. It's just that it'll be great up Arthur's Seat today.'

'Bloody freezing.'

'I suppose so, but I'm still going.'

I make a concession since it's Christmas, and all that. I put on my leather jacket. Eve, as Eve always does, overdoes the maternal bit and wraps a scarf round my neck, making sure there's not one piece of bare neck that the wind can possibly attack.

'Isn't it funny how memory plays tricks on you?' she says. (We've been out five minutes and I want to go home now.) 'You know, I never remember anything about winter in my childhood until I see the snow, and then I get all nostalgic.'

I groan inwardly. A childhood story. Just what I want to hear.

'There was this hill opposite where my mum and dad lived. I used to go there as soon as there was the slightest trace of snow, with an old tin tray. The speed it used to get to was incredible. Much faster than the rest of the kids there, with their fancy shop-bought sledges. I thought I ruled the world when I whooshed down that hill.'

'I had a red plastic one. It was the business, though. Everyone wanted a go on it 'cos mine was the fastest. But it was to do with the run before going downhill, and then the steering. Nobody could ride that sledge like me.'

'I bet I would have beat you on my tray.'

'No chance.'

'Betcha.'

'Never.' I'm wheezing when we climb Arthur's Seat until we reach the top. I think I'll leave Everest for another year. It's too cold to breathe through my nose. I've discovered this by a big inhale, until my nose gets that almost-fizzy feeling. Okay, I'll suffer this walk without too many moans, but I draw the line at frozen bogies. The cold parches my throat and a beer would be the business right now. Even a bowl of soup would do.

'Another thing about winters in childhood: it was never as cold as this.'

'It probably was. We just ran faster in those days.'

'God's sake, Will. You sound like an old man.'

And I feel it, I can tell you, climbing up here for what I see as no good reason. Eve slips and giggles at the same time. I take her hand and give her a yank up until she's at the same level as me. She's all girlish and excitable today. The wind and chilly air have made her cheeks flushed. She smiles, a grin from ear to ear. It isn't a loaded smile, loaded with connotations and innuendo, which a lot of smiles are, like my own. Mind you, all she needs is a pigtail and I'd be convinced she was six years old. Even her hat has kid-on baby pompoms. It's supposed to be one of those trendy ones, but on Eve it just looks like a kiddie's one. I'm surprised Ian wasn't done for underage sex.

'Wow!' Even, I have to admit that the view is pretty amazing. Jesus, I love this city. Okay, I hate the weather. For that I would prefer to be on the set of Baywatch with scantily clad females frolicking about, but I suppose you can't have everything. We try and orientate ourselves. We spot the Castle, Calton Hill and Princes Street. When we pan round to the right, we look down towards Leith, except there's no sunshine on it, and over the docks to the sea. More importantly, we look over towards the flat, and although the window isn't visible, we feel kind of proud when we see the block.

When Eve tries to locate Newington Road, to see if a

big black cloud lingers over Flower Power, I leave her to it and get a handful of snow and force it down the back of her jacket.

She's not really that mad, considering. There aren't many other people about. So she lets out a girly scream which echoes loudly right in my ear-hole. What follows is a pathetic attempt at a snowball fight. First of all there isn't really that much snow. And secondly, Eve is a pitiful opponent.

'You throw like a girl,' I have to complain.

She just stands there with her eyes closed to my bombardment. A few times she tries to throw a handful of snow in my direction. Pathetic!

'That's because I am a girl. Believe it or not.'

She ends up splodgy white, while I remain the sexy and mysterious colour of black. She does manage to steal my baseball cap, which she then fills with snow and puts back on my head. She's dead meat if it has an adverse effect on my hair gel.

The next thing I know she's lying on her back in the snow, splaying her arms and legs up and down, laughing away to herself as if she's just been allowed out for the day. 'Come and make a snow-angel,' she says.

Well, I worry a bit about dog shit and other things, but after checking, I join her. Plus there's no-one about to see me. Let's face it, no other mad fucker is going to come up here on a day like this.

'Eve?'

'Mm?'

'Do you ever wish you could change things?'

We're still lying in the snow. Lying still, though. Not moving. Scared to, really, 'cos we both know it would break this moment, and we don't want that to happen. Neither of us do. 'Cos this is the kind of moment that will always stay in our heads – Jesus! Must be all this Christmas shite, turning me into a sentimental sad git. Eve's been playing her Robson and Jerome tape too much.

'If I could change anything, it would be me. I have this theory: if I change, then everything else will just follow on.'

It occurs to me that with anyone else this scene would happen in a bed after rampant sex, moist naked limbs all wrapped around each other. But with Eve, no, it happens in a snow storm. 'Don't change, Eve. You're great the way you are.'

'You say that because you know me. But I'm not the kind of person people want to get to know. I'm not the kind of person who walks into a room and people turn to look at. In my own way, I'm very plain. I see girls all the time and just by looking at them I wish I was more like them. I don't imagine other girls look at me and wish they were like me. Do you?'

'But that's face value.'

'We live in a face-value society, Will. Everyone and everything is seen as how attractive you are, how many degrees you have, how much money you make. You're like that as well. You see a girl and decide whether she's in the to-be-shagged or not-to-be-shagged category. You're the biggest victim of it.'

'I would look at you twice if you walked into a room.'

'And ask, "What is she doing here?" My only chance seemed to be with Ian, and I've blown that one.'

'You're better off without him.'

'Am I? Here it's coming up to Christmas and all I can

do is dread the nights I'm going to spend alone with just the TV for company.'

'I'll be there.'

'No, you won't. You'll be out with Poppy.'

'Okay, okay. I'll spend Christmas Day with you.' Jesus, she's definitely worse than my mother for the guilt trips.

I begin to feel I'm lying in a puddle, so I get up and pull Eve up with me.

'What would you change if you could go back?'

'Not the size of my willie, anyway.'

'Will. How come you always manage to lower the tone?'

She's exasperated, I can tell. She suffers pretty bad from PMT, you know.

'I think a person is like a tree, Eve,' I explain. 'The person is the trunk and the branches are the roads which you follow.'

'That's quite profound for you. See when you put your mind to it, you're quite intelligent.'

'I thought it sounded like a pile of shite.'

She wears my baseball cap, which makes her ears stick out. I'm wearing her pompom hat, for the simple reason that my ears are cold.

'I'm so disorientated, Eve. I'm heading somewhere, but I don't know where.' I know I'm talking shite, but it's important shite, and it's important that Eve knows that it's important shite. 'Everything still seems to be out of my control. Suzie was out of my control, that's why I stopped it. I wanted control and order in my life. And now look at me. I still don't have it. And then I get to thinking that control is boring, control is middle-aged, and then I think fuck it, I'll end up where I end up and that's that.'

We head down the steep banks back to civilization. We're soaking wet from lying on the snowy ground for so long, looking as if we've pissed ourselves. We cross the road at the Commonwealth Pool and head for the newsagents. We buy the biggest bag of Doritos in the world and head back just in time for Home and Away.

EVE The mirror never lies.

The coldness, even though I've got the two-bar electric fire on in my bedroom, makes my nipples hard. Big nipples, erect from droopy breasts. The only erect thing on my whole body, which is the way I think it's supposed to be. Oh, to have small pert breasts, though, that wouldn't bounce when walking, ache when pre-menstrual, flap down towards the ground in obedience to gravity. Sometimes they're so heavy they could anchor the Canberra.

I've been thinking about my one advantage over the sticks. 'Men prefer women with a bit of meat on them,' as Ian told me. Then they invented the Wonderbra – which, if I ever dared to wear one . . . I'd never see my feet again.

Even so, the sticks still don't have to stand and do the bounce test every time they want to buy a bra.

A protruding stomach means that child-bearing will be easier. Padding to protect the baby, so they say. If I breathe in, I can feel my hip bones jut out and the stomach resembling a rugby ball disappears. Oh, to have hip bones as the corners from which Levi jeans can hang – instead of stretching across the belly and making the fly pop open. The T-shirt then worn baggy outside, instead of inside with a brown leather belt fastened at the last hole. I drag my hand over it, from hip bone to hip bone, as Ian used to do in moments of passion. His hand would squelch about in it and sometimes he would reach orgasm by the sheer feel of it.

Myself, I could never see what the big deal about it was.

And now, the bum. Oh, God. The by-product of blubber. Men's bums are small and pert or otherwise non-existent. I think a lot of that has to do with men clenching at every possible opportunity. Watch them, they're always at it – in queues, standing talking, there they go:

Out in, out in. Give the balls a scratch at the same time, why don't you?

Women's bums make up for it, though. If they're not squeezed into jeans much too small for them, which at least hoists them up above the knee, they're ingeniously covered up by long jumpers. Sometimes the jumpers don't quite hide the last ridge, however, and creased flesh is detectable through the cloth. Sometimes *even dimples of cellulite* are visible. We women kid ourselves on we wear long things for comfort. Forget the visible panty line. Forget hiding the whole thing. We like to believe we do it all for comfort, and not to attract men.

Why do we have bums anyway? Yes, I know we need a bit of padding, but surely an inch is enough?

My legs are okay, actually, even if I say so myself. When I rub my hand down the back of my thigh, I can feel the muscle. I know it's muscle because it's harder than a chicken leg. But even then it's an effort to make them hairless. Everything comes at a price, I find.

What else is there?

My face I'd rather not mention, as it tends to screw up in a self-deprecating manner. The nose is too broad, with wide nostrils. Lips chapped from the east-coast wind. And, of course, eyes. Everything complete. Nothing missing. Nothing unusual. Nothing to write home about.

After that?

Elbows? Bony and dry. Knees? The same. Hands? In need of a manicure. Feet? Pedicure. Ankles? Bony: tights always wrinkle.

Any more?

Really, I don't want to know.

My dressing gown soon enough disguises all the lumps and bumps under a swathe of terry towelling.

Lycra. What a godsend and a slap in the face at the same time. Yes, it's a wonderful creation to people like Will. They say it's like a second skin. Well, hey, you've got to have a decent first skin in the first place. They say it's elastic. Well, it's not as thick as an elastic band. It hides nothing. With Lycra, nothing is left to the imagination. Which is probably why Will and his cronies think it's the second-best thing in the whole world after the sports channels on cable TV.

Imperfections aren't as much disguised as accentuated. Lycra comes in all shapes and forms, and I'm just talking about the bodies here.

Okay, I confess grudgingly, it's a wonderful thing to hold you in and tuck you in, hold things up, and fit like a glove. But really, personally, I don't think it does the job as well as, say, some builder's scaffolding. If I am to be completely honest about it, then I'm afraid I think it's another marketing strategy to help already-large-enough egos or hold back in-some-need-of-boosting egos by half a century.

WILL Christmas Eve is Christmas Eve, right? And you've got to do something, even if it's just going for a bevvy with your mates from work, 'cos you get off an hour early and you think: well, it is the start of the holidays. The point is this: you've got to do something.

But our Eve is without her Christmas (get it – Christmas Eve? Christmas? Eve?). She's sitting in that living room of hers, curled up on the sofa with a bottle of Lambrusco in one hand and her other hand deep in the Quality Street.

But she's not going to make me feel guilty. I refuse to feel guilty. I know she's just doing it to annoy me. And it's working. But I'm not going to feel guilty about it. This guilt thing is a real pisser. First it's the mother, then it's the girlfriend, then it's the wife. It's right there eating away at me all the frigging time. And I get to thinking: well, she's not my wife and not my mother, so why should I feel guilty about leaving her in on her own? It's not my fault she's got nae pals.

'Don't leave the lights on. With a bit of luck, I might not be back.' I remember to check my pocket for the Mates bought earlier.

'You'll have to come back. The parents are coming tomorrow.'

'The thing is, Eve, they don't laugh at my jokes. So I don't see the point in me being here.'

A sigh. 'Please yourself, you always do anyway.'

See? Guilt! Every single fucking time!

And to make matters worse, when I close the door behind me on the way out I feel another huge sigh of disappointment from Christmas-less Eve land bang on my shoulders.

Not for long though, 'cos when I look at my watch,

I'm already late and Poppy gets a bit stroppy when I'm late.

EVE See when I hear that door slam behind him, I let out one big sigh of relief. I've got the wine, the chocolates and the remote control all to myself. I can toss the sweetie wrappers on the floor if I want to. I can even eat the whole box if I want. In one go.

WILL In I creep about five. All that good cheer towards your fellow men and women makes you a bit randy, you know. And I thought my luck was in.

It wasn't, but that's another story.

Eve is standing in the middle of the kitchen, just standing there, staring out the window. Except it's pitch black outside, so she can't see anything anyway. There aren't any lights on.

Well, being honest, I don't really see her. But, know how when you feel someone just standing there? Well, that's the way it is. The hairs on the back of my neck erect.

My Christmas good spirit ran out when I didn't get my end away, and looking at her standing there I just know there's bound to be another frozen-vegetable saga. Well, I can't be bothered with it. I'm fed up with her moans and groans. I'll just say things I'm bound to regret when I sober up a bit. It's just not worth the hassle. And I need some sleep.

Eve must have heard me. She must have, but she doesn't bother saying anything, so neither do I.

So I go to bed with my customary half pint of water

to ward away those evil demons of Hangover City. I'm sure they come in the middle of the night and breed on my tongue. And from there the bastards run haywire through my brain and blood, sapping all my intelligence and willpower. Bloody parasites! It's not as if they ever buy a pint. I can just see them sitting on my tongue. 'Why bother,' they say, 'when we can suck the sap from this sucker?'

The bastards must have known I was thinking about them, 'cos when I wake up after a few hours kip, a chisel couldn't have prised my tongue from the roof of my mouth. Maybe I should up the stakes from a half pint of water to a pint. But then I'll just need to piss all the time.

The TV is blaring, probably a deliberate ploy on Eve's part to wake me up. 'Have Yourself a Merry Little Christmas,' by Judy Garland. Jesus, all I want to do is stick my head under the covers again. But it's Christmas, and she's bought me a present.

Then, all of a sudden, I want to see Eve. It happens in one of those moments when you think you're thinking clearly, and then later, with hindsight, you see you weren't. But I want to walk into the living room and see her curled up in a ball on the sofa. At that moment when she turns and looks at me with those big puppy eyes of hers – half smiling, half pleading – I have to admit I feel a bit lost.

The problem's always been I don't know what she expects when she looks at me like this. I never know what to do or say.

'Don't look at me like that!'

'What?'

'Funny like.'

'Jesus Christ. Merry Christmas to you too!'

I flop down beside her on the sofa and grab the remote control from her hand. Judy Garland is shut up rapidly.

'Did I wake you?' she says, as if she doesn't know.

I've a limp piece of mistletoe behind my ear that Eve has been conveniently ignoring for a while. The least she can do though is give me a snog when I hand over her Christmas present.

'Listen, Will, it's not as if I don't want a kiss. I do,' she says. 'But do it here, please.' (Points to her cheek.) 'I know for a fact you didn't brush your teeth before going to bed, and kissing your mouth just now would be touch-and-go between a brewery and a sewer. So, no offence intended, but I think I'll give it a miss if it's all the same to you.'

Always the florist, she gives me a present which is perfectly gift-wrapped, all bows and squiggle-bits of ribbon. Mind you, it doesn't stay like that for long. Inside is a complete CD collection of James Brown recordings.

Of course 'Sex Machine' goes straight on the boogie box. It must be the alcohol but when Eve stands up and I see her tighten her belt of her bathrobe and tuck in that triangle of naked flesh exposed from her neck to the beginning of her titties, I grab her hand and force her into a dance. I'm on the couch giving it my all. I'm on my knees. I clutch Eve close to me forcing her into a ritual dance for the Godfather of Soul.

'That man is pure sex!' I shout.

The belt of her dressing gown unravels and flaps about. Underneath, her tartan PJs are hardly inspiring for me: the Love God, Will. But still I pull her close. And here we are swaying our hips together. I've got this image in my head of Patrick Swayze and Jennifer Gray in 'Dirty

145

Dancing'. But I know for a fact that I'm better-looking than Patrick. The only thing he's got going for him is his twinkletoes and pecs.

Eve tries to break free. It's just part of the innocent act, though. I'm only wearing an old T-shirt and a pair of boxer's. (On the front is Santa Claus, but where he sticks his tongue out, Will's willie is supposed to appear and on both cheeks on the back is written *Ho, Ho, Ho!*) For the first time ever, our legs touch. Okay, she's got her PJs on, but I have an imagination. It must be the booze. 'Cos I like it. Every time she tries to pull away, I won't let her go.

'Stop this, Will. The music's too loud. Think of old Mr McCormack downstairs. Let me go. You've squashed the cushions on the couch.'

Now, this may not be the obvious come on, and my only excuse is still the flow of ale through my blood. But when I come to rest my hands on the small of her back, and then her bum for the mere fraction of a second, well, naughty old Santa's tongue!

Right away she goes off on one of her tangents, jibbering:

'I'm not one of your tarts, Will.'

'Loosen up, Eve. It's Christmas, for fuck sake. We're only having a bit of a laugh.' Okay, okay, I know I shouldn't have touched the sacred bum of Eve, but for Christ sake!

'Just don't get me mixed up with them, okay?'

I adopt my I-surrender pose. 'Okay, okay.' Them? I don't know whether to be as chuffed as mint balls or mortally offended. Them? 'I'm a one-gal kind of guy, you know.'

'Well, whatever.'

I'm trying to avoid the guilt syndrome on Christmas Day but somehow I've only been up for half an hour and already I need a priest. This woman is driving me to be a Trappist monk! 'Look, Eve, I'm sorry. Carried away by Sex Machine, I suppose.'

The way she's hitting those cushions, I can tell she wishes it was me.

EVE He doesn't even have the decency to make a pass at me when he's sober. He's stotious. I'm surprised he hasn't keeled over or wet the floor yet. How dare he treat me like this? How *dare* he assume that I'm as easy a target as the rest of his conquests? He's just spoiled it. That's all. Totally spoiled it.

'That's what you honestly think you are?' I say. 'Don't you?'

He laughs, unconscious of the vile fumes from either end of him as he does so. 'What? A sex machine? Give me a break, for fuck sake, Eve. It's Christmas, and I can't be bothered with one of your high-and-mighty lectures. All right?'

'You do, though. Don't you? I'm not saying it's right or wrong. I just want to know. Just out of curiosity.'

'Aye, right! It's lads' talk, that's all. You know what your problem is? You take everything so seriously. It's just a laugh. A joke. It's wishful thinking, most of the time.'

I wish this wasn't Christmas Day. I wish it was any other day of the year, but not Christmas Day. It shouldn't be like this on Christmas Day. It should be like the ending of *A Christmas Carol*. All nice and good-natured, like the front of a Christmas card.

'You piss me off so much.'

'You're worse than my mother.'

'I hate you, Will.'

'No, you don't.'

'I do, Will. Sometimes I do. I think you're a pig who's only good for lying about in the shit all day.'

'Oh, say what's on your mind, why don't you? You're just pissed off with me 'cos I'm going out with Poppy.'

'This has nothing to do with Poppy.'

'Yes, it has.'

'Poppy isn't going to give you what you need.'

'Right now, Eve, I need a shag. And you're right in thinking that she's not going to give me her precious cherry.'

WILL 'What's wrong now?' Jesus, the headache is starting. The queasiness is starting. I'm farting horrors.

She shrugs. 'Nothing.'

'Yes, there is. I can tell by that look on your face. Say it. Say what's on your mind. You're dying to.'

Eve looks straight into my eyes and says:

'You deserve more than that.'

This kind of conversation always makes me feel uneasy. It's not as if I come out in a cold sweat or am desperate to leave the room or something. I just don't want to sit down. So I do the mature thing in the circumstances and pace up and down. I rant and rave about how I know I deserve more and maybe Poppy – with her cherry intact – is the girl for me. Abstaining now will make the event an Olympic triumph, when it happens.

'This time last year,' I say, 'I was helping Suzie get her

148

fucking drunken bitch of a mother into bed. I don't want to go back to that, Eve.'

'It doesn't have to be that way.'

'No? Well, if it's not that, then it's bound to be something else. Like measuring for a new fitted kitchen, visiting the relatives on Sunday afternoons or going down Princes Street on Saturdays to buy low-calorie coleslaw and tampons. Which, let's face it, I have no desire to do!'

Shit!

The hassle these pearls are causing, you can't imagine. Jesus, how the fuck was I supposed to know that Eve's mum got a set of pearls for the first Christmas she spent with Eve's dad?

Nobody thought about warning me. Here I thought I was being really nice for a change, when all of a sudden everyone gets the idea that Eve and me are 'together' – shagging, not to put too fine a point on it.

I blame Eve. This one is definitely down to her. It was her idea to have the parents round.

In comes Eve's mum. 'So,' she says in that *la-di-da* way of hers, wearing a lot of perfume and a bit too much lipstick, 'what did William give you?' Her eyes all a-flickering, and smiles that crack her face. 'Oh, *do* call me Flora, Will. You're almost part of the family, for heaven's sake.'

Right, so I get to thinking that I know exactly what's happening here.

Flora. What a name. Eve had an aunt called Fauna, you know. Jeez, that's even worse. Flora and Fauna.

But Mother Nature must have thought they were taking the piss out of her and killed off Fauna in a childhood accident. Now Flora expects Eve to meet a nice lad called Adam and let his serpent loose on her.

Anyway, I can't bring myself to call the woman something you spread on toast. I might as well call her *I-can't-believe-it's-not-butter*, but I settle for Mrs M. Aloud.

'Mrs Mum? Uch, that's lovely,' she sings.

I'm not such a heartless swine as to tell her I've actually nicknamed her Mrs Marg.

Okay, okay, I might be a wee bit too affectionate, but it seems like a good joke. Eve's pissed off, though. I can tell by the way she keeps snarling her upper lip at me in a really poor Elvis impersonation.

EVE It's his idea. Nothing to do with me.

'Here,' he says. 'Why don't we let them think that we are, you know, boyfriend stroke girlfriend, type of thing. I mean, if they've got the idea into their heads, then there's not much point disappointing them, is there? You know, it is Christmas Day, and, well, all my mum wants to see is me settled with a nice girl. She feels I'm lacking something since my dad died. What they don't know won't hurt them, and if they did know they'd be shitting themselves.'

He slobbers over me like a St Bernard that's drunk all its brandy. Wet kisses on my ears, over my face, sooking off all the make-up I hastily put on before they arrived. I don't think the joke is very funny, to be honest. I'm not a deceitful person and I hate to lie like this. But their faces give them away. Relief, it is, that's written all over them. The mums chatting as if

150

they're already choosing their colours for the wedding and my dad helping Will attach a plug to an electric razor.

'What's the afternoon movie?' Will asks. The funny thing is, as I look at him bent over the plug, his tongue sticking out the left corner of his mouth, he's so like my dad; you'd think he was *his* son.

'Pinocchio,' I say.

By the end of Pinocchio everyone is sleeping, apart from me. The snores mingle into some level of tuneless harmony – all inhaling and exhaling together; regular as clockwork. I shrug Will's head off my shoulder, where his slobbers have mixed with the dye from his purple paper hat (which fell over his face) and left a mark on my white blouse.

I go and put the kettle on, hoping that someone will wake up soon, because I feel a bit left out at the moment. I try and conform to the breathing rhythm but fail miserably with the inhales. Once an outsider, always an outsider.

A bottle of wine, half empty, sits on the draining board. I refill a glass that doesn't have the rim smudged by my mother's lipstick, and stand sipping it, looking out of the window.

Whereas the rain was a mere drizzle this morning, now it's heavy. So heavy that it bounces off the window panes. The sky is almost black in that claustrophobic way that always reminds me of Tuesdays: not quite the beginning of the week and certainly not close enough to the weekend.

My mum, when she sees the weather, will make an excuse to leave soon. I can just hear her:

'This weather plays havoc with the car battery.' Or,

'You know with your dad's eyesight we'd be best going before the roads get any worse.'

The streets are empty. Not surprising, really, when you look up at the skies. Not one person about. No children showing off new bikes and prams. No couples huddled together under a huge stripy golf umbrella, hurrying to their next port of call.

'It's pelting now,' Will's mother says, peering out of the window behind me. So close, she is, that I can smell the faint aroma of sage from the stuffing on her breath.

'Help yourself to some wine.'

She does. 'You know, Eve, I'm glad we've got a minute alone.'

'Oh?'

'Yes. I'd just like to say that I'm happy you and my William have got it together, eventually.' She snorts and some wine comes down her nostrils. She's quite hard to take seriously when she's wearing a lime-green paper hat and her new fuchsia-pink slippers that her only son gave her. 'To begin with, I was a wee bitty worried. You know, after Suzie and whatnot. But he's happy with you. His daddy always said you'd be the one to keep him on the straight and narrow. And at long last my boy is happy. It's written all over his face. He never was any good at secrets.'

Well, what does she want me to do? Am I supposed to clap? Shout bravo? Grab the woman to my bosom and shout Mama? I don't know, but I can tell she's waiting for a reaction. I don't say anything. I just run my hands through my hair. The disappointment on her face is evident.

She continues:

'Can I be honest with you, Eve? I know how much

William mucks about with his so-called friends, and whatnot, but you seem to be able to keep him in line. I always used to cut out potatoes from his meal when he was a bit hyperactive. Too much starch in potatoes, you know. I read that once in *Woman's Weekly*. He would sit there and eat his mince without his potatoes, watching me and his dad eat ours, knowing fine well why he didn't get any. Never got pudding either, as a matter of fact. Mind you, with all this fuss about BSE, I might have been better cutting out his mince!'

I gaze out the window. Across the road a motorcycle roars, and then stops as quickly as it has arrived, outside Number 45. Even from this distance I can see his smile when the girl opens the door, beckoning him in with a giggle and a kiss.

'I have to say, though, he never had acne. So some benefit came from the potato phase, I suppose.'

What about me?

I want that.

When is it going to be my turn?

I want him to look at me.

And love me.

Just like that.

Just with the click of my fingers.

Just by the way he'll look at me.

And I'll know he loves me.

'What would you say if I told you Will and I had no intention of ever getting married?' I play with my pearls.

She looks at me squarely. A mixture of confusion and disbelief.

'Look, Mrs McIntyre . . .'

'Liz. Oh, do call me Liz.'

WILL 'I'm glad we've got this minute alone,' she says. The lipstick's washed away by wine. And she's got that bleary-eyed look that I would call pissed and she would call tiredness.

We're alone in the kitchen, doing the dishes. I didn't volunteer, Mrs M. did that for me. I assume for this little 'chat'.

I wash the dishes, shoving my yellow Marigolds deep into the hot foamy water.

Eve's mother half inspects, half dries, giving one dish in three back to be re-washed.

'I half expected you to buy Eve a ring.'

'Well, Mrs M., you're really jumping to the wrong conclusion there, you know –'

'Why?' She interrupts. 'Is it not on the cards?'

'Look, Mrs M., after my last fiasco, I'm a wee bit wary of getting into anything like that.' All of sudden the ingrained grease marks on the oven tray seem really interesting.

'What do you mean, "anything like that"?'

'Well, you know.' I squirm a bit to get my shirt, which is sticking to my back, off it. Pints of sweat are pouring from my armpits. Jesus, this is worse than when my dad told me about the birds and the bees. 'Permanent.' Now she probably knows this word as a wave in her hair, so I squirm some more. The shirt remains stuck there.

'Uch, that was just the wrong person. Now you're with Eve, everything will be just dandy. You always did fancy Eve, even when you were engaged to that girl.'

'Her name was Suzie.' Scouring is not the word for what's happening to this poor plate.

'Whatever,' she sniffs *à la* Miss Piggy. 'I'm telling you, even before you knew it yourself, *I* knew. That's why you called the wedding off. Of course, I don't expect you to admit it. I know you're into all this macho stuff.'

What? Does this woman think that I chain her daughter to the bed and whip her naked backside with my belt?

Jesus, I can't get my Marigolds off quick enough to get away from this loony.

EVE 'Right,' I say, 'but what about every other time they come round? What are we supposed to do?'

'Don't invite them round. Ever again.'

I ignore this. 'Just turn the switch to automatic-lover mode? Pray tell me: how are we going to get out of this one, smart arse?'

'Watch that elastic on your knickers, Eve-sweetie-pie. We'll think of something.'

'What's this "we" malarkey? This one is down to you. *You* sort it.'

He ignores this. 'Just think of the positive side. From now on you'll not be expected to spend Sunday dinner with them. They'll just assume we're here, shagging like rabbits all the time.'

He dabs some more Jazz on to his chin, sleeks back his hair, dons his jacket and leaves me – to meet his girlfriend, Poppy.

8

EVE There's a Safeway's carrier bag hanging from the tree. It looks as if someone has tied it there.

I'm watching it from the window. When cars aren't passing I can hear the rustle of the wind against the bag. It's like a trapped bird there, caught in the web of branches, wriggling furiously, intent on escape. The wind gives it a heartbeat. A pulse, even. The green writing on the bag gives it trailing veins. It's alive, and caught. And not very different from any other living thing.

I hate January. I call it the month of discontent. The euphoria of tinsel and holidays is well and truly over. All that's left is a box of leftover turkey in the freezer and another hole in the front door where I hung the

157

wreath. January is a month of good intentions. It's a month when you give up chocolate and take up driving lessons, or throw out all old pairs of knickers and promise to phone your mother once a week. There's something very Lent-ish about the month of January. Well, the first week anyway. And then it's just back to normal, really, saying, *Mañana, mañana*. Okay, you say, there may be holes in these knickers, but at least they're thermal. And why do I have to do all the phoning? If my mum wants to talk to me, then she can phone here. And it's winter, so I can't give up chocolate. Nor can I start driving lessons. Say I skid on black ice, for example?

It's winter.

It's January.

The coffee machine's going barmy behind me, but for the life of me I don't have the energy to turn round and pull it off the hob. That's another thing about January. I'm always tired. I can feel tiredness sweep over me like a late May haar.

A guy goes by wearing a denim jacket and shades. He looks a bit of a prat, really, considering it's January and the clouds are about to open with sleety rain to mist them up. The girl he's with has a dyed-raspberry-red crew cut. It looks good in a rebellious sort of way and I wonder if it would suit me.

'Madame Butterfly', they're away to see at the new Festival Theatre, you know. He had to ask directions to get there. Never mind that we live no more than fifteen minutes away from it.

'Poppy's class,' he says. 'She likes the finer things in life. That's why she likes me.'

I don't know whether it's the hair, or hats, or black patent shoes she wears. I just don't know. It must be something to do with using *parfum* instead of *eau de toilette* and calling him William instead of Will.

Forever the traitor that he is, he bought eleven yellow roses from The Purple Gladioli. In January, as well. I gave him seven out of ten for originality.

And he did something that he's never done before: he stroked my cheek with his finger tips and placed one of the roses behind my ear. It's not until he's closed the door behind him, and I can't hear his whistling any more that I look in the mirror. He'd taken all the thorns off and cut the stem.

WILL Okay, I know everyone goes through phases. I'm the first to admit that I am a phase kind of bloke.

I've never quite lost the knack of leaping from one thing to another. Please let me be frank here – I don't want to. If it's not Superman, then it's football, and if it's not football, it's snooker. One night I dream of being Paul Gascoigne and the next being one of those strippers from 'The Tartan Terriers'. I go from chocolate to pakora to tortilla chips. It can last a day, a month, a year. It's weird, but that's the way it is. That's the way the cookie crumbles.

You grab life by the balls and then the next minute say you can't be bothered.

I'm going by the grab-life's-balls motto just now. Some sceptics would say that's normal for me. Well, I'm just like any other everyday sort of guy: I have limp-penis days as much as the next man. But not just now.

Between you and me, though, I'm not keen on opera or nouvelle cuisine. I'm not too keen on it and neither is my bank manager. All this for a shag? I ask myself. It'd be

159

cheaper going elsewhere, but you can never tell. I mean, Poppy's great. She laughs at my jokes. She's just a bit too fond of my wallet. Says she believes in gallantry. Says she likes being taken different places. Makes her feel grown up. But it's me who's paying for it all!

Least I'm not going through a wistful phase like Eve. Jesus, she's so fucking sad. All that staring out of windows, and sighing every so often, it kind of grates on your nerves after a while. But still she carries on, selfish as ever. Thinking about herself. She should be in one of those Merchant Ivory films with the heaving of bosoms and pruning rose bushes in the garden in Laura Ashley get-up.

I say to her:

'Do you know what your problem is? You think life is like one of those Jane Austen books. You think everyone uses paper doilies under their cake plates. That everyone knows a gâteau fork isn't for getting the last pickled onion out of the jar. That everyone's underwear is white cotton and nobody does number twos! You think every life should have a happy ending!'

'Not ending,' she replies, sighing as per normal. 'The end is death. That's inevitable. Meanwhile, a happy chapter. Everyone deserves a happy chapter.'

See what I mean? Irritating as fuck.

'You live in Cloud Bloody Cuckoo Land!' I tell her.

If she misses Ian that much then I don't know why she doesn't just phone him. It's not as if it broke up – more kind of dwindled out.

Listen, it's been a long time in coming, but things are going right for me. Well, for a wee while, hopefully. I have earned the right to be a smug wee bastard. The bubble is bound to burst soon, but just let me wallow

160

in it for another day or two. Until then I'm happy with Poppy. She's a great girl, and she's not a head-case like Suzie. Not yet, anyway.

In saying that, though, the map to the treasure chest of Poppy's knickers is well and truly hidden. But gimme time. Gimme time. All I need is the magic key to that chastity belt. Jason chased the golden fleece and I'm doing much the same. It may not be golden, but unless she shaves her pubes then there is bound to be a fleece.

It boils down to the *R* word: *R*espect. So she says, anyway.

Not the *L* word. Not *L*ove – don't be daft. What do you think I am? A complete fuckwit.

Love. It means nowt. It means zilcho. There's nothing there apart from a hard-on, heavy breathing and the obligatory purchase of polo mints. That's what love is. That's what it's all about. Nothing to do with companionship, or friendship, or togetherness. Don't you get it? Don't you know? It's all part of the cliché. It's sex, pure and simple. Don't get embroiled in all that Bills & Moon shite, 'cos it doesn't ring true. Don't complicate matters. There's no point. Why set yourself up for bruised testicles?

Yeah, butter them up, go for the flowers, go for the full whack, but don't believe it. Do it, but don't believe it. *She* should believe it, yeah, but not you. Don't put your hand into that fire, 'cos then your arm will disappear, and then the rest of you.

That's Eve's problem, and really 99% of the female population when you put your mind to it. Eve believes in it. Believes in love. But Eve believes in fairies at the bottom of the garden, for fuck sake.

EVE 'Right, that's me off.' I fling my bag over my shoulder and zip up my jacket.

'You going out?' he asks. I notice the hole in his left sock at this point. He lies on the couch, one hand clutching the remote control. A dirty plate of leftover Birds Eye chicken tikka masala is abandoned on the floor. His work tie hangs over the arm of the couch like a noose, still with the knot tied firmly in place. He never unties them, just pulls it on and tightens the loop with one tug. One tug too tight, and that would be that.

His toes bend back and forth, the big toe's nail flashing through the black sock. It's not until I look at it a second time that I notice it's covered in a pinky shade of nail polish.

I don't want to know.

He hardly takes his eyes off High Road.

'Mm.' I peek in my bag to make sure I have everything – keys, purse, cards. Keys. Purse. Cards.

'Where you going?'

'Out.'

Thinking he's missing out on something, he turns round to look at me. 'Where?' I watch his eyes look over the tracksuit and trainers.

'Just out.'

He laughs. 'What is it? Cardio funk? Step? What?'

'Nothing.'

'Why won't you tell me? I'll give you a lift if you just say.' He presses the mute button on the remote control. Davie Sneddon's Irish twang is cut short, so I know he definitely thinks he's missing out on something.

I just know he's going to come over and force his way into my bag. Running out the door appears the best option, but . . . he always was faster than me. 'God, Will, you're so childish.'

He looks like a hunting tiger. 'I just want to know what you're up to. Go on! Let me see.' He pulls my bag off my shoulder.

'Don't laugh at me.'

'I promise.' He sticks his nose in my bag, and I think of the bag lady rummaging through a bin in Princes Street Gardens. He rifles through a pair of socks, a bottle of water and a can of deodorant. He pulls out the pair of shoes by the ribbon, which he has managed to fray in doing so.

'Tap shoes?'

'Give me them back.'

'How long have you been doing this?' He's smirking in that way that tells me he's going to make a vicious comment: sooner rather than later, unfortunately.

'Ooh, ages,' I manage with a shrug. I'm hardly going to confess to him.

'Why didn't you tell me?'

'Why didn't I tell you?' I do a poor imitation of Will. 'Because I knew you'd act exactly like this. I knew you'd laugh at me.'

'Who's laughing?' He's smirking.

I grab the shoes out of his hand and shove them back into the sports bag.

'You know, Eve – or should I call you Shirley? You'll never meet men that way.'

'God, everything reduces down to men and sex with you, doesn't it? Grow up! Maybe I do it to get away from men for a while. We're not all love-starved and sex-starved like you, you know. If you must know, I've been going to tap-dancing classes for years. Stupid me

163

only gave them up when you moved in. God knows why. Now I'm late. Thanks a lot, Will.'

'Let me give you a lift then.'

I run down the hall, but suddenly turn back. 'You know, Will, this may surprise you, but I had a life before you moved in here. I did things. I didn't sit in every night, like I do now. God knows what the hell I've been doing the last few months. Believe it or not, my life does not revolve around you. I need to get my life back into some kind of order. And you know something else? I'm good at tap-dancing. I'm doing my blue riband now.'

'Thought that was a biscuit.'

'A medal!' I shout. My voice is getting all screechy, so I know it's time to make a dignified exit. 'Shit! Now I'm really late. So you'd better give me a lift after all. Just don't look in the window, okay?'

WILL Poppy first kissed me outside Argos on the Bridges. That in itself was romantic. But it's only an interlude. Just the commercial break before the feature film. No big deal. Nothing to write home about. No tongues involved.

The second time is in the Fiesta. I pick her up at home. Chicken out of meeting the parents and just toot my horn. Out she comes running – after blinds twitching.

'I like going out with someone with a car,' she says smacking a huge snogarooney on my lips. I can smell her perfume. It's a bit too peachy for my liking and it's too cold to open the windows. I'll just have to breathe quickly. 'Every other guy I've gone out with had to get their dads to pick me up if we were going out. And then collect us later when we wanted to go home.' She giggles, making herself comfy in the seat.

164

'No, this is more like it. I could get used to this.' Then she smiles.

Just as well it's pitch dark outside and she can't see the bodywork. The car's, not mine.

'One of them had a skateboard but I don't suppose that counts.'

'Have you had lots of boyfriends then?'

'A few,' she says, exhaling visibly in front of me. 'About twenty or so.'

The brakes screech to a halt, which is no mean feat in this ice. 'Twenty!' I don't believe it. 'How many is that a year?' Considering she's only nineteen we must be talking record-breaking stuff here.

She giggles a bit more. 'It was just messing about really. Kid's stuff. Experimenting. It's nice to go out with someone more mature.'

Is she talking about me? Mature? Next year's cheddar cheese is more mature than me! I pride myself on being immature. But if the lady requests maturity, I'm sure I can manage that.

We kiss at the red light until the car behind us beeps. The girly perfume grows on you, after a while.

EVE I've always fancied falling in love in a book shop. You know? Meeting someone in the crime section, and find you've got the same insatiable taste in murder. That really would be a match made in heaven.

I roam about the book shops now. Not deliberately on the hunt for a husband, of course. Not gently bumping into someone who happens to be flicking through *Sophie's World* and looks a bit like a boffin. It's not for that at all.

I'm not in any great hurry to go home any more.

Walking in and hearing nothing but the clink of my keys in my pocket is depressing. Very rarely do I get the Neighbours theme or Oasis blasting in my ears, and Will shouting, 'Where's my dinner?'

Now, when he comes into Flower Power, he picks up Poppy instead of me. She has said to go out with them, but I'm not playing gooseberry to anyone.

I don't like being the first back at night, when I have to switch the lights on and close the curtains. It seems so final somehow. So dull and boring. I say to myself, 'Well, that's that, then. Another day, another dollar.'

You get a buzz in the shops. I'm never on my own there. It makes me feel part of something. Like a well kept secret. Even when I'm flicking through a Danielle Steel. It's the closest I'll going get to being an intellectual in this city where every second unmarried person is some sort of student.

Bright, I think is the word. Bright, even though it's dark outside. Bright and interesting, and I just want to feel a part of that.

The good thing about Edinburgh is that there are lots of book shops. I don't have to keep going back to the same one all the time. Like some saddo who hasn't got a life at home.

Sometimes, if I'm lucky, I come across a signing session by some author I've never heard of. But I can pretend, stand there, smile falsely like all the other pseudo groupies. I can sip red wine while acting the number-one fan.

Anyway, tonight, someone is talking about aromatherapy. The medicine of the twenty-first century. Well, so it says on the poster. Learn how to massage your partner. Use natural oils to create an enjoyable ambience in your own home. Use aromatherapy techniques to combat stress. Become a whole person with essential oils. There's more than ten other phrases squashed on to a blackboard at the front desk. The big sell. *Massage Yourself* is squeezed down in the corner, in tiny writing, so I've got to be practically nose-to-board to read it. So much so, I can smell chalk. Why can't they put something like 'Boost masturbation with the aid of oils: no batteries required', if that's what they're meaning?

The wine tastes like cat's piss.

Why do people say that? How does anyone know what cat's piss is like, unless they've tried it? So someone must have tried it at some point if they say it tastes like cat's piss in the first place. Mind you, cat's piss might not be so clawy. I'm sure this stuff is taking the enamel off my teeth.

We're ushered downstairs to the dungeons below Millstone's shop floor. I try not to think about fire hazards or battery hens. Other folk have come in for a laugh before going on to the pub to discuss the pros and cons of organic carrot juice, no doubt. I sit in the last seat of the second-last row. Self-conscious, but not really uncomfortable. Yes, I'm surrounded by four walls. But at least they're not my four walls. Lights are dimmed; introductions conducted.

I wish I'd brought some sweets to suck.

Lavender oil and lemon grass are very popular, it seems. Strips of perfumed oils are passed around and I can't keep up since I'm the last in line, so always at least two smells behind everyone else. One's relaxing, the other's invigorating. I'm sure it would work – if I could decipher which was which.

They're now looking for a volunteer for a shoulder

massage. 'Preferably male, please, because it's better for the top half to be naked.' A few sniggers, but no volunteer steps forward. Least of all a woman not embarrassed to show off her accidentally grey-tone-dyed bra to over fifty people.

And then *he* steps forward.

'Give him a show of hands,' says the woman.

It's not until he's seated and I squint round the bad perm sitting in front of me that I see him properly. He's stripping off. Taking off his tie, then unbuttoning his shirt. The same way he used to do it for me. I'm pleased he's not wearing his thermal vest tonight. I watch the masseuse rub oil over her hands and then up over his shoulder:

'Remember, though, it's not like kneading bread. Gently does it. Let the oil seep into the skin.'

His eyes are closed. He's not wearing his glasses. Tonight must be a contact-lens night.

'Oh,' she says, 'that muscle is so tense. Do you have a stressful job?'

'I travel around a lot,' says Ian.

A bit of an understatement, if you ask me. I must have snorted, because the woman beside me turns to give me a funny look.

I'm trying to pay attention to what this Ms Haddington is telling us, but really I'm paying more attention to Ian's torso. There's no middle-aged spread yet. Although, on reflection, his nipples are certainly bigger than mine. What does this mean? Does it mean anything? He's a bit hairy, granted, but no-one is throwing up in the corner.

He sees me when he's buttoning up his shirt. I'm trying not to look like I've been gawping at his body instead of listening to the pros and cons of clary sage. Now I'll have to mill about afterwards to talk to him. I'll have to feign interest in *Boost Your Ego With Essential Oils*, which can bought at a bumper price tonight and signed by Ms Haddington. I hate that – *Ms*. It seems like a politically correct statement. No-man-can-tie-me-down, kind of thing. Plus it adds intrigue about age and whether the woman is married, unmarried, divorced, or living with someone. Miss or Mrs keeps things simple. Otherwise you're just plain nosy to find out what Ms signifies.

'Picking up some hints?' he says, over the bookstand, where arms are seizing copies of the book on either side of us like loaves of bread in the supermarket before a holiday weekend.

We move out of the way of the masses.

'Enjoy your massage, did you?'

'Just the ticket. All I need now is a gin and tonic and a good book.' He holds up a black and gold Millstone's bag. 'Came across this, just by accident. Glad I did, mind you.'

'I can smell it. Smells really good. Makes a change from Eternity.'

'Been stood up, have you?'

I think of my dress. My eye-shadowed eyes. Probably too much lipstick. So I immediately start panicking in case I've got lipstick on my teeth, my face is looking too pale, or too powdery from too much compact. My feet twitch and I can feel my tights wrinkle at the ankles. Down they go quicker than the Titanic. I really should go for Lycra ones, like Will keeps annoying me about.

But Ian says:

'You look nice, really nice.' He laughs at my visible discomfort, rocking back on his heels as he does so.

God, and my mind plays tricks on me. As always

169

when I least want it to. Showing me in full Techni-color the first time ever I saw him rock back on his heels and laugh at me. He's in my head, and in front of my eyes in the exact same way. I look into his eyes. I notice how his hairline is actually receding and I never noticed it before. I don't mind it though. Scraggy lines surround his eyes and I can't tell if laughter or tension has caused them. All he needs is a few more massages. It's good to see him. It's just occurred to me, like a huge right hook to my chin. It's good to see him.

He asks me if I've tried the new place in Buccleuch Street. The Balti Bowl? Somehow it seems impolite to refuse.

'Why didn't you phone?' he asks. The candle wax is taking a beating from his fidgeting. I look at the flame and imagine the candles in his bedroom, in his bland, arty-farty flat in Stockbridge.

'I didn't think you wanted me to.'

'I wouldn't have said, "Phone," if I didn't mean it. Of course I meant it.'

Keep to polite conversation, I remind myself. 'So, you think this aromatherapy works?'

'God knows if it's psychosomatic, but all I feel I want to do right now is lie down.' He takes my hand.

I get his meaning.

'Will's going out with Poppy,' I say. 'Remember Poppy? That girl who works with me? Well,' I laugh, 'eventually Will just wore the poor girl down until she said Yes. And now they're inseparable.' I shrug. 'I've just got to get on with my own life now, I suppose.'

Ian slowly nods his head. 'Why are you telling me this?'

I shrug again, suddenly feeling very tired of the charade. Knowing why I'm telling him, and not admitting it to myself or him. 'I just feel I should explain things.'

'Do you love Will?'

I can't keep up with the spring-boarding of this conversation. I feel as if it's a tennis match and I'm the ball.

The first time I wasn't prepared for this question. But I've prepared some pretentious off-the-cuff remarks to keep the vocal tennis match going. 'It goes way beyond love. It's really hard to understand, but I guess somewhere along the way we blinked and missed that stage.'

'Would you like it back?'

'Oh, come on! We'd kill each other. He'd get on my nerves, and I'd get on his, then we'd be bored with each other. It wouldn't be right.'

He leans across and takes my other hand. I can't help feeling surprised. And I wonder: is this going to be one of the romantic moments in my life?

'It's just, well, I don't want to step on anybody's toes.'

'Have you missed me?' I try to keep my desperation under wraps.

'Yes.'

'A little, or a lot?' Oh, God. Subtle, or what?

'A lot.'

'Good. Good.'

We'd had this deal, Will and me. I can't help thinking about it at this moment, while Ian is leaning across the table holding my hands. My feet are up on his chair and I can feel his thighs against my instep. How could I have forgotten about this? How could I for one minute think my world revolved round Will and forgotten about this? Forgotten how his thighs rest against my instep. How my head fits so perfectly on his shoulder. How our noses jigsaw so well together. How we talk. How we laugh. How he's the strong one and I feel vulnerable in a feminine kind of way. He makes me feel like a woman. And yet, even while I'm doing this, with Ian's thigh against my instep, Will is there, always there in the back of my mind, reminding me of the deal we made.

I wore blue-and-pink-checked trousers, and a blue T-shirt. Jesus, I thought I was so cool. Sitting there in Will's dad's greenhouse, sampling the hidden bottle of Whyte & Mackay. It burnt my throat, I remember that. Will was all in black: black jeans, black T-shirt and black biker's jacket. The whisky hadn't warmed me at all, and when he saw me shiver he wrapped his jacket around my shoulders. The very weight of it made me think of Will as being strong.

It was just after his dad's funeral. He didn't want me to be there. He wanted me to meet him in the greenhouse. It seems so decadent, when I think back on it, that we met in the greenhouse and shared the Scotch between us instead of making idle chitchat with old aunties. Neither of us wiped the bottle when we slugged. We were so confident, so sure of each other. It was nothing really, but it meant everything.

I let him talk, ramble, while I sat there listening. I could smell tomato plants, and to this day tomato plants remind me of death.

It was all reassurance, I suppose. But when he said – no, promised – that he would marry me if he hadn't met anyone else by the time we were both twenty-five, I was stupid enough to believe him. No blood oath, no shaking of hands, no kiss to consummate this promise; nothing. And yet, I believed it. Lots of things got in the way, though. Girls by the names of Beth-Anne, Laura, Suzie . . . and Poppy. His list is in a little black book he still hides underneath his pillow.

Mine is a Post-it note with two names on it.

'What do you say?' Ian asks.

'Every time I see you, you're always in a suit, with the tie tied properly, and the top button of your collar never unfastened. Don't you own a pair of jeans? Trainers? A fleece?' I'm trying to avoid answering his question.

'That's for you to find out. Anyway, stop evading the question. Will you, or won't you?'

I don't say anything. Look instead at the candle wax on the table.

'Is that a yes, or a no?'

Silence.

Can't even muster a giggle. I'm listening for the warning voice in my head. Nothing. So I say:

'Okay. Yes, it is.' Unfortunately it comes out more nonchalant than I feel.

We shake hands. The wax he's been pulling off the candle sitting on the table between us feels smoother than the skin on his fingers. It's also warmer.

WILL *How did we meet?*

Eve's probably the best one to tell you. You know, she'd add all those wee-bitsies that everyone wants to hear. Our eyes met across the crowded room, and so on. She'd exaggerate to make it sound something out

173

of one of her books, when really it was nothing like that.

I went to this party. I can't remember if I was invited, or gate-crashed, or what. I was sixteen at the time, and just ended up there after the under-eighteen disco at Oscar's. You know? You go with the lads, to pick up some bird with braces on her teeth. But you're pissed after drinking a bottle of cider at the swing park. You can't tell if she's got braces or not, until your tongue gets caught between the plastic plate and the roof of her mouth. Or worse, when it's one of those chain braces and your lip gets caught in it. And you're stuck. And then bleeding everywhere until it looks like you've got a big cold sore in the middle of your face. That sobers you up and then you look at the person you've been snogging and you wish you were still pissed. But then, with the cold sore and all, the game is blown, and no-one else wants to snog you anyway.

So in I cruise to this party and pick up the nearest bottle. It was green and looked alcoholic. Need I say more? I couldn't understand why everyone laughed. I mean, who in their right mind would take a bottle of low-alcohol wine to a party for experimental sixteen-year-olds? Right, you've got it, Eve. But she came out into the garden when she heard me throw up. I leaned on her then.

She says, 'I helped you because you were killing the rose bushes.'

But I know it's always been more than that. She fancied me. We may be way past all that now, but she definitely did then.

EVE He had on this hellish herringbone coat. When he threw up, it trailed in the mud. But his hand reached out and grabbed my shoulder to stop himself from falling. He leaned on me then, and he's leaned on me ever since.

WILL Jeez, now you want me to talk about Poppy.

Well, to be honest it's running as smoothly as the engine in my Fiesta. She's a nice girl and all, but, between you and me, she's also bit of a prick-teaser.

Right, any guy tries. That's the way of the world. You know, a bit of a touch there, a bit of a feel here, but when the girl says *Stop*, you do. No questions asked. She gives it the You'll-not-respect-me-in-the-morning treatment. Well, no. I suppose I won't. But when you're in the throes of passion, then the *R* word doesn't come into it. Well, it shouldn't.

It's all part of the game, yeah? You accept it once, twice, three times at a push, but Poppy's giving it this all the frigging time. She's nothing but a tease. I've tried every tactic in the book to get into her knickers but she snubs me at every turn. I've a good mind to say, 'Grow up, dearie.' Christ, if I'm that desperate for a shag, then I can go clubbing with the lads. No big deal.

She's just after crying, huge big sobs of the stuff, dribbling down her face, and demanding hugs. I kind of feel sorry for the kid. She's a changed girl these days. For a start, she doesn't laugh at my jokes. She doesn't want to even snog. And who could resist me? There's something big going on here, and I don't know what it is. But I don't want to know either. Jesus, I don't want to get involved with any psycho bitch. I've had enough of that.

Besides, I miss Eve.

Okay, I admit it. I admit it without my hands being tied behind my back. Without a gun to my head. I MISS EVE. I miss the nights when we'd share a few cans of lager and order out for a pizza. I miss that. I miss watching videos and arguing over what to watch. I miss her grabbing the remote control from me when I channel-hop at the adverts. The wee annoying things that made sharing worthwhile.

EVE There's a photo of me in Ian's kitchen, stuck right in the middle of the pinboard. It's there in amongst the telephone bill, a postcard from his mother in Italy and the take-away menu for The Spice of Life.

'Is that new?' I ask him.

He plunges the filter down the cafetière. 'Shit, I forgot all about that. Take it down.'

'Why? I like it. I like how you've got a photo of me in your kitchen.'

'But I don't need it now that you're here. I can see you. I can touch you. I don't need a photograph any more to remind me of how you look. I can see you for myself.'

He must feel the way I do. I hope he does. God, I hope he does. I want him to see into my brain, to see the erased Will, gone. Gone.

Ian snores.

I can't sleep.

He lies on his back, me tucked tightly against him. He needs a cotton reel glued on his back to make him lie on his side and hence stop the snoring. Will's mum probably told me about that at some point after reading it in *Woman's Weekly*. But I like lying like this. I can tolerate the snoring, as long as I'm tucked in beside him. Our breathing's in sync except when he blusters a snore every so often. My fingertips play with his chest hair. Chest hair! How glad I am to have it back. Did I honestly say that? Me, who thinks men have a cheek to complain about women's hairy legs and unshaven oxters – when they've got more hair plastered to them than the yeti.

The digital clock reads 5.05.

Or is it SOS?

WILL She comes in when I'm having breakfast. The football results are shite, so I think I can pay her some attention.

'You're back, then.'

'Will,' she says, 'why do you think you've never made love to me?'

Well, for a Sunday morning, she's certainly sharp. Sharper than me, sharper than the knife I'm holding. 'Dunno,' is all I can come up with.

'That's not an answer. I want to know.'

'Jesus, what is all this?'

'Don't you see it? We're drifting apart, Will. I need to know.'

Being the man that I am, I shrug and then giggle a bit:

'Never came up, I suppose.'

'Did you ever want to?'

'Oh, yeah. Loads of times.' Bloody stupid question really.

'Why didn't you do anything about it?'

I shrug. 'Because there's women and there's you. It's different.'

'But I'm a woman. I'm a woman too. Look at me, just once, and see a woman. Please.'

Well, you can pick me up with a crane if you like, because all of a sudden she unfastens her coat and she's not got a bean on underneath.

'Eve, for fuck sake, the blind's open!' I croak.

'Look! Look!' she shouts, still standing there starkers in front of me.

I force myself to look. And I'm not enjoying this at all. Come on, it's not as if there's anything wrong with her body. It's Eve's and it's nice.

But Eve.

Eve!

It's not right.

'Now kiss me.' She steps out of her coat and walks towards me. Her titties are heavy and kind of wobble as she walks. I can't keep my eyes off them. I just want to warm my ears in between them. Eve's nipples are round and brown, protruding like those brambles you used to steal from your neighbour's bush in his garden. And speaking of bushes, a triangle of light peeks through between her thighs. I've got a hard-on and don't want to stand up.

'Kiss me.'

Jesus, my legs are trembling and I all I can think about is the blind being open.

Plus, I don't want her to see my hard-on. But for fuck sake, what does she expect? A naked nymph frolicking in front of me, what does she expect? So I do stand up and put my arms around her waist. The skin is so soft, like a peach, with all those prickly little hairs standing on end. She licks her lips in preparation. That is one of the most erotic things I've ever seen. The

178

way she does it isn't dirty or suggestive, just necessary.

Anyway, we kiss.

Her lips are hot, her fingertips resting on my shoulders, cold. Her tongue licks my upper teeth. Tighter and tighter, my arms go around her. I want more. I want more. But then again, I always was a selfish bastard.

She tears herself away from me. 'Do you know how long I've wanted to do that?'

She's bending down, gathering her coat around her. For a brief second I can make out the dimpled flesh on her bum. So that's cellulite. What's the big deal? I kind of like it. 'For ever,' I say, about to shoot my load. 'For ever and a day.'

Her smile lights up her whole face. 'Thanks. I just wanted to do that once. Especially since now I'm getting married.'

9

WILL Fuck!

Fuck! Fuck! Fuck! Fuck! Fuck! Fuck! Fuck! Fuck!
Fuck! Fuck!

Fuck!

Fuck!

EVE This isn't how I imagined telling my parents I was
getting married. First, getting them to pay for the taxi.
Second, phoning the bank and Access to cancel my cards.
And thirdly, crying, wondering how I am going to get
back into my flat again without the Fort Knox keys.

It's not really my fault I left my bag on the bus. I have

181

too much on my mind just now without worrying about handbags!

'Well, I wouldn't worry about it if I were you. Will's got a set of keys. He'll sort everything out,' my mother says.

This makes me cry even more. 'I'm getting married.'

'You see,' she says smugly, getting the wrong end of the stick as per normal. 'I knew my pep talk with Will would work miracles.' She passes me a paper tissue.

'Not to Will. To Ian.' I try not to sound angry.

'Ian?' This is my dad. 'Who's Ian?'

'The man I'm going to marry.'

'So, you're not marrying Will?' My mother always takes the longest to understand punch-lines.

'No.'

'Why not?'

'Because I'm marrying Ian.'

'Oh, for goodness sake, we're just going round in circles here. George, get the brandy.'

My dad, ever dutiful, goes to get the brandy.

'You're pregnant.' It's not even a question. It's a statement. 'How will I live this down? I've always said I'd support you, no matter what. But pregnant. You know how disappointed that makes me feel. I'll forgive anything but that.'

'Mum, I'm not pregnant.'

'Then why aren't you marrying Will?'

'Because he didn't ask me. Ian did.'

'Ian?' This is my dad again. 'Is he the one who likes Formula One?'

'Yes.'

'Ah.' He nods his head in approval. 'He's the one that's been to the Monte Carlo Grand Prix?'

'I think so. Years ago.'

182

'Grand.'

I can just see them together in ten years time, sitting in front of the TV watching cars zoom round and round and arguing good-heartedly about how many laps there's been. Me and mum will be rustling up a Sunday roast in the kitchen while the kids play on a swing in the garden.

And pigs might fly.

'Is that all you've got to say, George? You want your only daughter, your only child, to marry someone who's been to the Monte Carlo Grand Prix in nineteen bumteen?'

'But, Flora, he had a really good view. Said he could see the whites of James Hunt's eyes even through his crash helmet. Imagine that.'

'Will once nearly had a drink with Graeme Souness.'

My dad snorts.

It's nice to know my future happiness revolves round the sporting personalities whom Ian and Will have seen from a distance.

'But why not Will?' my mum continues. 'You've always loved Will. Secretly, I know. But mothers do know these things.'

God, I can't cope with one of her mother-child umbilical-cord talks right now. 'It's not mutual. It wouldn't be right. We'd make each other unhappy.' I try to think of every other cliché I've read in books and magazines. 'We don't love each other the way other people love each other.'

My dad's still thinking about Formula One. I can tell by that glazed-over look on his face.

'Rubbish,' says my mum.

My dad pours another brandy for himself, quickly, before my mother catches him.

'We should be drinking champagne. I'm getting married, Mum.'

'To Ian?'

'Yes.'

'He's a bit well . . . nondescript, don't you think? This Ian?'

'No. He's just set in his ways, that's all. You liked him because he could get the bones out of the trout in one go, you said.'

'He's well brought up, I'll give him that.'

'You liked how he knew what wine to drink with what meat, and how he can do the crossword in the *Scotsman*.'

'That's right.' She mulls this over for a minute. 'He's got a house down in Stockbridge, hasn't he?'

'Uh huh.'

'He wears cuff links?'

'Uh huh.'

'Gold ones?'

'Only on special occasions.'

'He's not a bad catch, all things considered, I suppose.' She's counting the qualifications after his name. Ian Morrison £.£.£.£.£ . . .

Thinking about hats, I shouldn't wonder.

'Why isn't he here, asking your dad for permission?'

How do I tell my mother that things don't quite happen like that any more? I try to think of things to pacify her, but that's just going to set the ball rolling again. Short and straight to the point, that's what I'll aim for . . . 'America. On business.' I try not to sound like a petulant child but fail miserably. The pettish lip gets larger with every word.

'Club class?'

184

'Probably.' (Eve Morrison $.$.$.$.$.$ . . .) 'He would have got out of it if he could, but, you see, well, getting engaged just sort of happened on the spur of the moment. It was spontaneous.' I like the sound of that. Spon Taneous. Makes it sound romantic.

'Well, Eve, the only thing I'm going to say on the subject is that Ian is the kind of man who always wears starched shirts. You're going to have to be handy with a steam iron.'

WILL Eve always makes a huge amount of noise when she walks. God, how it gets on my nerves. If it isn't zips jangling on her jacket, her Doc Martens squeak or loose coins roll about jingling in her coat pocket. Every-single-frigging-day. It's enough to drive you demented.

And she's always going on about the things I did that got right on her wick.

She makes herself out to be some kind of perfect woman who never did anything to annoy anyone, ever. Which is just a heap of shite. God, she irritates the shit out of me with her prissy-ing about all the time. Don't get me wrong, everything is done with good intentions, but there's something so Mavis-Wiltonish about it that just rubs me up the wrong way.

She makes herself out to be a victim. A wronged woman. A woman-who's-been-treated-like-shit-by-a-man type of woman. 'I gave it my all,' I can hear her say. 'God knows how I tried. God knows what I put up with.'

But they all say that. They drone on about how they get the raw deal, how the man is a complete bastard who hits, shouts, screws around, drinks beer and whisky chasers, heats up kebabs in the microwave and – the biggest of all possible evils – leaves the toilet seat up. But if you leave it down and spray it, then that's wrong too.

There's no winning with women.

None at all. It's like you're the goalkeeper and they're queuing up to take penalties. Most of the time you never know what direction they're going in. And sometimes if you're lucky like the Brazilian goalie against Baggio in the 1994 World Cup – the ball may just fly over the goal post. But that's just if it's your lucky day.

Okay, I know you can blame a lot of it on PMT, hormones and all that shit. But it's all a big excuse for being a stroppy cow. Every bloke would agree with me.

When men are bastards, they come out and say they're bastards. To each other. Least they've got the guts to do it. But women. *Women*. Women don't say anything, apart from nag and moan then blame everything on the man.

Suzie, for instance, blamed the wedding (or lack of it) on me. Yeah, I admit I didn't turn up personally. I physically avoided the whole charade. And that's just what it was – a charade. I'm man enough to admit that. Least I'm honest about it. Me not turning up was the wonderdrug for some ailment that a dose of kaolin and morphine would have cured years ago. All that time I thought the feeling in my chest was love. Now I realize it was years of indigestion.

Anyway, I'm honest about it. Put it this way, if I hadn't been honest, I'd be an old married man by now, shuffling about in a cardigan and enjoying trips to B&Q on Sundays.

And that is the difference between men and women. Men simplify things, make things honest. At least in their own heads. Women complicate things, exaggerate things a hundred-fold, work it into a huge trauma and make a big deal about nothing. They stomp. They screech. They yell and throw things. Then cry. Then start all over again.

Take Eve, all this shenanigans with her at the moment. I have no idea what drugs that girl's on. Drugs are for mugs. And that's what Eve is – a mug.

Married? To Ian? Eve? Don't make me laugh. She'll do the same thing as me. She'll go through the motions of picking the dress, choosing the flowers, matching it all together, and then chicken out at the last minute.

She's like me. She's honest. Like a man.

God knows how she got herself into this mess in the first place. And I know she'll try and blame me. I know she will 'cos I know Eve. She'll say this fiancé fiasco is down to me. My fault. Don't ask me why. But as I live and breathe, get up in the morning and go to bed at night, it's bound to be my fault. Just ask her.

One minute she's with him. The next she's not. Then she's back with him. Marrying Mr-no-overdraft-tadger Ian. I mean to say, it doesn't make any sense.

Mind you, no-one ever said women did make sense, did they?

I thought she was happy being Miss Independent of the nineties with her own flat and everything like . . . tap dancing. It just goes to show. I can be wrong. Sometimes. Occasionally.

EVE It's funny being home. Well, it's not my home, because my flat's my home, but when I'm at my mum's, she likes her home to be called my home. I have two homes. I'm spoiled for choice. In one home I have the debts to prove it's mine and in the other I can be a permanent guest with free access to the fridge.

Everything comes at a price, though. They've got me feeling like a kid again. Here I am, waiting for the phone to ring. Waiting earnestly for Ian to phone from wherever the hell he is to enquire about my health and – oh, how could I forget? – to make sure he's got the parental approval for our forthcoming nuptials.

Ignore the facts that he doesn't know I'm here and also doesn't have my folks' number. Forget that, and I'm still sitting here waiting for the phone to ring. Every time it rings they look over at me, with cheesy grins, waiting for me to pick up the receiver. I should just let it ring out because I know it's not going to be Ian. But I can tell they already think I'm making a complete mess of my life, so I don't want to confuse them any more. So, instead, they think Ian is a complete bastard, even though I've told them he doesn't have the number.

'He's a businessman, for Heaven's sake,' says my mum. 'He'll have ways and means of getting in touch.'

'Telepathy?' I swing on my chair to annoy her even more.

This is driving me up the wall.

But I can't go back. Not yet. I can't go back to my other home, my own home, because at the moment it doesn't feel like my home. And it has nothing to do with my keys on the seat of the 31A bus.

More because Will's there.

That in itself is fine. I can cope with that. But he's sent me to Coventry since last Sunday morning. Since the Sunday morning he saw my naked body, and kissed me with his tongue practising cunnilingus on the roof of my mouth.

God! He's so infuriatingly childish.

I don't know what's bugging him.

Is it that I'm getting married?

Is it that I stripped off in front of him?

Is it that he kissed me?

Is it that I stripped off in front of him and he kissed me, when he's still going out with Poppy, and I'm getting married to Ian?

Which? What?

God, I don't know what's bugging him.

And meanwhile I'm mad with my future husband because he isn't telepathic. He's sitting pretty, completely unaware of all the stress he's put me under. And it's his fault. And Will's fault. And my parents' fault. God forbid that it should be my fault.

Ian will just have to practise his aromatherapy techniques on me when he comes back from wherever the hell he might be. Not that I know where that is. Why should I know? For God's sake, I'm only marrying the man. Nothing important.

Calm.

Calm.

I'm heading for the biscuit tin. And the bottle of gin. And some trashy film on Sky Movies. I don't care what it is, as long as it is complete crap and I don't have to think about anything for at least two hours. I'll even watch Jean-Claude Van Damme, come to think of it. That's how dire things are.

The only problem is my dad, who's watching some professional golf tournament on Eurosport and would rather be hung upside down over a pit of bloodthirsty rats than give me the remote control.

They say cars are extensions of manhood. But I think they've got it wrong. Remote controls are the thing. If

Freud was alive, he would call the remote control the pseudo penis. And he'd be right. They've always got to fiddle with some damn knob or other.

Calm.

Calm.

One. Two. Three . . . Eight. Nine. Ten.

Their concentration span is on a par with Will's. Boredom sets in within five minutes of watching one programme, so then they flick-flick up through the other 150 channels of equal downright crap. When I say *they*, I actually mean my dad. If you see a glimpse of something you might find remotely interesting, you must shout, '*Stop!*' Otherwise, the image quickly changes into a topless French quiz show or some Nashville alcoholic with a stetson singing so close to the camera you can count how many fillings he has. Or even worse: a repeat of George and Mildred.

He stops at an interview with Kevin Costner and Dennis Quaid talking about the film 'Wyatt Earp'.

'Did you know they were so worried about Dennis Quaid when they made this movie, the amount of weight he lost? One day a doctor had to be called on to the set because he collapsed,' says my mum.

'Really?' They must have channel-hopped to this before.

The interview goes on. A male-bonding scene between the two actors comes on.

'Did you know they were so worried about Dennis Quaid when they made this movie, the amount of weight he lost?' says my dad.

That's it.

I've had enough. 'Sorry for interrupting, but I'm getting that *déjà vu* feeling.'

'Why?' he asks.

'Because we had this conversation just two minutes ago.'

'Who with?'

I get up to go and pack my bag and phone a taxi. At least taking yourself off to Coventry means you don't have to listen to this drivel.

WILL And another thing, why did she have to take her clothes off? She could easily have sucked the face off me with her clothes on.

Jesus, I didn't even have time to clear my throat or brush my teeth. I didn't even have a stick of Orbit.

She shouldn't have done it. She knows it and that's why she's not talking to me. She's too embarrassed.

Well, so she should be.

She never should have done it. Eve's the one who crossed the line. Not me.

Tell me, what would have happened if Poppy had walked in? Okay, she didn't. We're talking hypothetically here. Or Ian? What would she have done? Would she still have pressed her tits against my chest? That's what I would like to know.

She's crossed the line. Not me.

That's it. I'm out of here.

She's shot herself in the foot this time and she'll be limping a long time before she catches a sniff of my aftershave again.

EVE I knew he'd leave.

The big wimp. Left the keys with the neighbour, which was lucky, all things considered.

I bloody knew it. Coward.
Bastard.

WILL I mean, it's now or later. Now seems as good a time as any. Let's be honest here, we can't go back to phallic innuendo over the cornflakes now, can we? We can't call porridge semen from a man with a particularly high sperm count now. It wouldn't be right.

Least at my mum's I can sleep at night without thinking I'm going to be raped in my bed.

EVE I've never been a groin magnet.

Hans Christian Andersen is a bloody liar. He said the ugly duckling changed into a swan. Well, I'm still waiting.

Why did he go?

Okay, I *know* why he left. I know why he packed all his stuff – even the pillow cases, for God's sake – and carted them back to his mother's. Doesn't his mother have pillow cases?

He knows.

And I'm not attractive enough for him.

He knows.

And I've not transformed into a swan yet. Will would say that's because I always was a late starter.

If I had ever in my life been a groin magnet, do you honestly think I would be in this situation?

I just can't believe he took the pillow cases. What kind of man takes the pillowcases? He thinks I'm jealous of Poppy. That's what it boils down to. He thinks I'm jealous because she's slim, attractive, witty, intelligent and has him. I bet that's why he's left. He probably thinks I'm marrying Ian to get back at him.

The only evidence left of him staying here, now, is the few tack holes on the walls from his Tarantino posters and the smell of Steve McQueen's cage still lingering in the air. He's even taken all the empty Irn Bru bottles from the kitchen. Cleared out all the TV dinners from the fridge as well. Every cloud has a silver lining, I suppose.

A *Sunday Mail* lies on the kitchen table. Probably not moved at all from where he put it last Sunday morning when he stood up with his penis poking out of his boxer shorts. It's opened at the lottery number page. Page 13, it is. Must have been unlucky, because the lottery ticket's scrunched up beside it.

The second Sunday in February. Sunday before St Valentine's Day. I should just have sent a card. Like any normal woman.

10

EVE The phone rings and for once Nathan answers it. I hear him *Mm, mm-hoom* his way through the conversation. There's a problem. If I listen carefully, I'll probably hear Nathan's heartbeat in double-time, doing the paso doble round his body. Instead, humming a little ditty to myself, I carry on with the freesia display.

'Well . . .' the Oscar-winning sigh of the year. 'That's the third phonecall this morning. You've sent the funeral wreath to a Mrs Gillespie for her fortieth birthday, Eve. Eve? *Eve?* Are you listening to me? Now, I know Poppy's off at the moment, but if you're overloaded with work, let me know, and I'll give you a hand. I'm not a complete imbecile, you know.'

'You delivered it.' Going into a huff and blaming him seems the obvious thing to do.

'Yes, but only to the place you told me to. Pull yourself together, Eve. Your mistakes are costing me a fortune in compensation.'

'Well, that's just typical of you, thinking of profit before anything else. As long as there's silk lining your pockets and not nylon, then you're okay.'

'What is this? A bad-hair day?'

The first step of the vicious cycle, I want to reply. Next, I'll get a prescription from the doctor for a mild anti-depressant that will make me sleep. I'll get addicted to those and my system will become immune. Then the only answer will be Valium. And I'll get addicted to that. Down, down, down, I'll go into the realms of even more depression until I kill myself twelve months to the day after Nathan said:

'What is this? A bad-hair day?'

'If you're so concerned about the money, take it out of my wages.'

Eyes are rolled heavenwards in a God-give-me-strength pose. 'Now you're just being obtuse.'

'It's not as if February is a bad month. Last week we had St Valentine's day.'

He sniffs:

'Well, just buck yourself up. It's not my fault Poppy's got the flu. You're supposed to be the image of the blushing bride-to-be, and look at you. You look more like the girl who had a bad perm and found a boil on her nose on the same day.'

I don't say anything. I just stuff the freesias into a pot of water instead.

*　　*　　*

I thought it would be good getting back to the pre-Poppy days of just me and Nathan. But funnily enough I miss her. There's no-one to eat bars of chocolate with or someone constantly changing the radio station from Radio Four (Nathan's choice, not mine) to Radio One for good dance beats. I miss her jigging about the place, telling me about the new skirt she bought or the latest trendiest colour of nail varnish that's on the market. What I don't miss, however, is her evasiveness about Will. She talks about men all the time. One sweeping statement after another. 'They're farting machines.' True. 'They're pigs.' 'They all want replacement mothers.' She never says anything about Will, though. It's the taboo subject. Probably scared I would clipe back to him. Or worse try to steal him away from her.

I suppose I should phone her or pop round and see how she's feeling. But Poppy's a work colleague. I'd hardly call her a friend. And I have to admit I'm too embarrassed about stripping off and kissing her boyfriend anyway. How could I look her in the eye after that one. Dear, oh dear, everything's a bit too complicated for my liking.

Besides, surely visiting Poppy is Will's remit. After all, he is seeing her. And it might not be the flu. It might be contagious. I might have to have week after week off sick, leaving Nathan to run the shop. On second thoughts, I'd better not go to visit her.

'I know,' says Nathan, in a spark of inspiration. He's got that excited look in his eyes. Almost popping, so they are. I just know he's not going to take No for an answer. 'Mother. That's what Doctor Nathan orders. Mother and

197

sea air. Tomorrow we're off to North Berwick. There's a craft fayre which Mother is just adamant to see.'

'Oh,' is all I manage to muster in the meantime, until I can think of an excuse. *Any* excuse.

'That east-coast wind will blow all the cobwebs away, Eve.' Agony Uncle Nathan. Just what I need. He wears a wee smug smile as if it is the ultimate accessory. Then he starts whistling 'Bridge Over Troubled Water'.

And I know I'm in deep dog poo.

So now I'm squashed in the back of the MG, all because I couldn't think of a better excuse than defrosting the fridge.

Calling the east-coast wind of mid February bracing is a bit of an understatement, but Hilary insists on the soft top being down. Her chiffon scarf blows behind her, as we speed along the coast road. Her sunglasses are moons of inky blue glass, covering at least half her face. I can't help thinking of Audrey Hepburn. And when Hilary steps out of the car to allow me to climb into the back seat, I half expect pedal pushers and soft pumps. Instead, it's a Miss Marple special, with a cape enveloping her body which she must sweep over her shoulder with a dramatic flourish every so often.

Old people fascinate me.

How they springboard from one topic to another in the same sentence and expect everyone to follow. I try and listen, concentrate on every word, because I can't help feeling she's got something important to say. But I catch myself, my mind adrift, thinking of Ian, thinking of Will, and not listening to what Hilary is trying to say.

Nathan's not listening either . . .

'Thermal knickers, that's what you need in this weather
. . . I really miss the shop, you know, Eve. I miss you
buying doughnuts . . . Isn't that terrible about the Scott
Monument. I think they should just leave it, mind, you
never know, we could end up with our very own Leaning
Tower of Pisa, right there in the middle of Princes Street
. . . I read the other day in the *Sun* that Princess Anne
is expecting a baby. You'd think she'd know better,
wouldn't you? . . .

'So she said to me, "Red doesn't suit you, Hilary. It
makes you look like mutton dressed as lamb." So what
could I say to that? Well, wait until you hear what I
said to her. My ears are burning with the thought of
it. I couldn't believe I'd have the gall, but sure enough
I did. "Maud," I said. "If I were you, I'd try a tighter
panty girdle, preferably tied tightly round your mouth!"
Well, the minister's face was a picture, I can tell you . . .'
Hilary has turned the front mirror round, so she can look
at me when she's talking. She says she doesn't want to
strain her neck with all this to-ing and fro-ing. It's a bit
off-putting, with her eyes watching me all the time, but
I think she's just checking that I'm listening to her.

'I've not seen the MG before,' I say.

'No. This is our Sunday car, isn't it, Mother? The Range
Rover's a bit flashy for North Berwick, what with the logo
on the side. You know, all work and no joy makes Jack a
dull boy, Eve. It would do you good to remember that.'

I say nothing.

The thought of Hilary and Nathan being the do-gooders
just waiting for me to divulge my problem, and for them
to firmly sort it out, is definitely keeping me tight-
lipped.

I can't bear it.

We get a parking space, looking out over the beach. A few people are wandering about, but not many: the customary family out for a Sunday stroll, kids, wellie-booted, sand buckets in hand, hoods up, gloves on. The dog, sniffing sea weed, wandering off, coming back to have one more sniff. The dad struggling with a kite made from binbags. His efforts to keep it airborne, failing. And the mother trying to keep everyone in earshot and eyeshot, keeping her family intact. The boy chases after the girl with a gooey spiderlike strip of seaweed. The dog follows, barking, tail wagging. The girl waddles on, crying, screaming, laughing. The boy shoves it in front of her face and she howls.

Waves don't crash upon the shore. They kind of approach and flop over upon themselves with a Sunday-afternoon laziness. The sea doesn't roar. It lollops and plops about with the minimum of effort. I wanted huge crashing waves today. I wanted to stand right in front of them and feel the spray upon my face.

I wander off on my own for a while. Even so, I can feel Nathan's and Hilary's eyes bore into my back as I walk over the dunes and down on to the beach. There they'll be, peering out of the already-steamed-up windows, clucking and shaking their heads, wiping the steam from the windows, and thinking how with God's help they will 'sort the poor girl' out.

A popping sound comes from my feet, as I stand on streamers of seaweed. How can people eat that stuff? How can they make soup from it? It reminds me of bubble-wrap. I remember how, when Will and I were going through our 'learning to play the guitar' phase, we'd soak our fingers in methylated spirits to toughen them up and pop bubble-wrap morning, noon and night to strengthen the muscles in our fingers. I can't remember who told us to do it – probably his dad, for a laugh – but still we did all that faithfully every day, as if it were part of our mission to become the Eric Claptons of Scotland.

I try and imagine him here, right at this very minute. He'd either be rushing to jump into the sea, mid February or mid June, season irrelevant, or like that boy: chasing after me with moist leafy seaweed to toss down my back, or something. And I'd be laughing and screaming at the same time, just like the kid sister. People would think we were teenagers.

Or lovers.

Ian? He would walk along beside me. We'd be holding hands, pointing in the distance to the boats, writing our names in the sand with a stick for the tide to just wash away. I'd like him holding my hand. There would be a calmness overwhelming us. I'd feel adult.

What would I prefer? What would I like the best? Will would be my Friday night and Ian my Sunday afternoon.

God, I'm talking as if they've both fallen at my feet and I have to choose between them. They're down on their hands and knees begging me to be theirs. Oh, yes? Now pull the other one: it's got bells on!

That's the problem. That's what I want. I *want* them both to be on their hands and knees for me. One has already proposed to me. I wouldn't mind if the other one did the same. Okay, I admit it.

Okay?

By the time I get back to the car, there's the distinct smell of egg mayonnaise in the air. Out comes the flask of coffee for me, and a box full of brown-bread egg-and-cress sandwiches is thrust under my nose.

'Well, I must say you've got a bit more colour in your cheeks now,' Hilary says. 'I've never seen you look so pale as you were before. Gaunt is the word. Anaemic, even. Are you eating properly? Periods heavy? Maybe you should be taking iron supplements.'

'Oh, for pity's sake, Mother!' pipes up Nathan, obviously embarrassed by the turn the conversation has taken.

All Hilary does is laugh.

And Nathan flounces away after slamming the car door.

'Good, that got rid of him!' says Hilary.

'I thought you wanted to go to this craft fayre.'

'Oh, let Nathan do that. He's got an eye for fine details, you know. Maybe, with a bit of luck, he'll meet some heathen and run away to Gretna.'

'Heathens in North Berwick? You're joking. This is pure blue-rinse-and-pearls territory here.'

We walk along the beach.

My second time, Hilary's first.

Footprints from my shoes are still sunken into the thick sand. I try and walk in them again, but we're going at such a slow pace, I'm left with one leg in the air, trying to balance while Hilary totters along beside me. I give up.

'I hear you're getting married. Congratulations.'

'Thanks.' I try to give my voice the air I imagine a fiancée should have.

'And Will's going with that Poppy from the shop. Oh, happy days,' Hilary says. 'Have I met this Ian?'

'Yes. Remember? He used to come into the shop on the last Thursday of every month to buy me flowers. Remember? Tall, brown eyes.'

'Mm, him. And Will? Have I met him?'

202

'No.'

'Shouldn't you be spending your Sundays with Ian? Choosing curtain material, or whatever?'

I laugh. 'He's away in America at the moment. On business.'

'Right, he's the one who's always gallivanting? Here, there and everywhere?'

'Yes, he's very ambitious.'

We reach the end of the beach. Behind us lie the dunes, in front of us lies the sea. I like this sandwiched feeling I have. That east-coast wind rushes through me, taking my breath with it. 'I bet the weather's not like this in America.'

'It must be hard for you. Him being away.'

'No. Not really. I'm used to it.'

'But you must miss him?' A rhetorical question. A cunning lure for juicy details, more like.

'When I think about him, yes I do. Really, I can never tell how much until we meet up again, and then I think that I have missed him.'

'It's not really solid ground to build a marriage on.'

'No. I suppose not.' I rub my hands through my hair.

'Nathan's told me the story.'

I know what she's getting at, and she doesn't even apologize for gossiping about me over the Horlicks.

'I've never told Nathan the story.' Actually I didn't know there was a story.

'My son is like a sponge, Eve. He soaks it all up.' She says this with undisguised pride.

There's not much point in keeping my mouth shut any more. Someone I can talk to. At last. So here goes. A deep breath and go for it. 'What am I going to do? Love doesn't even come into it, Hilary. Well, it may do, but I'm not sure.'

'Love? You don't want to marry for love. Don't be stupid. It will just end in tears. Look at me. Left with a six-month-old baby at the ripe old age of eighteen. That's what love did for me. Ran off with a bus conductor from Paisley, he did. Defaulted to The West Coast. The bloody traitor. Has Will got money?'

'No.'

'Ian?'

'Yes.'

'Well, there's your answer. Money's half the battle.'

'I'm not marrying Ian for his money.'

Her eyebrows knit as if she doesn't understand. 'Why else?'

'Because he asked me.'

'If you want my advice, sleep with Will and get him out of your system. It's only sex.'

I laugh. But it's a kind of uncomfortable laugh. So much for Christianity.

'Then you'll know the answer. But if you want my opinion, the expectation's always better than the actual event. You'll blink and miss it. You'll not reach orgasm, his penis will be too small and after one groan it's over. Hallelujah! Years and years of waiting – for it to be over in less than a minute. What an awful lot of time wasted. You know, I've not lived liked a nun in this lifetime.' She winks. A knowing, loaded wink.

I laugh despite myself:

'I stood in front of him naked, willing him to come to me, but he was more interested in the football results.'

'Forget him. What's Ian into?'

I want to say bondage, but I stop myself just in time.

'Matching paperback covers and clear work surfaces.' Fed up talking about me, I change tack once again:

'Why do you think Nathan's never married?'

'I hate to say it, and I suppose it's mainly my fault, but my son is nothing but a mummy's boy. He's not quite reached the bringing-girls-home-to-tea point yet. Which, when you think about it, is really rather sad. Considering he's forty-two.' She pulls out a hip flask from under her shawl and passes it to me.

By the time we wander back to the car, Nathan's already there: reading the *Sunday Times*; bits tossed all over the car.

I sit on the TV guide. The black ink is bound to imprint the title Culture across my backside.

WILL Well, give me a fucking break. I'm stuck at home again, totally bored out of my face and wishing for fuck sake that I was at least going out with Poppy tonight. But no, here I am stuck in watching Michael Barrymore and Heartbeat with my mother. Of course, she's in seventh heaven having her prodigal back in the nest. There she goes clucking away again:

'Do you want a beer?' she asks. 'How about a cuppa? I'll just go and put the kettle on.'

She can't understand that I can go and get my own fucking beer, or make a fucking cup of tea for my-fucking-self! No, she's got to do the Nurse-Bloody-Nancy bit.

I watch her fussing about the place and I just want to hit her. I want to put my hands on her shoulders and give her a good shake.

She says:

'Did she throw you out, then?'

'No.'

'Couldn't put up with you and your messes any more.'

'No. She didn't throw me out.'

'Or did you not pay your way? You always were a bit stingy with the cash. Just like your dad.'

'No, mum.' How can I tell her that last Sunday over my cornflakes, Eve walked up to me, stripped to the buff, and told me she was getting married? How can I say that to my mum? She wouldn't get it. She couldn't work her brain around it. Mind you, I don't know if I can either.

I've tried everything from counting sheep to 'pillows and billows' over and over again, and still I can't sleep. It's worse than the nightmares I had when Psycho Suzie was after me with an electric knife. That seems like a wet dream compared to this insomnia . . .

Even Colin's got a bint at the moment. He was always really handy for the last-minute game of pool down the local, if ever I was stuck before. That was before he had a life, mind you. Now he's got this barmaid down at Greyfriar's Bobby. God knows what she sees in him. He's one ugly bastard. But then, looks aren't everything.

Jesus, that's an Eve phrase. I need help. Fast.

My life has been better, it's got to be said.

So, as a last resort, I phone Poppy for a quick half and hopefully a quick shag in the back of my car up the Meadows.

But Poppy's not well.

'Glandular fever,' she says.

Okay, that's a fair excuse. If she said a cold, then I would not have been a happy camper. I mean, all you need for that is a Lemsip and a hot-water bottle. And believe it or not, although during the day I might be

Mild Mannered Mr Insurance, at night I'm Rampant Hot Water Bottle – enough to make anyone's bed overheat.

Glandular fever's infectious, so:

'See you around, doll,' I think. It's kind of a relief, really, since I've got a lot on my mind. Still I ask:

'You don't want me to come round and see you, do you?' because I think I should.

'No,' she replies. (Thank fuck for that!) 'There's no point. Kissing's off the agenda just now.'

Right, so all I am is a snog machine who happens to have a car. Great.

And the more I think about it, the more I think I won't phone back again. Ever. Just call it a day. I hate to have to admit this, but she's a bit too young and flighty for me. Giggling is nice to begin with. But constantly? It's enough to drive a man demented.

When we go out she wants to go to the studenty pubs which I hate 'cos they're full of tossers. But she thinks they're trendy. I'm sorry but maybe I'm getting a bit too old to wait in queues freezing my balls off to go into clubs. What's wrong with pubs where you can buy real pints of real beer?

The other day she asked me who Marc Bolan was. I mean, I'm not old. I'm hardly collecting my old-age pension, for Christ sake.

And she's still got a teenybopper's mentality. Saying how gorgeous Peter André's body is. Has she seen mine? No. There would be no comparison.

Maybe it's time to hang up the young studs and go for the slippers and pipe. Jesus Christ, at this rate I would have been better getting married. Least I'd be getting it regularly.

Eve and me always said we would never fall out or

drift apart. The way it works when you leave school, get trendier friends, and forget about the poor souls you used to hang about with. That's never happened to Eve and me. Okay, it used to embarrass me when she'd turn up to the pub in her Arran hat and matching mittens, but friendship is more than a ball of wool. Nothing came between us. Well, until Suzie, I suppose. But that was my fault. I know that. I know Suzie didn't want me to see Eve. She put her foot down firmly about that one. And I didn't argue. Maybe I should have done. That was mistake numero uno.

Jesus I must be bored: wondering what it would be like lying in bed with Eve. I wonder what her body feels like. If she snores, or sleeps with the corner of the quilt tucked under her chin. I wonder if, when she lies on her back, her tits fall down her sides and reach the mattress.

See, when it comes down to it I bet she's not much different from any other girl. I bet her and Suzie and Poppy are like peas in a pod. Acting all coy and then rampant nymphos under all that Laura Ashley get-up. Sugar and spice and all things nice – bollocks! That's what I say to that. *Bollocks!!!!*

I'll tell you something for nothing, though. *My* bollocks are fairly bulging. No sex in how many months? Things are dire. They really couldn't get any worse.

Except, the next thing my mum says is:

'You didn't try anything with Eve, did you?'

For fuck sake, I'm getting fed up with this. I try ignoring her, but from the corner of my eye, I can see her toe tap in time with Michael Barrymore singing 'I Will Survive' with some stupid tart in a silver dress. I want to bite her foot. My mother's, I mean.

When I used to think about my mum, I always imagined her to be sitting in front of the TV, knitting. The fact that she's never knitted even a tea cosy is beside the point. Now, I'll always remember her toe-tapping to 'I Will Survive'.

As I said, things have been better.

'If you must know, she's getting married.'

In my head, the knitting needles stop clacking or whatever knitting needles do. Her toe stops tapping in time with the music.

'Oh,' she says, 'I thought . . . it doesn't matter.'

'Well, yeah, it does matter, Mum. It matters quite a lot.'

I see Eve in my head, bending down to pick up her coat. I remember the cellulite, and the glimpse of black tufty hair of pastures new.

'It matters.'

EVE Poppy's been off for a fortnight. I don't know why. Her mum phoned and said it was the flu, then tonsillitis, then glandular fever. Well, we all know how you get that, don't we? Kissing the wrong boys. Need I say more?

But I've kissed him too. And I'm Al-healthy.

So who else has she been kissing?

WILL I'm passing, so I don't see why I can't just drop by. No probs. We're mates. Nothing ventured, nothing gained. I suppose.

She's wearing her tap shoes when she answers the door. Her face is a reddy-purplish.

'Oh,' she says, 'I thought you were the paper boy.'

'Can I come in?'

'You owe me money, by the way.' Her breathing is irregular and I would say it's from exertion and not just from my face at the door. 'For the papers, I mean.'

'Ah, right. No more *Sunday Mail*s now.' I follow her down the hall, the tapping of her toes still loud enough on the carpet. Nope, nope, it's not tapping. It's scuffling. When we reach the kitchen, scuffles become taps when we walk over the lino.

'I'm practising for my exam.' She presses the stop button on the tape recorder.

And thank fuck for that. Yeah, I've missed her, but not her crappy taste in music. Some Andrew Lloyd Webber thing, it is. She doesn't take her shoes off, still taps her way round the kitchen. 'I take it you wouldn't say no to a beer?'

I sit down at the table and watch her. No diamond sparkles on her finger. 'Where's your rock, then?'

'What?'

'Ring?' I point to my finger, where a signet ring used to be, and still flattened hairs give the game away if you look really closely.

'Oh, Ian had to go away quickly, so we haven't picked it yet. Anyway, I'm not sure if I want one. We might just get married straight off.'

'I've missed you.' No point beating about the bush.

'Oh?'

'Have you missed me?'

All I hear is her bloody shoes when she spins round. 'Of course I have.' She pours a can of Heineken into a glass for me. 'I'm sorry, well . . . about, you know.'

'No, *I* should be saying that. I shouldn't have left without saying cheerio.' The beer is cold going down.

Welcome, though. It's giving me strength. 'Things like that should never have come between us.'

She taps her way over to the table, and sits down. 'What things?'

'Uch, you know,' I shrug. 'Just things.'

'No.'

'Where's Ian?'

'America, somewhere.'

'It's a big country, Eve.' I can't help being snappy. I've been here less than five minutes and already she's pissing the hell out of me.

'I know. I know. He'll be back in a couple of weeks though. How's Poppy? She's still off work.'

I can't bear to answer that, so I do the manly thing and shrug.

'I see.' Her mind is working overtime, I can see it in her face. She's never been any good at hiding things from me. I'm close to giggling and I don't know why.

'You'll come to the wedding, won't you? You're my best friend. I'd be lost without you.'

'You should of thought of that before you did a strip-tease in my face.'

She laughs. 'For goodness sake, you're always giving it this big masculine act, when really you're as soft as fudge. When it comes down to it, you're nothing but a big prude. I always thought it was me, but it's you. It's you. Mr Prissy Knickers.' She shakes her head as if she doesn't believe it.

Bitch.

'The trouble with you, Will, is that you're appalled with me stripping off in front of you. You're appalled and scared because it's suddenly occurred to you that I'm something you've missed out on and you've waved the chance bye-bye.'

211

'Well, I wouldn't put it quite like that.'

'Oh, indeed?'

Indeed, my arse! Now she's really pissing me off. 'Things aren't going to be the same between us, are they?' I want to be back in cosy conversation. None of this reality stuff.

'They can't be. Time's marching on and we've got to go with it. Grow up, Will.'

'I don't want to. I'm the eternal Peter Pan, me. Jesus Christ, why do you think I called off the wedding with Suzie?'

'You were scared shitless.'

We both laugh before each taking a slug from our beers. A look passes between us that I don't quite understand. Well, I do really. But that's reality. I don't want to think about it. I say:

'Are you?'

'Yes, and no.'

'It could be the biggest mistake of your life.'

'It could be the best thing I ever do. Anyway, tell me, what else am I supposed to do? Marry you? (As if that was ever an option.) No, I'm sorry, I've offered myself on a platter for too long. You've made it perfectly clear you don't want me. A girl can only take so much, you know. You only want me now because you can't have me. I'm not at your beck and call now, and it pisses you off.'

I hate her. She's really pissing me off with all this women-speak crap. 'But I love you.' FUCK! Where did that come from?

Her eyes are puppyish when they look at me. 'Maybe. But it's the wrong way.'

Where in hell's name did she get all this crap from? 'You've been reading *Cosmopolitan* again, haven't you?'

'Will, I've spent half my life dreaming. Don't you remember how you used to say to me, "Eve, do you know what your problem is? You read too many books." Don't you remember that? Well, I've stopped dreaming. I've woken up and smelt the coffee.'

I can't think what to say. I can't look at her. The bottom of the beer glass suddenly becomes really interesting. The way it's all frosted is really cool. I wonder how long it takes to make one glass. The beer is almost gone and with every swallow the cut crystal is more distinct. Bored with that, I look around the kitchen. Nothing much has changed during my defection. Except the blind. 'Why have you changed the blind?' The new one is a cream roller job, and completely boring.

She shrugs. 'You get bored with the same view all the time.'

'I don't like this new side to you. You sound really bitter.'

'I hate being second best, that's all. And I'm not going to be it any more. You've broken my heart so many times, I lost count. And it's not Poppy. It wasn't even Suzie, although I didn't like her. It's the way you've always treated me: like a kid sister all the time, or one of the lads. I've never been a woman to you. You've never looked at me close enough to see I'm a woman. You'd come running back to me with tales of your sexual exploits, and/or a broken heart, and expect me to pick up the pieces.'

'Most of them I just made up because they're was an awkward pause in conversation.' I don't like all this honest talk. These things should never be said. It's the male rule. Never question. Accept. It's the oath of male allegiance. 'You never told me any of yours, by the way.'

213

'I never had any exploits. Ian has been my only lover. I got fed up waiting for you. I lost my virginity on my twenty-fifth birthday. The birthday you promised to take me out.' Her index finger points at me and then jabs the table over and over. 'Well, that was until you met "a hot bit of stuff" the night before. So I phoned Ian, who was a customer, and asked him out. I cried all the way through it. Ian thought he had hurt me, but it was you who had.'

'Jesus, I had no idea. A twenty-five-year-old virgin. Wow!'

'Typical of you to pick up on that.' She stands up, her tapping going to the fridge for some more beers, I hope.

'Sorry.'

'Let's do it. Let's do it now.'

Her back is to me. All I can really see is her arse when she opens the fridge door. It's at eye-level. It would be nice to rub my cheek against her cheeks. As long as she doesn't fart. I think I've picked up the words wrong. 'What?'

'Let's do it. I'm serious. Be my fling, for once.'

There's not a lot I can really say at the moment. My brain is doing somersaults. But when it's offered to you on a plate. Besides, the salami's fed up being slapped. It needs some one-on-one action. 'Okay.'

EVE 'I should warn you,' I say, proud of myself for keeping my voice in check. (It doesn't waver at all.) 'I haven't shaved my legs.'

'Neither have I.' He tries to laugh.

God, what are we doing? I'd stop if only I could back out. Half of me wants to, the other half is saying,

Hurry up, hurry up, get on with it, get it over and done with.

He must have doubts as well. He must. For God's sake, the very thing we've being trying to avoid for over a decade and now it's about to happen. Are we stupid? I can feel a nerve jump in my neck. Maybe, it's not a nerve, maybe it's a flea. I hit it, once, twice.

'I hope you brushed your teeth this morning,' I say.

'Come here,' he says.

'Hang on, I just want to finish washing these dishes.' The one good thing about having lino on the floor is that you can hear someone come up behind you. Straight for the neck, he goes for. How does he know that's my erogenous zone? Nibbles, nibbles; bites, nibbles. Even through my Marigolds I can feel the boiling water work its way under the nails to that sensitive skin which throbs with heat. I'm trying not to nuzzle my head against his, but it's difficult.

'Do you want me to be masterful?' His voice is husky. Put on, I think. And I can't help wondering if this is just part of the rehearsed speech.

'Whatever.' What in Hell's name am I *doing*? I should stop this. I really should. Masterful? *Master*ful? Does that involve thongs and whips, or what?

No, I'm not into that. I've got to think of Ian. I must think of Ian. This is too stupid for words.

Masterful, my foot. It's desperation, that's what it is. This is all Hilary's fault. She was the one who suggested it. I've got to blame someone else. It's not me. I can't cope with it.

I turn round and wrap my arms around his neck. Environmentally-friendly bubbles run down beneath his shirt collar. I'm trying to feel his cheeks with the rubber

215

gloves still intact. All I feel is the bits inside the gloves, like bits of rolled up toilet paper under my nails. A trail of bubbles runs down his cheek.

His eyes watch me.

'What are we doing?' I'm shaking my head as I say this.

He snorts a laugh. A bogey dangles from his left nostril. But somehow it doesn't put me off. 'Call it my wedding present. Call it inevitable. Call it fate.'

'How many other girls have you said that to?' My hand flicks across his nose and the offending bogey is no more.

'Fewer than you might think.' He takes my hands in his own, and slowly removes the Marigolds. 'I'm sorry, but I'm not into kinky sex.'

My hands could do with some hand cream but I don't suppose this is the time to mention the fact.

I can smell his beery breath. We're that close. When he kisses me, I can taste it as well. I like it. All softness, and moist dew transfers from his lips to mine. And if I had known this was going to happen, I'd have been using lip balm religiously every day for a month. We're stuck together with superglue, with moist beery-breath superglue. We're so close a sheet of paper wouldn't get between us. He pulls back, his eyes darting about the kitchen. He eyes the table and I suddenly catch on to what he's meaning.

I'd like it like that. Like that scene from the movie. 'The Fall Guy', except there's no cartons of milk on the table. There's nothing on it apart from some toast crumbs, which hardly count.

He's fumbling with my clothes while kissing me, trying to push my T-shirt up over my head, but is reluctant to

216

break from the kiss. He's walking backwards as he does so. I marvel at his concentration, doing three things at once. I'm walking with him, tripping over his feet, and I can't help thinking of it as a poor apology for a waltz. The tapping from my tap shoes is the only sound I can hear. I feel his breath on my cheeks. Occasionally as he exhales down his nose, I can hear a slight hiss, but the tapping seems to echo louder and louder in my ears. I think of Fred Astaire and Ginger Rogers. We certainly don't have their panache, but there's a certain rhythm in this dance towards the door, given a little imagination.

We're in the hall. The taps are muffled by the carpet. He stops outside my door. I pull back. 'No,' is all I manage. He understands. I draw the line at that. That's where I sleep with Ian. I couldn't do that to him. Anyway, he sees it as a chance to take off my T-shirt. 'I don't have my good underwear on.'

'I promise I'll keep my eyes closed.' He breathes hard, and begins to grind his teeth. I try to unfasten some buttons on his shirt, but he pushes me away.

Taking my hand, he leads me into his old bedroom. There are no sheets on the futon. Not even any pillows. He took them away that Sunday morning he left me. There's a lingering smell of Steve McQueen's bedding and cage. I stand in the middle of the room, looking about me, watching him as he moves to pull down the roller blind. It keeps springing back up and he can't get it to stay. I can't make out the curses he's saying under his breath. I sit down on the edge of the bed until I see my roll of fat hang over the top of my leggings.

Jesus, I must look a sight – with only an accidentally grey-tone sports bra, a pair of leggings (not disguising any bumps), and tap shoes. Sitting on the edge of Will's bed.

217

Around my mouth the skin feels sore from where Will's couple-of-days'-growth has scratched me.

He walks over and stands directly in front of me, pulling my legs on either side of him. He unfastens the red ribbon on one tap shoe and then the other. No more sound, not even the ticking of a clock. He sees me watching him as he undoes his shirt. I squeeze my hand between the slit of material to feel his chest.

No hair. He probably waxes it off.

His shirt is wound round into one long rope and with it he ties my wrists – not too tightly, just nice – and I don't know whether to object or not.

This must be the 'masterful' bit, as he forces me to lie down on the bed while he pulls off my leggings. Okay, they're a bit stretched around the hips, but really he doesn't have to make such a song and dance about getting them off. One tug should have been enough. But no. Instead, he lifts my hips and rounds his hands over my bum. Kneading my buttocks round and round like scone dough. Would it be wrong of me to say to him, 'Look, Will, sorry about this, but I've changed my mind?'

'Do you like foreplay?' he asks, in all sincerity.

I don't know whether to laugh, nod, shake my head, or say, 'Well, actually I prefer Tom Stoppard.' My bra strap falls off my shoulder and instead of pushing it back up, he pulls the whole contraption off, like some piece of heavy construction work, over my head. I hear my breasts bow to gravity when the bra departs my nipples. Will heads straight for the mole under my left breast, and I feel like saying, 'Leave that. It's personal property. It's Ian's.'

I pull his boxers off with my feet.

The next sound is a groan either from him or is it me or both of us together when he's inside me. My tied arms are around his neck. We're sitting. I've never done it like this before. It's not exactly comfortable, but all right for a change. We're so close I can't see him. I feel his breathing on my ear. His tongue licks my earring. All the noise is down to the thudding against the mattress. We're silent. I want him to talk, but I don't know what I want him to say.

It's over all too soon.

He rushes out to the bathroom within three seconds. Another vile habit.

'Jesus Christ,' he says. 'I'd forgotten how noisy these pipes were.' He stands in the bedroom, hands on hips, penis now limp, a mini roll of fat around his middle from excess beer; legs hairy, and not very muscular after all.

I wish I had a duvet to cover myself.

WILL I don't know whether to sit down on the bed, lie back down beside her, or get dressed. Jesus, what a fucking mess. I look at her there, turning all shy and embarrassed.

Her thighs are hunched up to hide her stomach. There's certainly more meat there than on a nine-pound Christmas turkey, but that's no big deal.

I decide on sitting down. I rub my hands up and down her legs, feeling the blunt tickly stubs of her hairs. 'So, are you going to marry superstud Ian then?'

'Yes.'

'Why?'

'He's actually Superman in disguise.'

'And you're Lois Lane. Ay, right.'

'You broke your promise to me.'

Promise? I made a vow never to make any promise to any skirt. 'What promise?'

'The promise we made in the garden shed after your dad's funeral. Remember? The one about being twenty-five and getting married?'

'Eve, for Christ sake, this is the nineties, marriage isn't the be-all and end-all. You don't have to be stuck in the kitchen rustling up grub from a tin of tuna and some kidney beans. You're independent, have a place of your own, all that stuff. I don't know why you want to change that.' Her legs are goose-bumped, but there's nothing to cover her up with.

'Loneliness. It's no fun if you've not got anyone to share it with. Besides, if someone's about I eat less chocolate.'

'I was here and you ate chocolate. Loads of it.'

'Exactly. Besides there's less chance of the person running out on me if we're bound by the law.'

If that was a dig, I'm fucked off. 'No, there's not. It's just cheaper than a divorce, that's all. And by the way, I didn't run out on you. You talk as if there was an Us. We were friends, and that was it. That's all there was to it.' I've had enough of this shit. I'm out of here. I'm history. I start putting my clothes back on.

'You'll not see me again,' she says.

Now I'm really pissed off. 'Why not?'

'You don't get it, do you? You still don't see. What happened today killed the very thing that made us special. Now we're like everyone else. We resorted to sex. Now we're just normal.'

'Welcome to the human race, Eve. About bloody time.'

I have one last look back to see her, still lying there in the same position, all foetal-like.

Cellulite isn't a turn-on after all.

11

EVE 'I'm sorry about St Valentine's Day,' he says.

He thinks I'm annoyed with him because I didn't get a dozen long-stem roses a fortnight ago. Too right I'm annoyed. If Ian can't remember St Valentine's Day when we're just engaged, what hope is there?

Maybe I won't marry him.

Maybe I will.

I mean, it seems right. Why shouldn't it be? We're compatible. In our own way.

But maybe I don't want to marry Ian. How do you know when you've chosen the right one? I mean *really* know.

It's not like buying a melon in Safeway, is it? That's

easy. A bit of a squeeze at either end and you know whether you've got a good one or not. You can't really do the same with a man. Well, I suppose you can. But look where I ended up the last time I did the melon-testing routine. Besides, I'm sure I'd be more than happy with the quality if I was to squeeze Ian at either end. But the trouble with the melon is that you don't really know what it's like inside until you've cut it open. Do I know what Ian's like under that everything-must-be-in-its-place wrapper?

Plus I have to consider the walking-talking-tits saga. Aka the look-down-the-front-of-my-blouse-and-compare-me-to-Pamela-Anderson affair. If it's happened once then it could have happened a dozen times. How many other lip-smacking scenes have I not been privileged to witness?

He could be the type who has a woman in every port. You read about it in the papers. Ian could already have a wife in America. A mad wife locked up in the Betty Ford Clinic.

He says, 'I'm afraid I'll have to invite business acquaintances, Eve, honey.'

What's this honey business all of a sudden? Next we'll be wearing matching jumpers and sending cute fat-bears cards to each other. He inhales through his teeth. 'It's too good an opportunity to miss.'

'What?' I look across the table at Ian. Supposedly the love of my life. The man I'm going to marry. And I see the crisp white shirt with the boring paisley-pattern tie and the navy suit and the well scrubbed face and the clean-shaven chin and the short-back-and-sides. And I wonder what I'm doing.

'To the wedding, stupid!' Ah, his favourite topic of conversation: our wedding.

'Why can't we run away to Gretna Green and get it over and done with?'

He laughs good-humouredly at my wee joke. Well, he thinks I'm joking. 'I'm afraid I'll have to mix business with pleasure. It's just not possible, hon.'

'What am I, Ian? Business or pleasure? You're marrying me, not the company.'

His laugh reminds me of a parrot's squawk. He gently squeezes my hand. 'Don't worry about a thing. Don't get all jittery. I'll organize everything – the cars, the reception, the kilts, accommodation. I'll sort it. Don't worry your pretty little head about it.'

All this before I talk to my mother. Things are going to get well and truly out of hand.

Ian takes a sip of the house Merlot, while I clutch my pint of Guinness in both hands, take a gulp and wipe the smudges of head from my lips with the back of my hand. 'I'll do the flowers.' Thankfully I can make a small contribution to my own wedding. Apart from turn up, that is.

He grimaces and pats my hands in such a patronizing manner I think about tossing my pint over his head. Is he always such a pompous, righteous, irritating git?

No.

The truth is I am pissed off because I didn't get a dozen long-stem roses for Valentine's Day. Didn't even get a card. Says he doesn't believe in these 'commercialism days'. Romantic tokens are not exclusive to one day, so he says.

Pretentious twaddle. Why can't he just admit he forgot?

I did get my ring though. So I shouldn't complain. He bought it in America. Says he knows this dealer. Says it's an investment. A sapphire when I would have chosen a single diamond. 'My future's so bright I've got to wear shades . . .' if you get the picture.

WILL First of all I phone Eve. Why not? She's my mate. Just want to see if she's okay. Find out about the wedding. If I'm invited. If it's still on. If she's dumped the big raving tadger. She's blowing her nose when she answers the phone.

'Got a cold?' I ask, trying to be polite.

'What do you want?' she sniffs.

So much for being polite, eh? 'I just wanted to see if you were okay.'

'I am.'

'You don't sound it.'

'Is that any wonder?'

What's eating her? Is she thinking of our shag-fest or has she caught Poppy's cold? 'Are you not well?'

'I'm fine.'

There's a pause while I wait for her to talk.

She doesn't.

'What you up to?'

'Having a girlie night in actually. Which you're disturbing. Not that it is any of your business.'

'What you crying about? Is it that fuckwit Ian? Has he dumped you?'

'No, he bloody hasn't!' She's getting a bit loud and screechy. 'Which is more than can be said for you. Couldn't even button up your shirt before you ran out. You are a prize-winning bastard. Of the first degree. Now if you don't mind I've got the last five minutes of Beaches to watch.'

Right enough I can hear Bette Midler warble in the background. 'And then I'm going to watch "Terms of Endearment".' Eve's nose-blowing sounds a bit like a foghorn.

And then she hangs up on me. Can you believe it? Didn't even ask how I was. Just hung up.

Fucking hell!

Next I phone Poppy. I know I said it was over, but needs must when it's the only poking potential in the pipeline. Her mum always answers the phone, sniffing, no doubt with her nose in the air, making this excuse and then that excuse. She's not well. She's ill. She's at death's door, for Christ sake.

You'd think I'm the one who made her ill, the way the parentals carry on. Chance would have been a fine thing. Nae such luck. Her dad answers tonight. Just for a change.

'Look, son, she doesn't want to talk to you. Find yourself another girl,' he says, his voice much gruffer than mine. Maybe I won't go knocking on the door quite yet.

As if I was the one in the wrong. Jesus. Have I missed something somewhere?

Not unless Eve's been talking to her. No. Jesus. Fuck. No.

Okay. Let's think this one through:

Maybe Eve's so desperate for me to go back to her she's turned into a complete bitch. Maybe she's been spilling the beans to Poppy about our shag. But that doesn't ring true. Poppy's been off work all this time. How could she have told her? Okay, there's the telephone, there are faxes, there's e-mail, there are even smoke signals. But it just isn't Eve's style. Besides, there's Future Hubby to think about, so I doubt if she's told anyone about our interstellar rumpy-pumpy.

I'm not worried. There's no reason to feel worried. Hey, *Carpe diem*, as Pavarotti once sang.

Saturday afternoon, the phone goes. And my mum answers it. 'It's a girl,' she whispers. When I know she wants to shout it from the rooftops. Her smile is one of relief. She no longer sees me as her saddo son who has nae pals and will end up taking her on bus trips to Troon for a fish tea as his big social event of the year.

It's Poppy. Wonders will never cease.

'I think it's safe to meet for a coffee,' she says.

'Can't,' I manage. Cheeky mare. Safe to meet for a coffee. That's a new one. *Safe* . . . to meet for a coffee. I'm half tempted to tell her to fuck off.

'What do you mean?' See? Stroppy. She knows about me and Eve. She thinks I should just run after her just 'cos I should feel guilty. 'William, I know I've not been in touch, but I've honestly not been well.' She does sound a bit croaky, granted.

'Well, you didn't get it from me!'

'Please. I could do with some fresh air. My mum's driving me up the wall. I'm going to kill her.'

That I can understand.

But the truth is, she phones on a Saturday afternoon when the Five Nations Tournament is on. England v France. Kick-off's in two minutes. I don't say this in case she thinks I'm just making excuses. Trying to get my own back. Scotland aren't playing, so I don't really give a shit. As long as England get gubbed by the Frogs.

Anyway, the chase is the best part. So I believe. Might as well dab on some Jazz aftershave and share a Danish pastry. There's no harm in it. And she did phone me.

Sucker or what? The next thing I know I've gelled my hair, had a shave and found a parking space down-town on a Saturday afternoon. Which is no mean feat. And it's a piss-awful day. My baseball cap looks like its got brewer's droop by the time I get to Waverley Centre.

'I'm sorry about St Valentine's Day,' is the first thing I say. This seems like a good point to start. 'The problem was I didn't know where the land lay, really. And I know you'll probably think that's nothing more than an excuse but . . .' Grovel, grovel, grovel. I will resort to *any*thing for the sake of getting into a girl's knickers.

'It's all right,' Poppy says. She smiles briefly before it disappears. 'It doesn't matter. I wasn't really in the mood for it anyway.'

She's still a bit pale. I'll give her that much. Not that I think some flower arranging would kill her. It's hardly brain surgery, is it? Fuck, I'm so glad I'm not living with Eve just now. She'd be a bloody nightmare, moaning about being overworked and underpaid with Poppy being off so long.

But if she thinks she's getting a snog today she's got another think coming. God knows where her tongue has been. That glandular fever didn't come from my saliva.

'It works both ways. I didn't get you anything either.'

'Bet you got a truckload of big soppy cards. You probably couldn't tell they weren't from me.'

Not even a snigger. Okay, I admit I'm not going to make it as a stand-up during the Fringe but for fuck sake, least I'm making a sodding effort.

I'm not saying this is a date from hell but she could pretend she's enjoying herself. It wouldn't crack her face. Her smile has taken her sense of humour and gone on a Sabbatical by the looks of it. Sitting there

229

sighing heavily every so often. All women are the bloody same. Psychos.

She takes a gulp from her coffee. A dribble runs down the polystyrene cup and on to her scarf. It's not my fault the waitress filled up the cups too full for milk. 'So you're back living at home again? What happened? Did Eve toss you out for not recycling your Irn Bru cans then?' She laughs a bit too falsely at her own joke and I wonder how many Prozacs she had before she came out.

And then – Jesus, she knows! She knows about me and Eve. That's what it is. Fuck! She's building up to a scene. Wants to humiliate me in a public place. Shit! Fuck! What am I going to do?

'Nah, she found some pubes in the soap, so we had to part company.' Witty repartee seems like the best solution. But my heart is pounding. Believe me, it's not with guilt. Or feeling bad on Poppy's behalf. I just don't like scenes.

I play with things when I'm nervous. The polystyrene cup is chewed and mauled. Teeth marks all around it.

'Will you shut up making those noises?'

'What noises?'

'You sound like a dog chewing and dribbling over a bone!'

'Sorry!' This comes out more sarcastically than I intended. Think the secret is safe though. Stick to small talk. 'So, when you going back to work?'

'Monday, I suppose.'

There's no conversation. I'm not interested in anything she says. And she's not interested in anything I say. Still wouldn't say no to a shag though. If it's on the cards.

'So, what happens now?' she asks. A forward Missy. That's what I like to hear.

One of the girls at a neighbouring table gives me the eye, looks me up and down and then smiles. She looks a bit like Suzie in a tarty Spice Girls kind of way. She's eating one of her chips a bit phallically. Nice. I smile back.

Poppy tuts, folding her arms across her chest.

'What?'

'Your silence obviously means you don't care one way or another. Well, I've explained how I was ill. I really wasn't in the mood for going out, getting drunk and getting laid, believe it or not. I can apologize until I'm blue in the face but I'm not going to. It's your loss. You're the loser.'

Poppy really should wear make-up, you know. I would normally say I prefer the fresh-face look instead of the don't-make-me-laugh-'cos-my-make-up-will-crack brigade, but I still think she needs it. Especially when she's hacked off. Pale, my eye. It's got nothing to do with contagious diseases. It's more to do with the lack of Polyfilla in the pores.

Changing the subject seems a good idea. Keep things on a fun easy-come easy-go level. I don't need any hassle. Can't be bothered with it.

'Do you wear a thong or hip huggers?'

'What?'

'Just wondering. It says a lot about a person: the type of underwear they wear.'

She rolls her eyes heavenward and smiles. Not much. Just a bit. 'What if I say none?'

Ah, flirtatious. Like it. Like it. 'Well, I would say a close inspection for proof is called for.'

She looks a bit uncomfortable. 'Look, can't we just be friends, William?'

Friends?

When we were getting on so well.

Friends? Right, that's it. The biggest insult a woman can give a man. Almost as bad as laughing at the size of his knob. 'Can't we be friends?' they say. Translated from bitch-speak, that means you don't stand a hope in hell's chance of getting near me, you ugly bastard!

'Sorry, done that. Had a girl as a friend and look how that turned out.' It's in the air before I know what I'm saying. I can't eat the words back. Only hope Poppy is suffering from temporary deafness.

'Have you and Eve fallen out?'

I knew it. I bloody knew it. Too nosy for her own good.

'No.' Short, sharp and to the point. Least said, soonest mended. As my mum says.

'She's only getting married, William. Don't be so pathetic.' She snorts and some of her coffee comes down her nose. Not one of her most attractive features, I have to say.

'Friends? Is that what you want, Poppy? 'Cos I want something more.'

'You want to get the leg over. That's what you want.'

'Mm. Perceptive.'

'Look, I really like you . . .'

Here we go. The fatal combination. Wait for the but.

'But . . .'

See what I mean?

'I just don't think I'm ready for anything like that just now. Sorry.'

'Ready? You make it sound as if you've been through the mill the last month or so. You've only had a bloody head cold!'

She looks down at the coffee dregs, rubs her forehead and says nothing.

The Suzie lookalike stands up and looks as if she's walking towards me. She isn't. But her smile is the classic come-on-take-me-I'm-yours. Even that's like Suzie. I give her one of my best boyish lopsided grins. She wiggles as she walks, or maybe her heels are too high. I like it. There's a slight hint of VPL through the white trousers. No thong, but certainly not granny hip huggers.

Sod Poppy.

Sod Eve.

I can get a real one. One who doesn't want to be *friends*. Jesus, I'm a bloke in need of some serious TLC. Forget this friends shite. I can get someone who'll *want* to sleep with me. Easily.

The Suzie bird walks by the table and squeezes past my chair. Her perfume is the same as Suzie's. Can't remember the name of it, which pisses me off considering I bought enough bottles of it! I have to strain my neck to watch her glide out the exit. If I were a gentleman I would rush up and hold the door for her. But I'm not. She'd probably just want to tell me about her periods anyway.

EVE Sometimes I just have to stop and ask myself, why me? Why is Ian marrying *me?* What can I offer him apart from nice table centrepieces for dinner parties.

Ian's perfect. Well, he likes to think he is.

My ring catches the light from the candle and sparkles. I rest it on his shoulder. My legs are hooked over his shoulders. And I try to arch my back as much as I can with him on top of me. I've read that it tells your partner

233

you're aroused and ready for penetration. Ian sees this as his signal to reach for the condom. It's classier than yelling, 'Fuck me, Big Boy!' that's for sure.

My legs flop down from his shoulders as he pulls the red tinfoil wrapper off with his teeth. I'm glad of this because all that position does is make me want to pee. They never list that in the *Kama Sutra*. They should. Marks out of ten for continence control. He's fiddling with one hand and then with both. I look at the ceiling in case I'm putting him off. There's a spider's web up in the corner. So much for perfection. Although they do say spiders only make webs in clean houses. How come they never visit me? I'm not dirty. There's nothing wrong with my house.

'Jesus!' he says. 'I'm sorry, Eve. Forget it.' He rolls off me and tosses the condom to the floor.

To be honest, I'm a bit perplexed. I mean, I don't know what's happened. Has he seen the spider and completely flipped? The quilt is on the floor and we're lying naked on our backs gazing up towards its web. Maybe he doesn't like spectators.

'What's wrong?' I ask, not really in the mood for rampant rumpo any more.

He doesn't answer.

Out of the corner of my eye I kind of peer down at his widget just to see if it's blown up or dropped off. It's still there but about the size of an uncooked chipolata sausage.

'Ian, what happened?'

'Nothing.' He sounds all grumpy.

'Well, something must have happened.'

'Nothing happened. Look for yourself and see. Look! Look!' He's not so much huffy as panic-stricken.

234

So together we look.

As if aware of this attention, his widget twitches once, twice, trying but failing to raise the flag.

'You okay?' I manage.

'Uh-huh.' Then he sighs and mutters something under his breath.

'Do you want to talk about it?' Communication is the key. So it says in those magazine articles. Talk it over with your partner, and it won't turn into a problem.

'No.'

I try another tack:

'Maybe all this wedding talk has put you off your stride.' I curl up beside him, toss my leg over his body. His skin is so soft. Every time we touch naked is a thrill. Even now.

'Maybe.' His arm pulls me closer to him. I can smell soap from his skin.

'Has it happened before?' I ask, trying to be all mature about it when really I don't want to know anything about his other lovers. He might compare us. I might feel inadequate.

'No,' he sighs deeply. He manoeuvres himself out of my grasp and reaches down to grab the quilt from off the floor. He hoists it back over us as if to cover up his embarrassment. I curl up against him again and scratch his chest hair with my nail.

'It's a common problem, so I've been told,' Ian says. 'Never happened to me before, though. Must have been the Merlot. Good for the heart, but bad for the penis, eh?'

'D.H. Lawrence was impotent, you know.'

'I'm not impotent. Once without a stiffy does not mean I'm impotent.' He looks as if he's about to sulk, so I reach up and kiss him.

A cuddle would do but before long the quilt is back on the floor, my legs are hoisted up over his shoulders and he's struggling in his wallet for the emergency condom.

It's a complete waste of time because by the time he's chewed the foil off it's chipolata night again.

'You don't fancy me any more, that's what it is.'

'That's rubbish.'

'You don't find me attractive. And why should you? I must look like a tub of lard compared to the Pamela Anderson lookalike.'

'Complete and utter codswallop!'

I'm not listening to him. It's my turn to reach down for the quilt. I notice how the studs keeping the quilt inside the cover have opened and the quilt escapes in large folds of white stuffing. It looks like a mound of blubbery fat. The similarity between this and my thighs does not escape my notice.

I do the mature thing – grab the quilt and turn over on my side at the furthest end of the futon, away from him.

He comes up and snuggles behind me. I'm sniffing on the verge of tears. Opting for the dramatic touch. Working with Nathan for all these years has taught me something. I can feel the stubble of his growth rub on my cheek. I can smell his breath. He strokes my back, rhythmically back and forward. I can feel his finger trace my spine.

'It's not you,' he murmurs, half whispering and half nibbling my ear. 'It's me.'

So, he admits it's his fault. He's not so perfect after all. Of course, I still think it's because I'm fat and frumpy. I probably need hours and hours of consoling and reassurance. (Grovel, Ian, because you didn't buy me twelve long-stem roses on Valentine's Day! Grovel, and then grovel some more.)

'You don't love me.' I sniff.

'Don't be stupid.'

'Is the thought of marrying me just too horrific to contemplate?'

'Of course not.'

The nibbles are really nice. Bastard.

I mustn't cry. I mustn't. Because then my mascara will run and he definitely won't want to marry me then.

And it occurs to me that I want to marry him. I really do.

And then another fleeting thought flits through my mind. Maybe he's put two and two together about Will and me.

Now, I cry.

Now, I really cry.

WILL My mum's moaning about the phone bill. Says I'm on the phone too long to all my floozies.

Floozies? I'll give her floozies. We're talking top-totty here. Poppy's back wearing her make-up and occasionally when we snog she lets me slip her some tongue. So much for being just friends, that's all I have to say. Obviously I'm just too charming and sexy and a complete shag to resist. Slow progress, but I always like a challenge.

And there's Eve.

She's bought an answering machine.

The message says, 'Sod off, Will, I don't want to talk to you!' Then the beeps. Charming, eh?

My mum says to me:

'I think BT have sent the wrong bill. There's a Dalgety

Bay number here. Who do we know that lives in Dalgety Bay?'

I'm out the room before she puts two and two together. It seemed like a good idea at the time. Ever since I saw that Suzie lookalike, that day when I met Poppy for a coffee, I haven't been able to get Suzie out of my mind. I'm a complete sad bastard, I know. Next I'll be warbling along to 'Memories'. I figured it wouldn't do any harm to enquire about her health. I mean, she's been through a lot recently.

'Twenty-six times!' my mum yells, hitting me about the head with the bill, for the want of her handbag. 'To enquire about that tart's health? Twenty-six times? You're off your bloody rocker, son! What's worse, she must be off her bloody rocker answering!'

It's not as if we've met. She has phoned me back on the odd occasion from her bath. 'I'm just changing the blade in my razor,' she laughs. 'And I thought of you.'

Yeah, well, she always did have a warped sense of humour. Sharp. Razor sharp, even.

'I'm just flossing my teeth' – her voice is a bit hard to work out – 'and I thought what I'd like to tie this floss round. You immediately came to mind.'

I'm in her mind. That's a good sign.

'What about that lass Poppy?' asks my mum. She's given up asking about Eve. That's definitely a no-no subject. 'She seems nice.' What she means by that is Poppy phoned me after checking the Michael Barrymore programme was finished.

Maybe I can start a harem.

I can always dream . . .

Okay, I'm having lustful thoughts about Suzie in her

bathroom. But that could be just because I'm not getting my end away. And sex with her was always the best.

I'm making tentative progress with Poppy. Who I have to say is quite nice. I like her. Think the anti-depressant drugs she's on are a bit high-dosage, with her mood swings. But apart from that, things are ticking along nicely. But that could just be the thrill of the chase. Sex may be better with Poppy than with Suzie. Hard but possible, I suppose.

Then there's Eve. Or there would be if she would talk to me. Haven't even got an invite to the wedding. Yet. Poppy got hers. Poppy's helping her with the flowers. I could have helped her with something.

I could have helped her get well away from that dick-head! That's what I could have done.

EVE Maybe I should be in disguise. An ankle-length mac seems a good idea. And dark glasses.

This takes military manoeuvres, precision timing and nerves of steel. It reminds me of the first time I had to go into Boots to buy Tampax. It's that level of embarrassment.

We've tried soft porn. As in those magazines on the top shelves of dodgy corner shops. Ian said he got them from a friend. Some friend, that's all I have to say, being sure it wasn't jam sticking the pages of 'Tits of the Month' together.

'You put me off!' Ian whined.

Well, I can't help it. I'm far from one of these anti-porn lobbyists, but it does nothing for me. The first reaction is disgust at the blue eyeshadow and then the second is a comparison between my body and Miss July's. I always come out unfavourably. For a start I don't suit red, so those crotchless knickers are a no-no as far as I'm concerned.

Then we tried videos. But that failed too. I mean, where's the storyline? They're hardly going to be a welcome addition to my romantic-comedy collection. One was Greek. A bit too anal for my liking.

So now we're touring round the bookshops looking for a sex manual to stop the widget becoming a terminal midget.

'Jesus Christ!' He yells down at it every time we try. 'I've always imagined myself as a bit of a stud. I've even thought about giving pints of my sperm for science. Not now, that's for sure. What's happening? What's happening, Eve?'

I often ask myself the same question. But Ian's temporary impotence doesn't really bother me, I have to say. It's given us a common interest. Something to do together. A goal to attain in the future. Something to work towards.

The woman behind the cash desk in this department looks like a God-fearing Christian, with her rustling underskirt and 1970s-style perm. I can't do it. I can't glance through these books while that woman's eyes bore into the back of my head and security cameras are alerted to the perverts in the corner.

'It's just massage,' whispers Ian. 'We're engaged, Eve. And this is legal. Calm down.'

A special kind of massage. Not like the massage Ian received in the basement of this bookshop no less than a couple of months ago. I just want the ground to open up and swallow me. Why can't we try Jackie Collins? Surely that would have the same effect.

Ian ends up buying a bag full of How-To books. The shop assistant sniffs, purses her lips and draws a crucifix across her chest.

'Bet she never gives her husband a blowjob,' says Ian matter-of-factly, and a bit too loudly. His complete lack of embarrassment doubles mine.

Then I'm subjected to complete mortification when the security alarm at the exit begins to ring. Everyone who turns round knows what kind of books Ian bought when the carrier bag is opened and every title pulled out and searched for the tag.

How to Make Love to the Same Man for the Rest of Your Life.

How to Give and Take Sexual Pleasure.

How to Reach Orgasm Every Time . . .

I flash my ring about to give the impression that my life isn't sordid. And really these are joke presents.

Later Ian says:

'If none of this works, Eve, I think we might have to see a therapist.' He's lying in bed, naked apart from his reading specs, and reading about The Clitoris.

'What? Talk about it?' Oh my God! He's been spending too much time in America, that's the problem. How-To books, therapists . . . next he'll be wanting to go on daytime TV to talk it over with Richard and Judy. 'To another person? A stranger?'

'It's nothing to be ashamed of, honey. If we act ashamed then this little glitch will turn into a problem.'

'It's not so little.' A joke I think will boost his confidence.

It does. He beams with pride.

I flick through another tome, having to turn the pages this way and that to work out the logistics of the positions.

I just know my legs won't bend like that. And I bet it'll make me want to pee.

It occurs to me that maybe I've bitten off more than I can chew. In a manner of speaking.

WILL 'I can't, William. Stop!'

It's the story of my life, this. Never quite hitting home base. Fuck! What is it about me? I've not so much as taken her top off or unfastened her bra strap yet. Her skirt has ridden up around her thighs. Her legs are wrapped around my back. Now is not really a good time to stop. She's wearing hold-ups for God sake! But I do. For what I think is a temporary measure until I reassure her that I'm fond of her, will ring her again tomorrow and really she is doing the right thing. Honest.

'I'm sorry. I really am, William. I'm just –'

'Not ready for this kind of thing,' I interrupt. 'Yeah, yeah, heard it all before.' Does she really expect me to be all sympathetic when my willie is poking out my shorts and dying to do some thrusting?

Then she starts crying. Just as I roll off of her. Crying really loudly and really hard. Talk about psycho, I have to tell her to shush in case she wakes up my mum.

I sigh (thinking why me? I really don't deserve this) and get up off my bed to refasten my jeans. I'm not a happy camper and this is just pissing me off a bit too much. I mean, it happens every time. A tease, or what? How much longer do I have to be humiliated in this way?

What has happened to my life? Where the fuck is it? It's down the fucking toilet, that's where it is. There was a time when I could pull almost anything. The only thing that's getting pulled these days is my leg!

My erection subsides almost as quickly as it appeared.

'Let me explain.'

I'm not really in the mood for a sob story. Really I have too many things on my mind. For starters, Eve is getting married tomorrow and I still haven't got an invitation. Jeez, we had sex. Big wow! I wouldn't have caused a scene. I wouldn't have laughed. I wouldn't have rushed into the middle of the ceremony to declare my undying love for her. *As if*!

'If I tell you, you have to swear secrecy, William. I haven't told another soul.'

'Yeah, yeah!'

'I mean it.'

'I swear. Jesus, just tell me for Christ sake!'

'I wasn't off with glandular fever.'

'Never!'

'I had an abortion.'

Woah! Big grown-up talk. Too much detail. I don't want to know this.

She sits up on the bed and pulls her mini skirt back down over her thighs.

'That explains things, I hope.'

It does. Still all a bit of a shock though. I would have preferred something like a lesbian affair. A confusion over her sexuality which I could help out with. Or at least add to.

I figure I have to be selfish here. The likelihood of getting the leg over with this girl is minimal. I'd have a better chance with a nun! I mean, I have other options. I don't want to get involved in all this grown-up shit. It's too scary. I'll have to act mature and responsible, give some sound advice. That would be a new experience. I'm better out of it. Not get involved.

'If I don't tell someone soon then I'm going to go mental. Every day is just so hard, you know?'

I don't know, but I nod my head as if I do and then sit down beside her on the bed. I don't think I have much option but to listen. She blows her nose. Too loudly, but I just don't think I can tell her to shut up. I mean, she might flip at any second. Tread carefully, Will, my man. Very carefully. She could go off the rails any minute now.

'What do you mean?'

'Well, working with Eve every day. Especially now since she's getting married.'

'Eh?'

'Something terrible happened.' She looks at me quickly and then away again.

Oh, my God, she was raped! Molested by her father? Maybe Nathan's proved he was a man after all.

'I had a one-night stand with someone.'

It's Nathan. Fuck me, it's Nathan! Lucky bastard.

'And got pregnant.'

Evasive. Too evasive. I want names. I want telephone numbers. I want pictures. I want to know why it wasn't me!

She's a bit edgy, rubs her neck and can't look me in the eye.

'Who?'

'It was a mistake, William.'

'Who?'

'Just one of those things.'

'For fuck sake, *who?*'

'Ian.'

12

WILL '*Ian*?'

She nods her head. Still can't look me in the eye.

'Ian? As in Eve's Ian? As in Fuckwit-tadger-features Ian?'

She nods again.

'You're bloody joking!'

Shagging the walking suit. Has she no standards?

A shake of the head this time.

'Fuck sake, Poppy!'

She tries to grab my arm but I pull it away. 'It wasn't like that, William! It was at Christmas-time when they were separated. And you were well . . . annoying me. It just sort of happened. It meant nothing.'

'You bitch!'

'Don't be like that. You're just annoyed because he got the leg over and you haven't.'

Well. If she must put it that way. Suppose I am. But Ian? *Ian.* This I can't believe.

There's a silence for me to work out dates and quick calculations in my head. But I was never any good at arithmetic. Or science – the chemistry of this shagfest is beyond me.

'It only happened the once,' she starts, obviously sensing my slow uptake. 'After a bottle of wine. He came into the shop looking for Eve and one thing led to another.'

'You had unprotected sex with Ian?' I just can't get over it.

'God!' She tuts. 'Give me strength. Condoms rip, William, you know.'

Oh, yes. Indeedy, missy. I do know. Patronizing wee tart that she is! Been there, done that, bought the sodding T-shirt! I've probably had more ripped johnnies than she's had orgasms. So she doesn't need to tell me about it.

'I didn't want the baby,' she says a bit too quickly. 'Bloody hell, I'm nineteen years old. It would have ruined my life. It was just one of those things.'

'Did you tell Ian?' Not for the sympathy angle, you understand, just to see what level of bastardom he's at.

'Yes.' She scratches her head. 'He was great. Booked me into a private clinic and everything. I really could quite fancy him if it wasn't for Eve.'

'Please!' Now I think I'm going to throw up.

'He was really sweet and kind,' she continues – an insult to any man if ever I heard one. Almost as bad as being called nice.

'What about Eve?'

'Eve doesn't know.' Now she can't look me in the eye. 'Please don't tell her. What she doesn't know won't hurt her.'

A red rag to a bull if ever I heard one.

EVE If I knew a priest I would talk to him. You'd think I was born a Catholic, with all this guilt.

I cannot marry Ian.

And it's not down to pre-nuptial nerves.

How can I marry him when he doesn't know about Will and me sleeping together? I'm not starting my married life on a lie.

I know sex is . . . well, sex. But it was much more than that with Will.

He hasn't even replied to his invitation. Surely that should tell Ian something.

'Ian?' I say down the phone, hoping he doesn't detect the tremble in my voice.

'Hi, hon,' he replies, thankfully not aware. 'Just think. This time tomorrow you'll be my wife. In fact' – I can tell he glances at his watch – 'in less than five hours.' He's excited. He pauses. 'It's not bad luck to speak to you before this afternoon, is it?'

It could well be, but I can't tell him that.

'I just wanted to hear your voice,' I manage, 'that's all.'

If Hilary was here she would grab the phone from me and tell me not to be so stupid. She'd say what he doesn't know won't hurt him. I wind the telephone flex around my forefinger. 'Don't you think it's weird that I haven't seen hide or hair of Will for a while?'

There's a silence down the phone. A silence when he might put two and two together. It would at least save me the bother of finding the right words to tell him.

'No,' he says, 'I haven't given it much thought, actually.' Might have known. Damn. 'I assumed he was pissed off because you chose me over him.'

Sometimes I wonder if Ian and I are on the same planet, never mind wavelength. I want to ask him why he's marrying me. But I know I'll sound all needy and pathetic. Still, I do. 'Why are you marrying me, Ian?'

He tuts good-humouredly. 'You know why.' Giggles a bit like a schoolboy.

I want him to say those three little words. I shouldn't need to prompt him. It is our wedding day, after all.

'Even if I had done something really bad?'

'Mm-hm,' he replies. 'Bad as in what kind of bad? Are you telling me you're not a natural brunette and dye your hair to hide the grey?' He laughs at his own joke.

If only it was as simple as that. 'Oh, well. I can't really say over the phone.' The flex is beginning to cut off the blood supply in my finger.

'Intriguing.' He's taking this as a huge joke.

'Can we meet at the hairdresser's?'

My mother's idea – the hairdresser's-stroke-beautician's. 'I see some dark hair on your top lip. Don't want that in the photos, do we?' she said. Get made up. Get nails done. Get waxed. Get moussed. Get conditioned. Get moisturized. Get so moisturized I could slide home again.

'Won't that be bad luck?'

'Why change things now?' I reply.

WILL Okay, let's not panic.

Oh, my God!

Oh, Jesus. Fuck.

What do I do now?

Okay, okay, she asked me to keep it a secret. 'Promise,' she said. And I did. But I didn't cross my heart and hope to die, so that's null and void as far as I am concerned. Besides, Eve has a right to know.

'You've got to tell her.'

'Why?'

''Cos she's making a huge mistake.'

'Who says? You? What a bloody cheek. Don't you dare tell her, William. If you do it's the end of us.'

Well, it was the end of us when she told me about her romp with Ian. I don't want his fucked-up leftovers.

Then she sleeps. Puts her head back on the pillow, closes her eyes and is out like a light in less than a minute. Obviously the weight has been lifted off her shoulders. She has told someone. The burden is halved. Now she can sleep.

Of course I can't.

I wake her up a couple of hours later. A couple of hours that I have spent fretting and pacing, and biting my fingernails and being cool, and being extremely pissed off and having reached no decision at all.

'You've got to tell her.' She tries to unhook my grip on her shoulders. My plan is to shake her into submission.

She yawns. 'No!' She manages to push my arms off her.

'If you don't, I will.'

'And spoil her day?'

'Better than spoiling her life.'

'Jesus, William. What are you going to do? Hold up the ceremony? Do the big Dick Turpin act? More Dick than

Turpin, you are.' She rubs sleep from her eyes, smudging her eyeliner in the process.

I could be a mean fucker and nickname her Chi-chi. But then it occurs to me that this is the closest I'm ever likely to be of getting her into my bed. Bummer.

She rubs her tongue over her teeth. She'd be better brushing them. Her breath is fairly stinking.

'Don't take this the wrong way, but it has nothing to do with you.' God, she can be stroppy!

'You shouldn't have told me, then.' It's really hard not to go beserk at her. Acting as if she's just told me that she picks her nose or farts in the bath. Jesus Christ, this is big news. This is huge. What am I supposed to do? Forget about it? Fuck, this girl lives in Cuckoo-cuckoo-land.

'Right, that's it. If you're going to be like that, I'm off.'

Now I'm pissed off. 'Like what? How can you act like this when you've just killed Eve's fiancé's baby?'

'I prefer "terminated",' is her icy reply. Then the nonchalant shrug. 'Life's a bastard.'

EVE I've changed my mind. I don't think I'll tell Ian about my affair. Besides, it was hardly an affair. One afternoon of kisses, gropes and a bout of the other does not qualify as an affair in my book.

He opens the door of the salon and I see his face. And I know I can't spoil his day.

'So?' he starts, after kissing me on the cheek.

My mother's in the back getting her French manicure. Thank God. She'd be checking her pulse for palpitations if she saw Ian here.

I keep one eye on Ian and the other on the beautician's

door, which is no mean feat considering my head is rollered and stuck under a huge extra-terrestrial-style hairdrier.

I have to say I'm not really looking my best at the moment. My face is red from the heat of the drier. And blotchy from plucking and waxing. The curlers loosen off with every blast of heat. I tried to tell my mother that I'd look like Shirley Temple. But I was wasting my breath.

WILL I can't say I follow her because I know where she's going. I just give her a five-minute head-start and then make my own way to Flower Power. Eve's picking up the bouquets at noon. Or so the Tart Without The Heart told me.

Synchronize watches. 11:27 and 15 seconds. Thirty-three minutes until confrontation. A doddle. As long as the car starts.

Not that I know what to say. Or do. But something will come to mind between now and then.

It's hard being inconspicuous in an orange Fiesta that makes more noise than the Book of Records' loudest fart.

There's a display of some large tree things outside the entrance to the shop, so I can hide behind them if need be.

I'm too early. Shit. Least it gives me time to think up a plan. Except my brain is blank. More than normal, I mean.

I've changed my mind anyway. I don't think I'll tell Eve about Poppy and Fuckwit.

I'm not her keeper. 'If she wants to balls-up her life then let her go right ahead. No skin off my nose. I nip

251

into the nearest pub for a quick half to think things over.

EVE I feel like a contestant on Countdown. The clock is ticking noisily by and I have to do something. Or say something. Except it won't be as easy as asking Carol Vorderman for another vowel or consonant.

He sits stroking the veins on the back of my hand, just looking at me and not talking. He obviously doesn't have a lot to say. I do. The problem is finding the right words. Plus I'm treasuring these moments of quiet before my mother bursts forth to cause a rumpus.

The Bee Gees sing in the background 'You should be dancing, yeah!' and I tap my foot along. Puts me in the mood for a party. Just as well I'm going to one this afternoon.

The beautician's door opens and I shove a shower cap on Ian's head as his cunning disguise to fool my mother. He laughs and pulls it off.

'She's superstitious,' I tell him. 'If she sees you here she'll go mad. You know what she's like. She'll be wanting to throw salt over her shoulder or tie a knot in a piece of string, for crying out loud!'

He glances at his watch too.

Tick, tock. If I'm going to do it, I have to say it now.

But I've gone to all this effort with my hair and nails and everything. It would just go to waste if I told him. I don't want to spoil things. I'm not good at scenes.

'I have to go and get ready. What's this terrible secret you're going to tell me?' He's not taking this seriously; looking at me with ghoulishly large eyes and twitching his fingers in the air. 'No, no, let me guess. You and Will are having an affair?'

A silence falls across the salon. Even the Bee Gees seem a bit surprised. Their high-pitched voices are almost a scream. My heart begins to pound. The hairs on the back of my neck stand on end. My armpits feel sticky as Sellotape.

This is it. My moment to confess. I open my mouth –

And he laughs. Throws his head back and laughs whole-heartedly.

I shake my head in disbelief. *A joke*? He was joking? Another roller falls out from the violence of my shaking.

I can't look him in the eye. If he had half a brain or at least a modicum of common sense then surely he wouldn't have cracked a joke like that. I can't believe I'm going to marry someone so stupid.

I open my mouth and nothing comes out. My confession has grown roots inside me.

There's no point telling him. Especially when he's in this mood. 'Damn, you have me sussed, Ian.' I laugh falsely but he doesn't notice.

He kisses me just as the hairdresser bustles towards me armed with a tin of hairspray the size of the ozone layer. The beautician's door opens wide for my mother to come out blowing on her new nails.

'See ya at three o'clock, hon,' he says walking out humming 'I'm getting married in the morning' under his breath.

And I watch him walk out. Still mute.

Damn. Loused that one up good and proper. Big chicken. That's it. I had the perfect opportunity and messed it up.

But I couldn't tell him. I just couldn't confess. He seemed so happy. It would have ruined his day.

My mother's getting blowed-dried now. A bouffant do. Shame it's not her mouth because she's driving me up the wall. 'Cheer up,' she says, laughing at her own joke:

'You're going to your wedding, not your funeral. Ha, ha, ha.'

I *hate* people who laugh at their own jokes.

She keeps running to the toilet, making a show of herself, claiming she's got the runs. God knows why. All she has to do is sit there and dab at her eyes with a tissue when I say 'I do'. It's me who's taking the big step. The giant leap. It's *my* life that's going to change. Why don't I have the runs?

I decide to escape to Flower Power for the bouquets. An escape to sanity. But then again, there is Nathan flouncing about when I open the door. Poppy's looking a bit drained and I wonder how much of a hard time Nat the Rat is giving her.

When he sees me he puckers up his nose. 'You look like Shirley Temple,' he says eyeing me up and down. I can tell he's thinking, 'Mm, more Ugly Sister than Cinderella.' Pig.

He ignores my flaring nostrils. On second thoughts, though, I disguise my growling into a pseudo cough in case he changes his mind about not charging me for the flowers.

He curls a bit of ivory ribbon around his finger before tying it around the lilies and gyp. Very classy even for one of my designs.

'Shirley Temple?' Poppy sniggers. Then she launches into 'The Good Ship Lolly Pop'.

WILL Okay, I've had a beer. And a chaser. And guess what? I've changed my mind. The more I think about it, the more it sticks in my throat. Eve has a right to know about her disloyal prick of a boyfriend. Well, he wasn't exactly disloyal 'cos they had split up, albeit temporarily, but it's a secret that I think she should know about before she gets in too deep with Tadger-Features.

I'm going to tell her.

No. Better idea. I'll get Poppy to tell her.

I'm just the innocent bystander in all of this. Let Poppy tell her. It would be better coming from a woman. Then they can get all gushy together.

I stop for a second before opening the door. Just to reconsider. But then I push open the door with a deep breath to see Poppy and Eve bent over a bunch of white flowers.

Too late now to change my mind.

Eve is so surprised to see me that the pins in her mouth fall out when her jaw almost hits the floor. Her head is a hideous mass of curls.

'You look like Shirley Temple.'

'*Shurrup!*' she screams, scooping up the pins and jagging them into the flowers.

Poppy looks a bit surprised too. In fact, she looks as if she's going to commit murder.

'Is that what you came to tell me? That I look like Shirley Temple?'

'No.'

'You're wanting a button-hole. You're coming this afternoon, aren't you?'

'No.'

Her head shoots up and the curls bounce. 'What do you mean?'

'I didn't get invited.'

'You bloody did! I sent the invitation. Licked the stamp myself.'

'I didn't get an invitation.'

'Typical! Must have got lost in the post. Will you come?'

'No.'

'Why not?' She finishes tying the flowers. Then she looks at me as if she's far too busy to be bothered about this (i.e. me) at the moment. Poppy stares, scared to move a muscle. Suddenly my throat gets a bit dry, and I say:

'I am not a hypocrite.'

EVE Not a hypocrite. What does he mean by that?

Oh, my God!

He's come here to tell me that he's in love with me. That's what he means.

He's going to say it. He's going to tell me not to marry Ian because he wants to marry me himself.

I think I'm going to faint.

'What do you mean by that?' My voice wavers a little. I'm coming out in hot and cold sweats. I have to cling to the table for support.

What am I going to do?

This just complicates things even more.

Yet another cat amongst our pigeons.

WILL Shit! I thought this would be a lot easier than it is. I feel self-conscious standing in the middle of the floor with this motley crew gawping at me. Nathan appears and yells at me to get out:

'You're nothing but trouble. And you're certainly not welcome in here.'

I don't know what to do with my hands. But I can feel them clenching into tight wee balls. Just a pity I don't have a set of knuckle-dusters for his poncy face.

'Shut up, Nathan!' shouts Eve. 'Will, tell me what you mean.' Her voice has that pleading tone. And her eyes are like a puppy's. I think perhaps she's getting the wrong end of the stick here.

My hands are clammy. I feel sweat run down my spine. 'Just what I say. *I'm* not a hypocrite.'

'Don't you dare!' pipes in Poppy. 'You do and I'll . . . and I'll . . . and I'll cut off your pathetic little balls.'

No need to be insulting about it.

'What's going on?' Eve asks. She's getting a bit impatient with these interruptions.

'You have to tell her, Poppy.'

'Tell me what?' Even more impatient.

'I'm not going to, William. And if you do, you're a dead man.'

Huh! An empty threat.

'Tell me *what?*' repeats Eve. Now a little perplexed too. She laughs a bit uncomfortably, as if it's a joke.

EVE Will stands there and says:

'You can't marry Ian.'

'Don't, William. I'm warning you,' says Poppy through gritted teeth.

This is it. Now he's going to tell me that he's in love

with me. Bugger Poppy, standing there telling him not to. She's just jealous.

'Why not?' I manage. I'm not saying I'm coaxing it out of him, but he seems a little slow to get to the point.

'He's not right for you,' he says. He stands awkwardly, rubbing his neck.

Maybe he wants us to be alone. But tough tamales, I have bouquets to finish for my wedding. If he wants me to jilt Ian then he's going to have to tell me in front of Poppy and Nathan.

'Just say what's on your mind.' Then suddenly I'm angry. I mean, how dare he? Do this to me? Turn up here and turn my life upside down. Expect me to drop everything for him. Especially today, of all days. Bloody cheek! 'As per normal, you're timing is spot-on. Couldn't you have said something earlier?'

'I didn't know until this morning.'

'Know what?' I look from Poppy to Will and then back to Poppy again. I may be slow, but is there something going on here? 'Tell me, for pity's sake.'

Poppy yells:

'Don't! I'll sleep with you if that's what you want.'

Will stands there and ponders this option. Sod. Told you she's jealous. Then he shakes his head. 'Too late for that, sunshine.'

My heart lurches.

Poppy can't meet my eye.

Will looks speechless. For once.

Nathan looks as white as a sheet. It's like we're frozen in time. When really it only takes ten seconds or so.

My heart lurches again.

'Poppy?' says Will. 'Come on. Be fair.'

'No,' says Poppy. She's adamant.

'Stop this nonsense,' says Nathan shaking in the corner with frightened eyes. 'You're just upsetting everyone.' Probably working out how much money has been wasted on the flowers if I decide to run away with Will.

Everyone ignores him.

'Will you just TELL me? I'm a grown-up. I can take it on the chin.' I try to make a joke of it, when really I feel sick. I close my eyes, expecting to hear Will's declaration of love.

But there isn't one.

WILL Just then the door bell tinkles and everyone looks round to sees who it is.

'Ian?' yells Nathan in disbelief. 'It's bad luck to see the bride before the wedding!' he says, meanwhile manhandling (well, sort of) poor Eve through to the back.

Nor is his the only smacked gob. Me, I just want the ground to open up and swallow me. Or to make a speed-of-light beeline out the door.

But a man's gotta do what he's gotta do.

EVE 'Let *go* of me,' I protest, elbowing Nathan in the stomach.

'What's going on here?' asks Ian. His face looks stern. He knows. The penny has finally dropped about Will and me. That's what it is. What am I going to do?

Damn. Will won't say anything now.

Not that I want him to.

I'm marrying Ian. I really am. I've made up my mind. Will's too late.

He's just too bloody late.

WILL Fuck!

This isn't what I expected. I really don't want to cause a scene. Well, I do. But I also don't want to be punched in the face by Ian. He's a big bloke. Hardly Mike Tyson, but certainly no weed.

'William knows, Ian,' says Poppy. 'He wants to tell her.' Her voice is a bit tearful. She glowers at me as if she could attack at any moment.

Ha, ha. Got him cornered. 'You what?' He doesn't believe it.

I notice Nathan rushing to the door and turning the sign over to Closed, and firmly snibbing the bolt. Shit. Bang went the quick getaway.

'Yeah, that's right.' Blasé seems the best stance. I do my Superhero Pose – standing sticking my chest out, hands on my hips. 'Poppy's told me, and I think Eve has the right to know.' Even my voice sounds deeper.

'The right to know *what?*' demands Eve. Her curls bounce. Her face is a bit too pink for my liking.

'Jesus wept,' says Ian rubbing his hands through his hair. He had come in whistling 'I'm getting married in the morning'. Now I think he'd be lucky to get away with 'Went To Mow The Meadow'.

I look at Eve, who looks on the verge of tears.

All of a sudden Nathan grabs my elbow and pushes me towards the door. I try to shrug him off but for a puny wee poof he has a fair bit of upper-body strength. He's digging his fingers tightly into my arms. I know I'm going to have bruises. Just as well I'm not a violent man. But so help me God, if he touches me again then that's it, he's dog meat.

Poppy rushes for a tissue and gives her nose a good blow.

Jeez, the way everyone's carrying on you'd think it was me who got someone up the duff.

Ian slithers over to Eve. He begins to stroke her shoulder. He even touches her curls, for fuck sake. Then he kisses her. Full tongue.

It's now or never. Right, if they don't have the balls to tell her, then I'm bloody going to.

'Ask Ian what he was up to around Christmas-time. Ask him who he was shagging.' I manage to get Nat off me. I have sharp elbows for a man and I tell you he won't be singing baritone for a while.

Poppy gasps.

Eve stands staring at Ian, then turns to me. She shrugs his slimy hands off her.

My voice turns into a shout:

'Go on. Ask him.'

EVE I don't need to ask him.

I know. I can see the guilty looks on their faces.

'It was an accident,' starts Ian. 'We had separated. I came looking for you –'

'And found her,' I point at Poppy.

Sniffling beside me, she cowers back as if I'd strike her. Yes, I'm shocked and hurt. She isn't his type. He doesn't like girls who wear eyeliner. But I still won't thump her. Partly because my feet are glued to the floor.

'We weren't together, Ian. It's okay.' I feel weary with all this. I just want to marry him and get on with our lives.

Bugger Will. If that's the best he can do, well, he can just sod off.

'It was only the once.'

'Fine.' Don't think I'll be discussing sex with Poppy over a white-wine spritzer in the future though.

'I got pregnant, Eve,' pipes in Poppy, the bitch from hell. Her whingy voice is barely audible.

Hang on a minute. This is different. This I can't quite take in. My knuckles are white and sore from clinging on to the desk so tightly. I don't mean to be melodramatic, but really . . .

'What?' It's so ridiculous I almost laugh. The thought of his body pumping away on top of her? Ridiculous. I don't believe it.

'I was having a termination. I wasn't off with glandular fever.' Her chin is down at her chest. If it was up to me it would be scraping the ground.

'What?' yells Nathan in disbelief. 'I have the sick lines here,' running towards the filing cabinet.

I'm aware of Ian stroking my hand. 'You were having an abortion?'

I don't believe it.

Ian stops the stroking for a second. He obviously thinks there's going to be a scene. Then he restarts in double-time.

Her tone is cutting:

'I prefer "termination", actually.'

Cold hard-hearted bitch. Ian won't find anything attractive about that.

'Why didn't you tell me?' I whisper to him.

Bitch from hell says:

'We didn't want to hurt your feelings.'

We? Well, Poppy can go and boil her head for all I care.

I don't want to talk to her. Or hear what she has to say. Never mind look at her.

You'd think Ian was proposing the way he gets down on one knee and takes my hands in his own. 'I didn't find out myself until after that night we got back together. I didn't want to lose you. There was no need for you to know.'

WILL No need for her to know? What a complete dickhead.

She's going to soak it all up like a frigging sponge. I can just tell. So much for women's lib. This is the 1990s, isn't it? Not the 1890s. Jesus Christ! How can she be so fucking stupid?

'It was an accident. A mistake. We both knew it.'

Poppy too bends down beside Eve.

'It's over, Eve. I never meant for this to happen. Believe me.'

Bitch. Bet she did. Coming to me like that, confessing to her sin, knowing fine well I'd try and tell Eve. Bitch.

'Really, I'm so sorry. Go on and get married,' she continues.

Eve sits there and lets the snot-nosed tart stroke her arm and tell her what to do. I feel a bit out of it, standing, instead of kneeling down and stroking her like a fucking cat! I clench my teeth in a effort to keep my trap shut. I can't really hear anything over and above Nathan slamming filing cabinet drawers and rustling bits of paper.

But the clenching doesn't help. I can't stand this bag of shite any more. 'Come home with me, Eve,' I say.

'No.'

What? She's turning me down. I'm offering her a way out and she's bloody fucking-fuck-fuck turning me down? I don't believe this.

That's what she wanted. That's what she's always wanted.

EVE 'No,' I repeat, before I know it.

Cheek of him. Thinking I would just drop everything for him. Probably thought he was doing the right thing, but God Almighty, we had an affair too. Only we weren't caught out. That's the difference.

'You are a hypocrite, Will.'

'What do you mean?' The lights are on but there's no-one in. Then I can see it dawn on him. He gulps. I see his Adam's apple bob.

'Look!' says Nathan, shoving the sick lines under my nose. 'She's lied. And her doctor. What is this world coming to when the medical profession falsifies sick lines for its patients?' He stomps and flounces. The pouty lip is well and truly out. He's just hacked off because this was gossip he didn't know.

'What comes around comes around,' Will says with a shrug. 'Is it confession time?'

Nathan, obviously still put out, snaps:

'Is this a florist's, or a chapel?'

'Confess to what?' quizzes Ian.

'Nothing,' I say. 'Will's little joke, that's all.'

What's the point? Dragging up the past. I'll let it go. Let Will go.

We look at each other closely – Will and I. I bite my bottom lip to stop me saying anything or doing anything, since everything I would certainly regret.

WILL She's looking at me with gooey eyes like an Andrex puppy. Her curls have gone a bit flat. Thank fuck. She doesn't look so much like a poodle now.

'What's this confession?' asks Knob-end.

I ignore him. Which is hard to do considering he's all over Eve like a rash.

'Aren't you coming with me?'

She's biting her lip to shreds. All she does is shake her head.

Fuck her, then. I couldn't give a shit.

Someone must have pressed Repeat on one of the buttons up Ian's back. 'What's this confession?' he whines.

'Why not?' I press her. Am I a glutton for punishment, or what?

'If I don't marry Ian today, I'll marry him another day.'

Pretentious shite.

Fuck her, then. I couldn't give a shit.

'*Tell* me,' he moans. 'What's this confession?'

Jesus, will he not just give it a rest?

The way I see it I have two options. I can tell Ian, with graphic details of course, about our romp in the sack. In which case Eve is well and truly fucked. Or I can keep quiet. In which case Eve is well and truly fucked too.

'What is this confession?' Of course, if Fuckwit suspects what me and Eve are thinking of saying, then he'll be seeing it as him getting off the hook.

Bollocks to that.

EVE Tell him, Will. Tell him. I dare you to.

If you're going to do it, do it now . . .

No. Don't tell him. Please don't tell him. I double-dare you.

I don't want you to tell him.

Please don't.

WILL Eve could appear in The X Files with eyes as large as that. She's practically eating her lip. Knob-end's gripping her hand tightly.

Bastard.

But I ignore him. It's the best thing to do. His whiny voice, 'Confess what?' is just getting on my nerves. Git.

Here goes. Fuck! I'll just have to let rip. Take the bull by the horns. 'You can't marry him, Eve. Jesus, look at him. He's a boring bastard.'

'Just because he doesn't drink lager. Doesn't mean he's boring, you know.' Her hand goes limp in his grip. Then she pulls it out of his grasp. 'He's been all over the world.' She can't look at me. Or him.

'And he's still a boring fuck.'

'Will!'

'Right, that's it,' says Fuckwit. 'You've said enough. I've let you stand here and slander me. I've let you stand here and try to ruin my wedding day. One more word out of you and I'll use your head for a loo brush.'

Well I'm shaking in my boots with that one. But better not push him too far. Above all I want to come out of this palaver with my pride intact.

'So tell me what you want to say and then disappear out that door for good.' This must be his business tone of voice, steely and really, even if I have to admit it, a bit scary.

Now the pressure's on. But I can't say it. I can't tell him about our fuck. Fuck knows I want to. Just to see him crumble. But the look on Eve's face warns me not to. She's chewing that lip faster than a tart would give head. Plus I don't know what kind of business he does. He could be a loan shark used to using knuckle-dusters and a sledgehammer on kneecaps for all I know. I have to think about me and my bone structure in all this crap. I like my nose where it is, thanks very much.

Fuckwit walks towards me. Shit. His chin is in line with my eyeballs. His voice is almost a whisper:

'Go on. Tell me. Or are you too much of a wimp to say it?' Threatening like.

I begin to feel a bit queasy.

'You know I've let you carry on like this because I had the audacity to think that you cared for Eve. Stupid me. I even thought you might have loved her. Ha!'

Knuckle-duster? Feather duster is more like it! This guy is a prize wanker. Jesus, surely Eve can see it. Or is she blind as well as stupid?

'Bet she hasn't told you she's only marrying you because she doesn't have me.' True or not, it seems a good come-back line.

'You bastard!' He makes a lunge for me but hasn't bargained for my Prince Naseen swerve.

EVE '*Stop* it.' I know I sound schoolmarmish but this is getting us nowhere.

They're standing clenching their fists into tiny balls, jaws set and ready to brawl all over the floor if need be. I confess I like the idea of two men fighting over me. It's a thrill I've always imagined since playground days. But

267

now it's actually happening, it seems a bit absurd. And I have to stop it, however half-heartedly.

They both turn round to look at me as if they've suddenly remembered what this is all about.

'Ian, if you want the so-called confession, you'd better sit down.'

'No, I'll stand if it's all the same to you.' Petulant child. He's still snarling at Will. And Will growls back. The similarity between them and a cock fight is not lost on me. Every pun intended.

My wedding is slipping away. My dad's arm guiding me down the aisle seems further in the distance than ever. Might as well just let it go. Give up everything. I go forward two steps. Now I go back three.

'Three times the bridesmaid, never the bride,' they say. But I haven't ever been a bridesmaid either. Just for once I would have liked to wear flowers in my hair and not looked like a hippy.

'Ian,' I try to take his hand but he won't let me. My voice attempts to sound soothing and calm. I think I fail. Maybe at long last he's worked it out. 'Will and I . . .'

WILL I can't believe she's actually going to do this. She's actually, really, honestly going to tell him. Fuck me with a barge-pole.

For once in my life I'm stumped for words.

EVE '. . . had an affair.'

WILL An affair? Is that what it was? Jesus, what a pile of shite.

One afternoon of headboard banging and the next thing I know it's 'an affair'.

EVE Silence is golden.

Ian says so much by saying nothing.

'Thought as much,' is his final say-so. 'I was just seeing if you would own up to it.'

I can't quite believe this. 'All this time you were testing me? You knew? Today at the hairdresser's, when you joked about it –?' I'm so shocked I can't even finish the sentence.

He nods but can't look at me.

Sod. Pig. Bastard. Now I'm all for punching him too.

But then he slumps down on the stepped display area beside a bucket of carnations. His head is placed in his hands, and he ruffles his hair a bit. The carnations run across and tickle him on the face. All he does is punch them out of his way. My anger evaporates. I feel quite sorry for him. But not enough to go over and apologize profusely.

There's a big sigh from behind us. Nathan stands shaking his head:

'What a to-do. What a mess!'

But I've worked with Nathan for years, so I can see the glint of excitement in his eyes. This afternoon has turned into all his birthdays on the same day.

WILL YEEEEsss! Ya dancer! That's my Evie! Can't help feeling a bit smug about things now. 'Can we go home?'

'Home?' she snaps. That's my Evie too: snappy mare. 'You keep saying that. What home are you meaning, exactly?'

'Your home. The flat.'

'Have you lost your marbles? Have you finally flipped your lid?' Now she's in rant mode. Jesus, wish I had never opened my mouth. 'Do you not remember you moved out? Actually ran out, is more like it.'

Well, I'm not going to tell her that my bags are already packed and sitting at my mum's. All I'm going to say is that it would only take a quick jaunt in the shag-Fiesta.

'I can come back.'

'Ha!' This is Ian. He's taken on a dramatic martyred role. Twat. Looking torn between tears and cutting my willie off with the secateurs lying on the counter. Don't know what Eve ever saw in him. '*We*'re getting married today, or has that escaped your notice?'

'You still want to marry me?' asks Eve, half in shock, half in surprise.

'Well . . .'

'Do you know something?' pipes in Poppy. Everyone had forgotten she was there. 'You are all pathetic. Pa-the-tic. Don't know why I ever bothered with any one of you.'

I'm beginning to dislike this girl.

'You still want to marry me?' repeats Eve, as if it's not quite sunk in yet. 'I passed the test, so you still want me?'

Poppy is obviously invisible.

So am I.

'Don't be like that, Eve, honey. You know I want you.'

They can't do it. They can't go ahead and get married now. They can't.

They can't.

EVE He still wants to marry me. After everything.

God, that says a lot about the man. He must truly love me.

'I can give you much more than him,' says Ian, picking one of the petals of the carnations to bits. 'Just think how happy you were when he wasn't about.'

Was I happy? I can't remember. I can't remember anything. Nor think of anything. I'm all confused. I wish everyone would just go away and give me time to think.

I look down at my engagement ring.

Just to think I woke up in a good mood this morning. Today was the start of a new life for me. And now all I can see in the future is my two-bedroom flat, struggling to pay the mortgage, and Sundays spent watching Eastenders Omnibus.

'He's a loser, Eve. He's the kind of bloke that won't amount to anything. He'll never have money. He'll never achieve anything. His epitaph will read, He's dead, so what?'

Maybe I know Will's a loser. Maybe I know he'll never achieve anything. But that doesn't give Ian the right to insult my friends.

'At least Will can get a stiffy.' The words are out before I have time to think about a suitable retort. It's tough when the tongue works faster than the brain. And you're hurt and annoyed and trying to make other people feel guilty to pacify yourself.

Will snorts with laughter:

'He can't get a stiffy? What a fucking retard.'

271

Nathan gasps and gulps, clutches his chest as if he's having palpitations.

Poppy, obviously feeling just as bitter, starts:

'Well, that was never a problem with me.'

Smug cow. She drifts in the general direction of Ian, who is sitting sheepishly in a statuesque state. It's like a child's game; them on one side, us on the other.

Then suddenly I'm angry.

So bloody angry.

How dare she side with him? How dare they just assume that I wouldn't mind about the baby? Am I supposed to shrug and say, 'Shit happens'? Well, no. I'm not doing that. I pick up the first available thing to hand – which is, unfortunately, my wedding bouquet – and toss it at them. Every rose, every single lily, every bit of foliage, one after the other, wishing the thorns would rip their eyes out. Try to pull the wool over my eyes, would they? The ribbon doesn't go far and falters in the air before descending slower than Poppy's knickers.

Tart.

What do they see in her? Tell me, please. Nobody has ever told me. And I really want to know. She wears eyeliner for God's sake. There's more to women than having pert breasts and wearing tight clothing. There's nothing dignified about matching your lipstick with your nail varnish.

Everything happens so quickly. Ian's arms are protectively covering his head. Poppy screams and cries, fighting off the flowers. Will moves towards me as if to stop me. I must be on a roll because the next thing I know I've picked up a bucket of water with half a dozen wilting irises in it and tossed that at them too. I hear the splash of water and then the drip drip plop of water running off the step-styled display area. So shocked is Ian that he falls off the edge, pulling over the bucket of carnations on top of him. He now looks as if he's wet himself, a big damp patch covering his groin.

'That's probably the best excitement your dick's seen in months,' laughs Will.

Nathan rushes for towels. Poppy whimpers then looks as if she's going to pounce on me. I look around hurriedly for another bucket, just in case.

I mean, I've just had my hair done, wedding or not. And my make-up. I don't want to end up looking like Poppy the Panda. Above all I must keep my dignity intact.

WILL Then she collapses in the chair as delayed shock sets in. Poor Eve looks so done in now. Bet this day gives her a few grey hairs. Of course, she'll say I caused them.

Probably have.

But there's always Henna.

Nathan comes back with a bundle of towels. His face is scarlet, at exploding point. I see water splashes down the front of his pink cashmere jumper. That explains it. Least the colour of his face co-ordinates with his crew-neck.

Poppy grabs a towel from him. In her hysteria her eyeliner has achieved the baby-panda look. That's the second time I've seen her like that today. I'm so glad I never had her. Shagging endangered species could lead to funny hybrids.

Eve looks on the verge of a nervous breakdown. She sits on the chair with her arms wrapped tightly around her body, muttering away to herself. I go and try to massage her shoulders. I'm surprised when she lets me.

Another shock is when Poppy rubs the towel on Fuck-wit's tadger. And he lets her. Never says a word. His hair's dripping. His face is puce coloured.

There's snot on the end of his nose.

And she goes for the groin first. Now that's class. 'Get you dry,' she says.

Get him even wetter, more like! The way that stiffy's bursting through his zip.

EVE He's getting an erection. He's sodding well getting an erection. My eyes are drawn to it like a magnet. You can't very well miss it.

'Oh my,' says Nathan.

'Oh fuck,' says Will.

Maybe I should have tried those red crotchless knick-ers. Maybe I should wear eye-liner and offer myself on a plate. Everything I went through. The humiliation of positions and porn when all she has to do is rub him with a towel!

I feel old and shabby and done. And I just want to go home. Climb into my pyjamas and eat chocolate biscuits.

I can hear it now, the sniggers when they hear my marriage was called off because I couldn't give my fiancé a hard-on but the girl who got pregnant by him could. Amongst other things.

'I'm so sorry,' says Ian when he sees everyone's eyes on his groin. He can't even pretend to be sorry when he's sitting there with a grin from ear to ear as if he's just been reunited with a long-lost friend. 'It's not too late, Eve.'

My voice is regretfully a bit high-pitched, when really I'm trying to control the mediocre dignity I have left:

'It sodding well is!'

'Is that it?' he wails. 'The wedding is off?'

'Uh-huh.' I could yell too much has happened, we can't go back or this is for the best. But I don't.

I feel Will kneading my shoulders a bit roughly.

Poppy's got a grin on her as well. She glances at Will with such a smug look on her face I almost leap out of the chair – claws out, newly manicured – to slap her hard across the chops.

'Eve, honey, come on.'

'Don't call me honey.'

I know they'll leave and go to have sex. Probably in what was supposed to be my marital bed. Roundabout the same time that I was supposed to vow my life to Ian. Hopefully this time with a durable Durex though.

Maybe I'll become an nun. Maybe I'll try celibacy. Or what about lesbianism?

WILL The wind has been taken out of Eve's sails and put up Ian, in a manner of speaking.

'That's it. That's the end,' she says quietly. Tadger-features still hears her. He doesn't even have the decency to look embarrassed. His eyes roll. The bastard looks as if he's going to cream his Ys any second.

'It doesn't have to be,' he pleads. 'We can leave now. Go home. Go to a hotel.'

Yeah, probably some sleazy joint with neon flashing signs and candlewick bedspreads. Seen enough of them in my time.

Besides, I think Poppy would have something to say about that. She's made it crystal clear what she's after. Could fancy him, she said. Now I get the picture. *Definitely* fancy, more like. She's not stupid. After all, he's got a bigger car than me, and no overdraft. She's got it all sussed. You got to admire her for that.

'Go. You go. I stay.' Has she lost the ability to speak? 'It's over.'

'We can't end it like this,' he whines.

Oh she bloody well can. Now fuck off.

'Go. You go. I stay.'

'Eve, honey, we're supposed to be married this afternoon.'

'No!' Eve's breathing is deep. 'That is the last time you call me Honey. No more.'

'You mean to tell me you're choosing him over me?' Fuckwit points at me.

'Well, there's no way on earth I'm going to marry you now.'

'But, Eve . . .' Then he slumps back down on the wet seat. Squelching but resigned. Sighing but still turned on.

EVE Then he walks out. Just like that. Poppy follows him. He doesn't say he'll phone or pop round for a chat, or anything. He doesn't kiss me on the cheek or give me a hug. He doesn't thank me for the time we had together or apologize for anything that has happened. All he says is, 'Cheerio,' as if he's just paid the milkman.

Cheerio, for crying out loud!

Then again, I don't suppose there is a lot to say. No doubt he would just sound like a walking cliché anyway. But better that than going without saying anything.

But at least when he walks out his crotch is still wet. Serves him right.

I watch them through the window. Ian walks in front. Poppy must call out his name and he stops to wait for her. He bloody well stops and waits for her. She runs up to him, her legs splaying in those heels. She's giggling a bit. Then the window steams up with my heavy breathing. And I don't think to wipe it off.

What's my mum going to say? All those guests at the church. Now I know how Will felt all those months ago. She's probably still sitting under a drier in the hair salon. She'll look like an afro-ed poodle by now. This could give her a heart attack. She's always telling me she suffers from angina.

I turn round to see Will and Nathan watching me.

'Well. That's that, then.' Sorry, but that's about as flippant as it gets.

'Her P45 will be in the post,' states Nathan, arms clasped beneath his chest and lips pursed. 'I don't know why you convinced me to take her on, Eve. Nothing but trouble. Didn't I tell you that at the start? You know I never like to say it, but I told you so, didn't I?'

I'm not in the mood to argue with him. All I do is nod.

'Let's go home,' says Will, reaching out his hand for mine.

WILL Jesus knows why I put up with her. She drives me up the frigging wall. But least she doesn't like Barry Michaelmore, or whatever his name is.

Do you know what the cheeky mare says?

'It's my home, Will. You're the lodger.'

'Come on.' I try to take her hand.

'And don't do that,' she snaps, smacking my hand

away. 'Leave my hand alone. I don't know where yours has been. I can guess and I don't like it.'

Bloody cheek!

Natty rushes us out the door claiming Flower Power was still a florist the last time he looked and not an amateur dramatic society. He could sook lemons for Scotland, so he could. Bloody cheek! And him the biggest drama queen of all.

EVE Amateur dramatics?

Bloody cheek! Nathan's the biggest drama queen of all!

He's not worried about the rest of the day's trade. He just wants us to leave so he can get straight on the phone to Hilary and his cronies. Probably have a 'soiree' to tell them all the juicy gossip.

Will passes me one of the miniature roses from the floor. Water drips from it. The scent is still strong. And it was from my wedding bouquet. I'll keep it as a souvenir.

'Tell you what, though,' Will starts as we're ushered out the door, 'your underhand throw could do with some practising. Do you have anything in the freezer?'

WILL God, she's a stubborn mule. For the umpteenth time I try to take her hand. She always smacks me away. I try to put my hand around her waist or shoulder.

'Quit it! You're annoying me.'

'Listen, Eve,' I don't know how to ask this. I take a deep breath. 'Well, you know how, we . . . you know . . .'

'. . . Made love?'

'Jesus, Eve, don't say made love. That's for saddos. Have you not learnt anything? Say shagged. Or fucked.'

'Okay. Shagged. Fucked.' A bit too loudly for my liking, walking along Newington Road like this. A few people stop and give her a funny look. She pays no heed.

'Uh-huh, well, you know, how we didn't you know . . .'

'. . . Use contraception?'

'Don't say contraception. Jesus, Eve. Say johnnies, or rubbers, or something.'

'Okay. Johnnies. Rubbers.'

The same people stand and look.

Shit! This isn't going to plan. I wish I had kept my mouth shut until we were in the car.

'Well, you're not, you know . . .'

'. . . Pregnant?'

The scariest word in the whole world. 'Uh-huh?' I'm out in a cold sweat just thinking about it.

'Maybe.' She smiles, gives a slight shrug. Carries on walking as if I've just asked her the time of day.

Now the palpitations start. 'Ah, fucking hell! No way!'

She still smiles. In fact she's laughing at me standing rooted to the spot, feeling like I'm going to spew and waving my arms in the air.

'That really would be Sod's Law, wouldn't it?'

My heart's pounding. I think I'm going to faint. How can she be so calm about it? This is a tragedy. '*Sod's Law?* Sod's Law, my arse. It's a bloody nightmare, that's what it is.'

EVE Maybe if he would shut up for a minute –

279

WILL 'It's mine, isn't it? I mean, it would have to be, wouldn't it? Ian only having a marshmallow. Fuck! It's mine.' I clutch my hair in big handfuls.

'Mmm,' is all she says.

'I'm too young for this. Jesus, Eve, what are we going to do? I mean, yeah, one day maybe. But now. Shit. This can't be happen –' Something occurs to me and I stop mid-rant to look at her:

'You're pregnant with my kid, and you were going to marry Ian today?'

EVE He looks so worried, it's kind of sweet. And I say:
'Sharrup and give us a kiss.'